ON THE LINE

ALSO BY S. J. ROZAN

THE LYDIA CHIN/BILL SMITH NOVELS

China Trade

Concourse

Mandarin Plaid

No Colder Place

A Bitter Feast

Stone Quarry

Reflecting the Sky

Winter and Night

The Shanghai Moon

Absent Friends

In This Rain

ON THE LINE

S. J. ROZAN

MINOTAUR BOOKS ❧ NEW YORK

This is a work of fiction. All of the characters, organizations, and events portrayed in this novel are either products of the author's imagination or are used fictitiously.

www.minotaurbooks.com

The Library of Congress has cataloged the hardcover edition as follows:

Rozan, S. J.

On the line : a Bill Smith/Lydia Chin novel / S. J. Rozan.—1st ed.

p. cm.

ISBN 978-0-312-54449-2

1. Smith, Bill (Fictitious character)—Fiction. 2. Private investigators—New York (State)—New York—Fiction. 3. Kidnapping—Fiction. 4. Chin, Lydia (Fictitious character)—Fiction. 5. Chinese Americans—Fiction. I. Title.

PS3568.O99O6 2010

813'.54—dc22

2010030457

ISBN 978-0-312-60924-5 (trade paperback)

First Minotaur Books Paperback Edition: September 2011

10 9 8 7 6 5 4 3 2 1

For Bennie

ACKNOWLEDGMENTS

My agent, Steve Axelrod
My editor, Keith Kahla

Betsy Harding, Royal Huber, and Tom Savage, for setting me on the right track

Pat Picciarelli, for keeping me out of trouble

Steve Blier, Hillary Brown, Monty Freeman, Max Rudin, James Russell, and Amy Schatz, for years of weekends

David Dubal, for inspiration

Jonathan Santlofer, for support

Nancy Ennis, for coffee

Tom Savage, again, for his way with names

Ed king and Tom Phillips, the world's best runners-up

1

Crashing dark chords smothered the cell phone's impertinent chirp, but the ringtone was "Ride of the Valkyries," so it penetrated, and I stopped. I was learning a Brahms sonata. After weeks it had started to come together into something I could feel good about. So good that I was up working on it at what is, for me, early morning: half-past eight, with a mug of powerful black coffee, and a big, bright, late fall morning beyond the windows.

I hate interruptions when I'm at the piano; hate them so much, I used to turn the phone off. Now, though, I just ignore it if it rings. Except for this one number, the reason I leave it on. I leaned from the piano bench, grinning, and reached for the phone, which was still squeaking out those opening Valkyrie notes. In my world, Wagner only trumps Brahms when Wagner means Lydia Chin.

"Hey," I said. "What's up?"

Silence, unlike Lydia; and an odd tone to it. Then she said, "Nothing good."

Those two words contained darkness: anger, fear, and something else. Warning? My skin went cold. "What does that mean?"

The answer didn't come from Lydia. It came from a different

voice, relaxed and mocking in rhythm, but inhuman in tone: thin, robotic. Deliberately, electronically altered. "It means, asshole, your girlfriend got jacked."

I was on my feet, heart pounding. "What the— Who are you?"

"Come on, you don't know me?"

"What's going on?"

"Jesus Christ! You fucked up so many guys you can't keep track!"

"Who are you? What do you want?"

"No." In a flash, joviality gone, the metallic voice dropped. "It's what you want. You want your girlfriend to live. Or am I wrong?"

"You're right, and—"

"Then find her. It's a game, get it? You find her, she lives. You don't, she dies. You following that?"

"Whoever the hell you are, leave her alone. You have business with me, bring it on."

"It's *on,* buddy boy. And if I were you I'd get down to it."

"Get down to what?"

"What did I just say?"

"How am I supposed to find her?"

"Well, lucky for you, I'm going to help. Clues, evidence, all that shit. I know you like that shit. So we'll have fun. Now get going."

"No. This is bullshit."

"Then your girlfriend dies."

"How do I know she's not dead already?"

"You just talked to her!"

"I heard two words from a woman, and you have Lydia's phone. That's all I know."

"Jesus, look! The son of a bitch is in the game already! Instant offense, whoa, I like that. Okay, good, I'll go along. Here, sweetie. Talk to him."

"Bill?" It was Lydia, which I'd known, rock solid, from those first two words.

"Are you okay?"

"So far. I don't know what's going on, though."

"Stay cool. I'll find you."

"I know you will. But Bill? I don't want my mother to worry. Looks like Tony, his birthday party, looks like I'll miss it." She stumbled over her words. "If I don't show up he'll call the apartment. Could you make some excuse? He already thinks I'm a ditz. Tell him he'll have to get a little older without me."

"Aw." The robot voice sliced back in, dripping acid. "How sweet is that? Doesn't want her mama to worry. Well, her mama's gonna have lots to worry about, you don't get your ass in gear."

I spun, stared wildly around the room, as though he might materialize and I could lunge for him. Forcing myself still, I said, "I want to talk to her."

"Sorry, you just did. One to a customer."

"As this bullshit unfolds, whatever it is."

"And by 'bullshit,' you mean . . . ?"

"This insanity! Your so-called game!"

"'Insanity'? 'So-called'? Oh, man, where's your sportsmanship? Respect for the opponent, all that. You know, maybe I don't want to play with you after all. Nah, on second thought, forget it. Of course, that means I pop your girlfriend. But I guess you don't care. So long, sucker."

The line went dead.

My heart had been speeding. Now it stopped. My breathing, my power to move, it all stopped. What the hell had I done? Played chicken with a madman, and lost. Lost Lydia. I stood rooted, for a second, an hour, a lifetime.

No! The words I couldn't get out crashed around inside my skull. *Not like this! This can't be how it ends.* Do *something. There's got to be—*

The phone, Lydia's music, rang again.

"*Lydia? Are you—*"

The robot voice: "Not her. Me. You in or out?"

"Goddamn you—"

"Smith?"

"Screw you, you bastard, I'm in." I realized I was soaked in sweat. "You think this is a goddamn game, I'll play." I took a breath, and did it again: "But only if I can talk to Lydia. So I know she's all right. You touch her, you motherfucker, I'll kill you."

"Oh, oh, listen to him! Big man! Know what, I really should forget the game and kill her right now. What could you do about it? *What,* asshole? But I'll give you a chance. I'll play fair."

"I talk to her. And you don't touch her." I dug in, praying my instincts were right. "Or I don't play."

"Are you listening? Who's in charge here? You don't find her, she dies. And you know what? You don't play, I hurt her a lot and then she dies."

"That's your rules. My rules, as long as I'm playing, you don't touch her, and I talk to her."

A hell of a gamble, going head-to-head with him like this. I didn't know who he was or what was going on. But if what he wanted was to kill Lydia he could have done that already, and he hadn't. This "game" mattered to him.

"Hmm," he finally said. "Okay, why not? But my rules: not whenever you want. You don't get what you want in life, do you? Fuck knows *I* didn't. Which would be *your* fault, motherfucker, if you remember."

"I don't remember. Tell me."

"No way! This is awesome! Oh, hey, did I mention you have twelve hours? A game's no fun without a clock. But we don't need no stinkin' refs. Cops come, cops even *think* about coming, she's toast. I mean it, motherfucker. First badge I see, pow pow pow! You got the rules?"

"And I talk to her."

"When you do something right. Like a reward. Oh, I love that! Yeah, good. I'll call you. But if you're thinking she can coach, fuggedabahdit. She has no idea where she is. And her phone, now that we got your attention, it's trashed. I mean, you don't think I'm that stupid?"

"I don't know who you are, so maybe you are that stupid."

The slashing laugh again. "Taunting! You could get called for that!" Then the instant hard freeze. "Okay, that's it. This is crap. Let's get down to it."

"What am I supposed do?"

"You're so smart. Figure it out."

And he was gone.

I hit call back, but got Lydia's voicemail. I cut off and waited. He'd have heard it ring; he'd know I wanted to talk. But my phone stayed silent.

2

"*MOTHERFUCKER!*"

My roar rattled the window frames. Or I thought it did. Or I wanted it to. I had to pull my arm back, stop myself from hurling the silent phone through the glass. *You'll need that, you stupid bastard. That, and any brain cells you might have. This isn't about you and it's not about this son of a bitch. It's about Lydia.*

All right. All right, stop, light a cigarette, think.

Who *was* he, this son of a bitch? What had I done to him—or what did he think I'd done? Obviously he knew me well enough to know he could get at me through Lydia, but that wasn't hard to figure. Anyone could see she was way more to me than a partner. She was less than he seemed to think—she was not my girlfriend—but that was her choice, not mine, a choice I lived with because I had to.

Though maybe her choice was right. Maybe getting too close to me was a bad idea. Any number of people over the years would tell you that. And look at the trouble she was in now, trouble that wasn't hers but would come down on her if I failed.

Except I'd already failed. She was somewhere locked up with a lunatic, I had twelve hours to find her, and I didn't have any idea how to begin.

I stabbed my cigarette out. *Focus! Christ, Smith,* focus. I closed my eyes, opened them. All right, yes, I had one idea, one thin thread. Lydia's phone. I knew fuck-all about cell phones, but I knew hers had a GPS. Even if this bastard trashed the phone, if he didn't pulverize the chip, could it still be traced?

I had no idea. But I knew someone who did.

I loaded my .38 and strapped on my shoulder rig. I checked the GPS on my own phone, made sure it was off. I didn't know how hard or easy it would be to follow me that way, but if it was possible, I didn't want it done.

I clattered down the two flights from my place to the street. At the bottom I took a breath, stepped outside. Nothing. Which is what I'd expected. Chances were he wasn't waiting to take a shot at me. What would have been the point of calling, of grabbing Lydia, then? But when your nerves run high you can plow into some bad mistakes. I'd done it before. I wasn't going to do it now.

It was morning, late fall, bright, cold, quiet. Braced for trouble, I looked around. Was he here, was he watching? That would mean Lydia was close, too. Across the street a guy rolled kegs into a truck. Two hipsters rounded the corner and a stocky woman trotted past the other way. No one seemed interested in me and I didn't find trouble. But I found an orange plastic bag dangling from the doorknob of my street door.

It could just be garbage someone was too lazy to carry to the corner. So they chose my shadowed doorway from all the places on the block, to leave it? Maybe. But "get down to it," the voice had told me twice. A peculiar phrase. And when I got down—downstairs—nothing was out of place, but this.

I unhooked the bag and went through the contents, only touching things on their edges. Maybe it was just garbage: a crumpled Starbucks cup, a punched Amtrak ticket stub, an empty American Spirit pack, a grocery store receipt. You drink your coffee, clean out your pockets, shove your trash in a bag.

And hang it on my door?

I took the bag and headed along the block.

Carefully. Even if he wasn't here, he might have someone working with him. At the corner I crossed against the light, watched to see if anyone else was in a big hurry, too. No one was. I jogged to the subway, got on an uptown train, rode two stops and at the third jumped off as the doors closed. No one fought through after me, so I climbed to the street, satisfied I was alone.

I came out on Sixth Avenue in the Village. While I searched for what I needed—a working pay phone—I tried to focus, to calm down. My skin, blood, the air I breathed were crackling. If I didn't get a hold of myself I'd be no good to anyone. No good to Lydia.

On the courts behind the Fourth Street fence a basketball snapped from passer to cutter, who kicked it out for the shot and score. Like *that,* I told myself. This bastard says it's a game. Narrow the heat, concentrate it, the way you do in a game. The way you do at the piano. Nothing matters, nothing *exists,* but this.

I lit a cigarette and drew in smoke.

Lydia had been telling me something.

It was like her to want her mother not to worry, not to know she was in trouble. But there was no point in heading off a call from Tony, her brother Andrew's boyfriend, asking where she'd been. He knew. She'd been at his party. That party was two weeks ago.

Looks like I'm going to miss Tony's party, she'd said. No, not exactly. She'd stammered: *Looks like Tony, his party, looks like I'll miss it.*

Looks like Tony.

The son of a bitch looked like Tony.

I almost let out a whoop right there on the sidewalk. Go, Lydia, go! What else? *He'll have to get a little older without me.*

A little older.

So. This bastard was big. Short hair. Ripped bodybuilder muscles. In his late thirties—a little older than Tony.

And, *He already thinks I'm a ditz.* Not Tony; Tony knew better. The lunatic. She'd set him up to underestimate her.

I felt my breathing even out, my shoulders loosen.

In this nightmare, Lydia someone's prisoner, my job to find her by doing I didn't know what, the person I'd most want working with me was Lydia.

And it seemed she was.

Here was a phone. I pushed my quarters in and punched the silver buttons.

"Wong Security." I was surprised to hear a woman's voice, but I didn't have time to care.

"Let me speak to Linus. It's Bill Smith."

"Mr. Wong is busy at the moment—"

"Tell him *now.* His cousin Lydia's in trouble."

A moment later: "Dude! Hey, what's goin' on?"

"It's bad, Linus. It's Lydia." I gave him a brief rundown: robot voice, Lydia's phone, orange plastic bag.

"Oh, shit! Dude, that's wack! Lydia, man? I'll kill that freak!"

"I need your help."

"Anything, dude. But first, where you calling from? A phone he could know?"

"No, a pay phone. Outside my neighborhood."

"Good thinking."

Any other time, that would have made me laugh: praise from a tech head barely old enough to vote.

I asked, "Can you trace her phone? He said he was trashing it. But the GPS—"

"Gotcha. If he doesn't smash it, yeah. If I can't, at least maybe I can find the cell tower. You know, closest to where the call came from. What service does she use?"

A truck's air brakes blasted and I jumped. "Jesus, Linus, I don't know! How the hell am I supposed to know that?"

"Hey, dude, chill out! I'm trying to help here."

I rubbed my eyes. "Yeah. Sorry. I don't know what she uses, but I use Verizon. She gave me the phone, so probably—"

"'K. I have a dude at Verizon, I'll get on it."

"And no cops, Linus."

"Dude! This is me you're talking to! Cops. Where are you?"

"In the Village."

"*Where,* dude? I'm coming there."

"No, you're not. This guy's dangerous, whoever he is, and if he got over on Lydia, he's smart, too."

"Whatever. You're not doing this alone. You know that's what Cousin Lydia would say."

"She wouldn't say, *Get my kid cousin involved.*"

"Yeah, but you did that already, so too late."

"Linus—"

"Dude! The shit in that plastic bag: you got any idea what it means?"

"No," I admitted.

"See? You need fresh eyes. I got 'em."

"It could just be garbage."

"He said he'd leave clues."

"Tracing that phone is the most important thing right now."

"What, and you think I have to be here to do it? Seriously? Why do you think they call it a mobile phone?"

I looked up and down the street. People walking, talking, going about their business. On the court, a basketball went up, a sweet arc, but it rimmed out. I asked Linus, "You have a car?"

"What's that, the price of admission? Yeah, I do."

"Okay, you're in." I looked around. "There's a coffee shop on West Third by the basketball courts. I'll meet you there."

In the twenty minutes before Linus blew through the diner's door I had three cups of coffee punctuated by a trip outside for a smoke. I tried Lydia's phone twice but it got me nothing. If anyone had come near me I'd have punched him; if I'd had any idea what to do or where to go I wouldn't have stayed. But I was as lost as could be.

I worked Lydia's description over and over in my mind, and the robot voice, and the words. I couldn't get close.

The bag, then. I could send it and the junk in it to a private lab to test for prints, but that would take time and anything they found I'd have to get a cop somewhere to run for me. Likely there wasn't much. Who wouldn't know not to leave prints? Or even more likely: even if this crap was clues, none of it was his. He'd dug it out of the garbage and it had prints all over it, a dozen different strangers' prints. That's how I'd do it, if it were me.

When had the bag been left? Anytime last night, this morning. I hadn't been out since around midnight; it's a shadowed doorway. How long had this bastard had Lydia? No way to know. Unless she could tell me.

The diner's door opened. Linus Wong glanced around, spotted me, slid into my booth. He was dressed skateboard-ready, baggy cargo pants and a short-sleeved tee over a long-sleeved one. His hair was buzzed short sides, long top, and he had a gold earring in his left ear. When I first met Linus, four years ago, he was a high-IQ high-schooler, always in trouble because hacking was more fun than history class, video games better than gym. After a fistful of suspensions, two expulsions, and a larceny charge—eventually dropped—for changing the entire junior class's grades to As, he fought the school system to a draw, got a GED, and last year set up an e-security firm in his parents' Flushing home.

"Dude," he greeted me.

A thin young woman had come in behind him and now slipped in beside him. She had a few inches and maybe a few years on him, meaning in this state she was old enough to drink. She wore spiked blond hair, thick black boots and a short plaid skirt, multiple eyebrow- and earrings, plus a stud in her nose, but none of those was what I noticed first. First came her electric blue eyes. Next was the air she carried: the tight-coiled joy of a runner at the starting blocks.

"Who's this?" I said.

She gave me a sharp grin. "Trella." This was the voice that had answered the phone.

"Friend of mine," Linus said. "She's good at stuff."

Before I could speak the waiter appeared, finally hopeful for more from this booth than the tip on a cup of coffee. Linus ordered a Coke. Trella asked for coffee and coconut cake. "With the cherries," she said. "Not the plain one." I'd been watching the dessert carousel go around for twenty minutes; I knew everything in it. I hadn't seen Trella, walking past, give it so much as a glance.

"Couldn't find the phone," Linus said. "That chip must be history."

"Shit!"

"But my dude found the tower. Number 378V72, lower Manhattan. Fulton and Church."

"That means the call came from near there?"

"Six blocks in each direction. But that was, what, an hour ago?"

Meaning: the haystack, though still huge, had gotten smaller. But the needle might have been moved.

"The voice, Linus. Electronically distorted. Does that mean he's someone like you?"

Linus looked at me blankly. "Like me, what?"

Trella rolled her eyes. "Like you, what. No," she said to me. "That's a voice modulator. You can get one at Best Buy."

The waiter clattered cups and plates onto our table. Linus said, "What else you got?"

"Lydia told me what he looks like." I repeated what she'd said and what I thought it meant.

"Yes!" Linus pumped his fist. He turned to Trella. "See? I said you'd like her."

Trella leaned forward, glowing eyes on me. "So what does it tell you?"

I could only shake my head.

"No idea at all, dude?" Linus asked. "Zero, nada, none?"

Trella said musingly, "If you heard him talk—"

"I told you, the voice—"

"Not the voice. His phrases, how he strings words together. A voice modulator doesn't change that. And you know kind of what he looks like. But you still don't know." As she spoke she dumped spoonfuls of sugar into her coffee. She stopped at eight, sipped, and added another. "Then it's got to be someone from a long time ago. But he's only coming at you now."

"He was in jail!" Linus said. "He was locked up and he just got out! Man, that would suck, being locked up. No wonder he's pissed at you, if you did it." Linus, who'd spent half his childhood grounded, spoke with authority.

"I had the same thought," I said. "But I still—"

"That's why he didn't just kill you." Trella looked up suddenly. "Or her."

"What?"

"He doesn't just want you dead. You made him suffer over a period of time, and now he wants you to. That's why the game. That's why the clock."

"Who did you send to jail, dude? That's your business, right, sending freaks to jail?"

"More than one guy. Some of them I probably don't even know about."

"Give me a break. How can you not know?"

I clenched my teeth to keep from snapping at him. Why would these kids know this? "What I do, half the time you never learn the outcome. A lawyer, a relative, someone hires you to track something down. You find it, turn it over to the client, that's it. If it helps put someone away, he might blame you, but you might never know."

"It may not be a professional thing, anyway," Trella said. "And it might not be he was in jail. Maybe somebody whose wife you slept with or something. Broke his heart, took him years to plot revenge. Or someone who went into the army to get away from you."

Linus gulped Coke. "Into the *army*? Dudess—"

"I'm just saying. Lots of possibilities. This is getting us nowhere. Let's see what's in the bag."

I'd been over the contents of the plastic bag at least a thousand times while I'd been waiting. I still harbored the suspicion it was someone's garbage. But I didn't have a better idea. I dumped it out on the table. "Don't touch it," I said. "There's a lab I use, I'm going to messenger it over. Maybe there are prints."

The two of them exchanged an *oh please* glance. "No one's that dumb anymore," Trella said.

"I have to check anyway."

"Whatever."

"That Amtrak ticket's to Philadelphia," Linus said. "You think you're supposed to go to Philadelphia?"

"And do what when I get there?"

Trella craned her neck. "Where's the receipt from?"

"Fairway."

"Which Fairway?"

"You mean, Broadway or Harlem? It doesn't say."

"Or Red Hook."

"There's a Fairway in Red Hook?" Fairway's a legendary New York market. For half a century there was only one; then they opened another, in an old warehouse in Harlem. But Red Hook?

"Red Hook's cool, man," Linus informed me. "Art galleries and shit. Cutting-edge yuppieville. About to be, you know, the place to be."

Trella, still focused on the table, shook her head. "Won't happen. It was hip for a while, but the minute Manhattan got affordable again, those yuppies were outta there." She frowned; the hardware in her eyebrows shifted. "But they do have a Fairway." She pointed her fork at the receipt. "He bought milk and sugar."

"For his coffee?" Linus gestured skeptically at the crumpled cup. "At Starbucks they give you that."

"Coffey Street," I said. Both kids looked at me. "There's a Coffey Street in Red Hook."

"Dude, I thought you didn't know about Red Hook."

"Not about cutting-edge yuppieville. When I was a kid in Brooklyn we used to drink in Red Hook. Out there we didn't get carded."

"Do people know that about you?"

"I don't know who knows. It's no big deal but it's not something I keep secret."

"So this guy could know."

I regarded Linus. My finger went to a scar beside my eye. "I got this in a fight out there. Four stupid Irish kids in a waterfront bar, trying to prove how tough we were. I almost lost the eye. I tell the story sometimes if I'm drinking with guys and they start looking for someone to punch."

"That bar—was it on Coffey Street?"

"No."

Linus deflated.

Trella tapped her fork against her front teeth. "I wonder what is? Look, guys. Suppose we're right, he means Red Hook and he means Coffey Street. So what about these?" She waved the fork over the ticket and the cigarette pack.

Linus had his iPhone out. He swiped his finger across the screen a couple of times. "Shit! No street view."

"What are you doing?"

"Google maps, dude." He turned the phone to me. On its screen was a map of Red Hook. Some streets were traced in blue, but not Coffey. "Street View, we could've seen what's there. But let me try something else. Maybe there's a place on Coffey Street named Philadelphia." A few more swipes. He shook his head. "Maybe American Spirit." He started to poke at the iPhone again, but I stopped him.

"No. Try one forty-three. The number, one forty-three." The

biggest print on an Amtrak ticket doesn't give you the station, the price, or the date; it's the train number.

"One forty-three Coffey Street," Linus said. "It's a bar. A hookah bar. Fatima's. Says here, full bar, Middle Eastern food." He looked up. "Strong Turkish coffee." Back to his screen: "Individual and group hookahs. Twenty-two kinds of tobacco. Whoa, dudes! Says, all pure, all premium. No additives."

We were out of there in seconds, me dropping bills on the table and sweeping the trash back into the bag.

That's the claim to fame of American Spirit cigarettes: pure, premium tobacco. No additives.

3

There was only one car on the block outside the diner: a decrepit Ford Fairlane in a no parking zone.

I said to Linus, "Give me the keys."

"No way, dude."

"Especially no way, dude, because it's my car," said Trella.

"If we're right and this lunatic is there—"

"Then you need someone to watch your back."

"I don't want you kids anywhere near him."

"Let me put it this way." Trella faced me, deadpan. "I'm going to Red Hook. You can come with, or not. You could take the subway, but this'll be faster. Or you could take a cab. But I drive better." She yanked open the driver's side door. Linus raised his eyebrows at me and got in the shotgun seat. After a second, I climbed in the back and hadn't shut the door before Trella rocketed away from the curb.

"You know how to get there?"

In the mirror Trella threw me the look you'd give to someone asking if you knew how to spell your own name.

The streets of Manhattan, the Brooklyn Battery Tunnel, the BQE, all about a thousand miles long. It nearly killed me to be sitting in the back, not gunning the engine, not cornering, passing, getting there. But for the same reason I hadn't called Linus from my home phone or my cell, I wasn't about to use my own car. It was a safe bet the guy at least knew what I drove, and for all I knew he'd bugged it. If we were right about Fatima's, he knew I was coming. This way, though, maybe he wouldn't know when I arrived.

Jittery as I was, a part of me was watching how adroitly Trella drove. She took the route I'd have taken and she took it fast, weaving, jumping lights, pushing the edge but not so far we risked getting stopped. The car's body was a wreck, the suspension was shot, but the engine purred. Trella shifted smoothly, probed the traffic ahead, sliced through gaps cleanly when she found them. Linus, belted in beside her, sat relaxed, never tensing or pulling away the way passengers sometimes do when the driver goes fast and cuts close. I guessed they rode together a lot, and I guessed she always drove.

Linus, fiddling with his phone, said, "Dudes. This Fatima's? Looks like it's closed. Lots of sad posts on iDine."

"When?" I asked.

"About a year ago. Must've been hot, people missing it a lot. Doesn't look like anything else opened there yet."

After that, no one spoke. Trella stayed focused as a surgeon. Linus watched the world fly by. I sat forward, chainsmoking through the fifteen-minute eternity from lower Manhattan to Red Hook. When I lit the first one, Trella narrow-eyed me in the mirror, but instead of saying anything she hit the master button and lowered all the windows.

Finally we were off the BQE, onto Columbia, up to Coffey. As we crossed Van Brunt I said, "Roll down the block, slowly, like you're lost. Don't pay attention to the place and don't slow down when we pass it."

I wanted an idea, the lay of the land. The bastard was expecting me, but he might not be expecting two teenagers in an ancient Ford, probably lost on their way to Red Hook Park to buy dope. Me, I was just the shadow in the backseat.

If a gentrification wave had broken over Red Hook, it had receded leaving no mark I could see. Single- and two-family houses, scattered four- or five-story apartment buildings, empty lots. Brick, or wood siding, or asphalt shingles hammered on when the wood began to rot. Everything I saw was what I'd seen when, younger than these kids, I used to come here looking for trouble.

Whatever cutting-edge yuppiedom had planted its flag here must be centered on Van Brunt, the commercial avenue. Only the most optimistic would open a bar on a side street. But apparently Fatima had been a hopeful sort. One block up, two buildings from the corner, we passed it.

Hopes can get dashed. This was a dusty and derelict place. Kept company on one side by a weed-choked lot, the three-story building nestled on the other side against its larger neighbor and dreamed of vanished glory. In the front window, ghostly through grime, an unlit neon hookah floated; in each of the upstairs windows, a smaller painted version of the same hookah flaked off the glass.

From across the street I could see the heavy chain and padlock on Fatima's front door. What I couldn't see was any point in trying it. At the corner, on my direction, Trella turned right; at the next corner, right again. I said, "Stop. Let me out here. And you guys stay away."

Without a word, Trella pulled to the curb.

I got out and headed down the block. Gentrification or not, in the middle of the morning Red Hook's streets were still empty. No one was in sight when I reached my goal, a one-story building I'd spotted from around the block through the overgrowth of Fatima's empty side lot. Set back from the line of front stoops, flanked by a pair of dark, narrow alleys separating it from the houses on either side, it looked to have started life as a garage. A spray-paint mural on the roll-down door and a giant sheet-metal rat on the roof announced it was an artist's studio now. The artist wasn't here, though. The psychedelic door was locked tight—I knocked, then tried the handle—but before he'd gone off the good citizen had put his recycling cans out. I recycled one into a ladder: hauled it beside the building, climbed on, grabbed the roof's edge, and swung myself up. I crouched, inched across the tar paper, crunching scraps of tin and glops of solder. I passed under the rat's haunch and, at the back of the building, dropped to my belly to give Fatima's the once-over.

The concrete apron behind the defunct bar was strewn with rusting carcasses of ductwork and kitchen equipment. Weeds like a fountain sprouted in a stack of tires. But I saw what I'd been hoping to see. Clipped to the back of the building, Fatima's had a fire escape.

I swing over the edge and dropped into the studio's slim backyard, scrambled up and over the chain-link, and dashed across the overgrown side lot. If the lunatic was watching the back he'd see me easily, but I was banking on him expecting me to come from the street.

If we were right, and the bag on my doorknob was anything besides someone's garbage, and he was here at all.

The ladder from Fatima's fire escape hung too high for me to reach. The metal wreckage in the backyard would clank and scrape if I tried to drag it over, but there were those tires. I could climb on them. The weeds bowed as I pulled the tires off and piled them under the ladder. I had to hope the top hook was good enough that when I grabbed the ladder, it would hold. Those ladders are made to drop when that hook's released and when they drop they make a hell of a clang. But there was nothing to do except hope, breathe, and jump, so I did.

The ladder shook but it didn't move. My arms shook, too, as I hauled myself up the half dozen rungs it took to get a foothold. When I got to the platform I crossed fast, took the rusted steel stairs to the next platform two at a time. I was thinking to go in at the top. That way, wherever he was—and I was betting, on the ground floor, just inside the door—I'd have both surprise and height.

At the top of the fire escape I flattened against the wall and inched to the window, peered around the jamb. Soot streaks clouded the glass but the room was a floor-through and sun slanted in the windows in the far wall. It didn't show me much: curved lumps of abandoned furniture, exhausted drapery on a bent curtain rod. It was the desolate end of someone's dream but it was all as still as a photograph and that's what I wanted to know.

This had been a bar, and the fire escape was its emergency exit. By law, when the place was functioning, these windows had to be unlocked. Had anyone cared enough, when Fatima's dream ended, to lock them up before walking away? Gently, I tried the flaking wood window frame. The window rode up without protest, too dispirited to care.

I eased over the sill, gun drawn. Nothing moved. No one burst out suddenly, no one dove through the weightless dust to slam me, throw me down. My own pounding heatbeat was the only sound. Motionless, I surveyed the room: floor cushions velvety with dust; beaded lamps and beat-up chairs; a low table where a hookah sat with its mouthpiece tubes curved, perky, pathetically ready. A sagging railing on the left showed me where the stair was. Beyond it, a sofa faced the front window. If someone were hiding in this room, that would be the only place. I took wary steps that way, had my gun out straight as I drew close enough to see over the sofa's high back.

Someone was there.

Someone was lying there, face down. A woman, in jeans and a black leather jacket. One hand over her head, fingers tangled in her short, black, Asian hair.

Blood rushing in my ears, I stepped around the sofa, knelt beside her, touched her.

Ice.

I put a hand on her shoulder and I hesitated. I didn't want to turn her over. I didn't want to know.

As though hypnotized, as though my hand were someone else's, I did turn her, toward me, slowly, gently. Sunlight bouncing off the floor showed me her face. It was twisted in pain.

And it wasn't Lydia.

My heart slammed to a stop, then started again, double-time. I sprang up, spun, gun raised, swung it left, right. He had to be here. He'd have wanted to see this. Where was he? But no. Not in the shadows, not in the slanting light. No creak of footsteps on the stairs, no searing laugh. I was alone.

Bending to the body, I took her pulse. No help for her. I looked her over. On her agonized face, blue eye shadow, dark lipstick. Beneath the leather jacket, a soft red sweater; red stitching on the jeans, and red sneakers, one on her foot, one on the floor. No purse. Who was she? *I'm sorry. I'm sorry.*

I stood. The bastard might be here yet, downstairs, waiting. Or maybe he'd never been here. Maybe *I* wasn't here. A vertigo of unreality unsteadied me. An Asian woman, a stranger, dead where I'd expected to find Lydia, where I'd come based on paper-trash oracle bones read in a diner with help from a hacker and a girl Goth. Maybe this was a bourbon-fueled nightmare and would be over as soon as the distant sirens I was hearing got close and loud enough to wake me.

They got close, they got loud, they cut off as the squad car with its flashing lights squealed to a stop in front of Fatima's. I wiped away window grime, saw a cop charge around to the back while another stood, gun drawn, at the padlocked front door. For a brief moment, nothing. Then a shout, the guy in the back yelling to his partner. He'd found my pile of tires, seen the open window.

The cop in front strode to the car, spoke into the radio. Then he straightened, clicked on the traffic-stop loudspeaker, looked up at the building. Straight at me, if behind the grime and the painted hookah, in the shadows, he could have seen me. "You up there! Police! Come out. Hands empty and where I can see them."

I searched the tin ceiling. Was there a hatch, a way to the roof? I didn't find one. And what if there was? The building next door was a floor taller. The empty lot was thirty feet down.

I heard a thump, felt a shake.

The cop in the back had leapt for the fire escape.

He shouldn't have done that. He was supposed to wait for his backup. A growing siren told me they were on the way.

Pressed in the shadows beside the rear window I'd climbed in, I watched him do what I'd done: edge to the window, peer around the jamb. He saw the same stillness and he did the same thing:

climbed over the sill, gun out. But he held his as per regs—two-handed, stiff-armed—so my Colt smashed both his wrists when I swung it down. He started to yowl. I didn't want noise so I kicked him in the stomach, knocked his wind out. I sprinted for the window, flew down the fire escape. I didn't bother with the ladder, just leapt over the side of the lower landing. I jarred my bones on the cracked concrete, jumped up, and had made it to the artist's fence ready to climb when the yard filled with cops.

4

Nothing worked, but I had no right to expect it to. I told them I was a PI. They took my gun. I told them I had no idea who the dead girl was, when or why she died. They cuffed me. I told them I had just found her, it had thrown me, and when the cop showed up, armed, I took him for the lunatic I'd been tailing. Since the cop was in his blues that was thin, and since he was standing on the fire escape, unable to climb down, holding both swollen wrists close to his chest, one of his buddies punched me for him. I pulled my head back, rode with it, but I still got the stars, would get an ache in my jaw as soon as my adrenaline cleared and let other sensations through. I braced for another but the sergeant, on the radio calling for the detectives, the ambulance, and the crime scene team, grabbed the buddy cop's arm. He growled, "There's windows everywhere, Collins. Just walk him to the car." His eyes told me I was goddamn lucky about the windows.

Collins vised on to my arm. He and the injured cop's partner, the guy who'd been at the front, hustled me through the side lot. Weeds pulled at our ankles. The injured cop was still on the fire escape and the sergeant stayed in the yard to keep an eye on his man, and on the exit route of anyone inside. Both cops stayed out of the windows' line of fire because they hadn't searched the lower floors yet and it was possible the lunatic was still there, though they were pretty casual about it because they didn't believe in the lunatic: they thought he was me.

I hadn't told them about the call, the laugh, the game, Lydia. I'd have to decide what to do fast, though. The no-cops rule had been broken in a big way; I wondered if the bastard knew that, and what he planned to do about it. Whether or not he knew, while they kept me on ice—and assaulting a cop can get you on ice for a long time—the clock was ticking. Nearly two of my twelve hours gone, and I was nowhere.

There was one cop I could count on to believe me, a cop I'd have called at the beginning if I hadn't been worried the anonymous madman might have some kind of pipeline into the department, might find out somehow: Lydia's best friend, Mary Kee. She was a Fifth Precinct detective. I wasn't sure she'd be able to spring me loose but I couldn't think of anything else that might.

"I need to make a call," I said.

"That comes a lot later, asswipe." Collins yanked me forward.

"If you're arresting me it comes now. If you're not, take off the cuffs, I'm leaving." I stopped walking, tried to tug out of his grip.

He brought his nose close to mine, exhaled tobacco breath. "Now hear this, motherfucker. Next move you make, if it's not into the car, it's interfering with an officer in the performance of my duties and I *will* break your head. You're not being arrested. You're being detained. Get in the fucking car."

I knew what this was about: the longer they held me without charging me, the more pressure would build. When the detectives finally showed I could demand to be arrested or released and they'd have to do one or the other, but these guys in blue were well within procedure to shove me in the car for now. And the detectives could take as long as they wanted at the crime scene before they talked to me.

Which meant if I got in that car I could be there, caged, silenced, and useless, for hours.

"What I was doing here," I said. "Someone's life depends on my finishing it."

"What about that girl? Her life depend on it, too?"

"I didn't kill her. I—"

"You know what? Shut the fuck up."

"Let me see the sergeant." It wasn't that I thought the sergeant would believe whatever I said—which, keeping in mind the no-cops rule, would be what? I didn't know—but to cover his own ass on the off chance I was telling the truth, he'd likely pass me up the line. That would mean having the detectives talk to me as soon as they got here.

"Sergeant don't want to see you." Collins slipped his baton loose, pulled on my arm again. I didn't budge. He glanced up; I could see him weighing the windows everywhere against the joy of bashing my skull. I was aware of taking a big risk for not much reward. The best this could buy me was a talk with the sergeant. The more likely outcome was I'd get caged in the radio car anyhow, battered and bruised, and still waiting, still useless. I just couldn't think of another way to play it.

But little miracles happen every day.

An engine roared down beyond the end of Coffey Street. At first I saw nothing; then a blur as a car raced by up Van Brunt, some testosterone-hopped kid grandstanding for his friends. Laying down rubber, the car vanished behind the buildings on the corner. Then a screech, a thud, squealing metal, tinkling glass. A horn blared, wouldn't stop. Sirens, buzzers, and beeps exploded from impact-triggered car alarms all up and down the block. Traffic in both directions started to pile up. Drivers too far back to see what had happened or too callous to care leaned on their horns.

"Fuck!" The injured cop's partner stared at the traffic mess. "Stay with him!" Collins nodded, tightened his grip on my arm as the other cop charged off. The sergeant swung around the corner of Fatima's lot to see what was happening, looked at Collins, and ran off that way, too.

Well, all right. Saying a prayer for the grandstanding kid, that he was uninjured and would also win the lottery, I snapped my leg and kicked Collins in the nuts.

He made a strangled noise and folded. I kicked him in the chin for insurance and took off running in the opposite direction. When I hit the corner I spun right, pounding pavement, hoping anyone interested in anything in this neighborhood was interested in the car-crash racket a block over. At the next corner I cut right again. I was hoping Trella and Linus had stayed put, but I must have used up my miracle quota. The block was empty. Likely they were down on Van Brunt, gawking: what kid could resist screeching rubber and shattering glass?

Which left the problem of the handcuffs. Working cuffed hands from back to front when you're my size is close to impossible. I'd tried it once when I was much younger, managed it, but almost dislocated my shoulder. I'd do that again if I had to, but maybe I didn't have to.

I ran full-tilt down the block back to the rat-adorned studio of my artist benefactor, where I slipped into the alley between it and the house next door. I was remembering the scraps all over the roof, hoping the guy was too monomaniacally galvanized by creative energy to clean up anywhere.

Was he ever. The alley, shadowed and tight, was littered with curls, shards, squares, and strips of tin. I dropped to the ground and felt around behind me, fingering and chucking sharp scrap until I found what I needed: a thin, narrow band. Manuevering was awkward but I'm a pianist. The rest of me is getting older, stiffer, but my fingers still move. It took under a minute to slip the shim under the pawl and jack the left cuff open.

I brought my hands around, popped the other cuff. Still on the ground, I took out my cell phone to call Mary Kee, see if I could cut a way out of this.

When I turned the phone on the first thing it did was beep that I'd missed a call. There was no message. My heart pounded. I hit callback, but the number was restricted and the call didn't go through.

Cursing, I thumbed my contact list for Mary's number. It had just come up when a black-windowed Escalade rolled across the mouth of the alley and stopped. I froze, there in the shadows, waited for the car to drive on. It went nowhere. Instead, its door slid open and disgorged two gigantic Asian men, one with a shaved head, one with a ponytail. Moving as inexorably as fate itself, they converged on my alley.

I took off but it was all over fast. The alley ended in the neighbor's backyard, wrapped by an incongruous plastic slat fence, too high to jump. I leapt anyway, grabbed the top, but Shaved Head tackled me, pulled me down. I had a good grip: three slats cracked, a dozen more bent.

Shaved Head must have weighed three hundred pounds, so there wasn't much point, facedown in the crabgrass, in my struggling to shake him off. But I found I was doing it anyway, until I felt the cold barrel of Ponytail's gun pressed to my temple. One of them duct-taped my hands behind my back; neither of them spoke a word. Hauling me to my feet, they hustled me up the alley to the SUV. Shaved Head had to turn sideways to fit.

The car door slid silently open again. The two giants tossed me onto the floor. Shaved Head climbed in with me, Ponytail swung in front beside the driver, and we were off.

I twisted, made it to one knee, trying to get up.

"Sit down." That casual order came from someone on the seat beside Shaved Head. Next to the giant he looked like a wraith but my bet was he was a normal-size guy. Asian, thirties, handsome square face, short slick hair. Not someone I knew.

Shaved Head prodded me with a huge round boot, not hard, just translating. "Mr. Lu said sit down." His voice rumbled like the A train. He pushed me down, pinioned me between the seat back and his boulder knees.

"What the fuck?" I said.

"What the fuck is right," said the smaller guy. "What the fuck happened to Lei-lei?"

"Lei-lei?"

"Don't give me innocent, you stupid shit!"

"Wait." I was catching up with myself; maybe this did make sense. "Lei-lei? Short hair, leather jacket, jeans, red Keds?"

"That why you killed her, you didn't like her shoes?"

"I didn't kill her."

"Fuck you didn't. All I want to know, you do it for kicks because you're some kind of sick fuck, or you're working for someone?" Shaved Head had spoken with a Chinese accent but all I could detect in Lu was Great Lakes, Milwaukee maybe. A homegrown businessman employing immigrants: it would've warmed my heart if I hadn't had other things to think about.

"I didn't kill her. Some lunatic did, and he's going to kill a friend of mine if I don't find him."

"A lunatic? A fucking *lunatic*? Oh, shit! Ming, what do you think? That's a good one, right?"

Either Shaved-Head-Ming chuckled or I was feeling an earthquake.

"Wait, I know," Lu went on. "You're about to say I need to let you go so you can find him! The lunatic. Am I right? I like it. I haven't heard it before." He leaned forward, eyes black ice. "The find-the-lunatic part. The let-me-go part, I've heard. Now listen, you son of a bitch. I'm pissed off but I'm not unreasonable. Lei-lei was valuable. That means she had a value. You killed her—"

"No."

Ming's boot thudded into my hip, sent pain stabbing from my toe to my shoulder. The bone didn't break only because he had no room to swing that sledgehammer leg. Lu studied my reaction. He seemed satisfied, settled back on the seat. "You owe me. Now, if you're just a weirdo who kills girls for fun, that's one thing. She was young, she had some years left, she was a good earner, but I'll be honest with you, she wasn't top of the line. Net, she'd have been worth maybe another hundred thousand before I'd have had to cut her loose. What do you think, Ming? About right?"

Ming grunted assent.

Lu nodded. "If you're flush, that's great. Pay your debt, walk away. Otherwise, you can work it off. You like to hurt people, kill people, that's lucky, I can find things for you to do. You can work with Strawman and Ming."

From the front seat, without turning, Ponytail-Strawman gave a thumbs-up.

"On the other hand," Lu leaned forward again, "if you're working for someone and this was some kind of message, you better read it to me, because I don't get it."

"Look," I said. "I know how it sounds, but I was set up. I'm a PI. My wallet's in my jacket."

At a nod from Lu, Ming went through my pockets. He passed my wallet to Lu.

"This lunatic grabbed my partner," I said. "He told me I could find her at that place, that bar on Coffey Street. When I got there she wasn't there but your girl was. Dead. I need to find him." To sweeten the pot, I added, "When I do, you can have him."

Lu looked up from fingering my license, gazed at me thoughtfully. Maybe I was getting through to him.

Or maybe not. "So you're working for someone. Now tell me who." He tossed my wallet to the floor, flicked my license after it. "That Italian slob, Canelli, thinks he's Tony Soprano? Or Fatboy Cho? Ugly girls and a lot of ambition, Fatboy. Or someone else, someone new? Just tell me. And why bring her all the way out here, Red Hook or wherever the hell this is? What's that supposed to mean to me?"

"I'm not—"

"Oh, shut the fuck up!" Lu considered me. "If you were just a sick puppy, just rough trade, got a little carried away, if that were it you'd be jumping at this chance to come on board with me and work it off, doing what you like to do anyway. But you're sitting there whining about lunatics. So your boss, he's someone you're scared of. More than you are of me. Must be someone pretty impressive." He rubbed his chin. "If you think about it, can't really be Fatboy, then." Ming grinned as Lu leaned past me, tapped the driver's shoulder. "Let's go home." He settled back, spoke to Ming. "There's no room here and this may take time. Though I wonder what he's so scared of. What could his boss do to him worse than what you and Strawman can do?"

"There's no boss," I said.

Ming shook his head and tapped his lips with a warning finger the size of a dynamite stick.

"I didn't kill your girl," I said. "You can beat the crap out of me, it won't buy you anything. Or you can—"

Ming's backhand knocked me over. Before my sight cleared he'd materialized the duct tape and taped my mouth shut. I tried to twist, shove him off me; he just smiled and socked me. Through the ringing and the throbbing I saw him raise his fist: *Again?* Three hundred pounds of Ming slamming me, or not, it was my choice.

The car, which had been rolling steadily, now sped up, made a few turns, swooped downhill. I couldn't see through the blacked-out windows but when they'd tossed me in, the Escalade had been headed west and my sense, even with the turns, was we were now going north. If that was true, the swoop was the expressway, and we were going to hit the bridge any minute. My best chance, though it wasn't a good one, would be when we reached our destination and got out. Or when I came up with a way to make Lu believe me.

Or when I got another miracle.

A siren crescendoed fast from behind and a flashing red light penetrated the murky rear window. Lu's driver swore, slowed, stopped. The siren stopped, too, but the light kept flashing. Inside the car, some quick rearrangement of steel as three guns slipped into a lockbox. Lu kept his. That made him the only guy in the car with a carry permit, and no doubt the licensed owner of the other three guns. The driver rolled his window down and smiled thinly. "Something wrong, officer?"

"Let's see your license and registration, sir." It was a female cop, an emotionless, traffic-stop voice.

A voice I knew.

The driver handed his paperwork out the window to Detective Mary Kee.

5

It was a miracle, but that didn't mean it would end well. Mary ordered the driver out of the car. He looked back at Lu. I could see Lu running the calculus: waste her and speed off with me, or cooperate and try to convince her—maybe with a mix of fast talk, grease, and Asian fellow feeling—that the story on the beat-to-shit guy in the back was, they'd stumbled across a dangerous fugitive and were taking him in. If he picked door number one he'd keep me but he'd have burned a cop. Even in his business, that's got to be a bad choice. Door number two, he risked Mary taking him and his boys, too; or she might let them off, but he'd lose me, his link to his dead girl. How much did that matter?

I decided I didn't like her odds. I tried to pull away, kick something, warn her. Ming lifted off me and I thought I was getting someplace until I realized it was just for leverage. He drove his fist into my stomach and I couldn't move. Or even breathe. Choking, I fought the gray fog that rolled in, was dimly aware of Lu leaning close. "This is not the end," he whispered. "Tell your boss I'm coming for him." Then he sat up and nodded. The driver, and Strawman with him, got out. I heard Mary telling them to spread their legs, hands on the hood. She tapped on Lu's window and he powered it down.

Even in civvies, her braid swinging, even short as she is, Mary's impressive, with an in-charge cop swagger. To me, strangling on the floor of the Escalade, she was the Eighty-second Airborne. "Please step out of the vehicle, gentlemen."

Lu echoed his driver. "Is something wrong, Officer?"

Mary's voice hardened. "Please step outside." Lu climbed down, assumed the position. Ming gave me a souvenir squeeze on the windpipe, setting off a storm of tiny silent stars. Then the weight lifted from my chest as Ming followed his boss.

Mary called, "You in the car! I said you, too!" I hauled myself up, half-rolled out, half-fell. Mary watched me, no flicker of recognition or sympathy. To Lu, she said, "What's this?"

Lu didn't respond. Mary leaned down, yanked the tape from my mouth. I drew deep, heard her ask again: "What's this?"

"Rough trade," I rasped, kneeling in the gravel, trying to fill my lungs with air. "But I changed my mind. These guys aren't my type."

Mary cuffed everyone except me, collected everyone's IDs, including mine from the floor of the car, took the only gun she saw, which was Lu's, and disappeared behind her wheel. A minute later she came out. "Mr. Rough Trade," she said. "Come with me."

I staggered to her unmarked car, dropped into the back. She leaned in the window, eyes burning. An explosion was on the way, but right now all she did was ask, "Just tell me, do I arrest them?"

"No."

She strode to the Escalade, unlocked Lu's cuffs, clipped the plastic cuffs off the others, gave everyone back their IDs and Lu his gun. I heard her tell them their playmate was wanted by the NYPD, did they know that? Lu widened his eyes, *Ooh, scary.* He gave her the abashed smile of a man whose kinky pastimes had been found out, thanked her for saving him from what certainly could have been a bad situation, a wanted criminal!

"All right, you're free to go. And get that brake light fixed. I won't ticket you now but the next cop who stops you will." She gave Lu a stony stare. "Sorry for the inconvenience." From the back of her car I saw the Escalade fill, heard the doors slam, watched the perfectly intact brake lights dwindle as the car slipped into traffic and headed over the bridge.

Mary got in her front seat, turned to face me. "Now, what the hell is going on?"

"Jesus Christ, I wish I knew. Where did you come from? This can't be coincidence."

"Who told you it was? I got a call."

"You— What call?"

"A woman named Trella Bartoli. She said you were in trouble and Lydia was in worse trouble and you were in an SUV headed north along Conover in Red Hook. Gave me the plates. Said as a cop I wasn't supposed to know about this, except Linus Wong said to call me. Since as a cop I happened to know there's a warrant out on you for assaulting two officers and for homicide, I put out a call on the SUV without saying why, got a likely on it from a sector car, came over the bridge, and got lucky. Now tell me what's going on or I swear I'll call it in."

That she hadn't called it in already was the best news I'd heard in a while. I turned. "Can you take the tape off?" I knew she could. I wasn't sure she would.

"Why?" But she leaned across the seat and did it.

"I don't know how Trella knew about Lu and his boys. But what she said was true." I slumped back against the seat, slipped out a cigarette, found my hands trembling as I lit it. I pulled in that nicotine, closed my eyes, let it flow.

"No!"

My eyes snapped open at Mary's shout.

"Don't pass out on me. You're hurt, I'll take you to a hospital, but you have to tell me what's going on." She started the car.

"No. No hospital. I'm fine." She snorted at that, but turned the car off, faced me again. I rubbed my eyes. "A couple of hours ago, I got a call. Someone, I don't know who, but he's crazy, grabbed Lydia. He's holding her until I—well, now I don't know what." I ran the whole thing down for her.

Anger blazed in her eyes, the kind that flares to hide fear. "Why didn't you call me right away?"

"I don't know who he is, Mary. He could even be a cop. Or not, but have ears in the department. He said no cops. I was afraid he'd know."

"You didn't think I could've kept it quiet?"

"Of course you could. That's not the point. I couldn't afford to chance it."

"So you called a couple of teenage superheroes. Fantastic. And your friends in the Escalade?"

"Lu's a pimp. The dead girl was one of his. He thinks someone hired me to kill her as some kind of message to him, but he's not sure what it says."

"How did he find you?"

"I don't know."

Leaning over the seat back, she scowled silently for a few moments. Then: "What are you supposed to do next? To find Lydia?"

"I don't know that either. He said he'd call me, and someone did, but my phone was off and—" I stopped. My phone was ringing, not Lydia's ring, but a blocked number. I pulled it from my pocket, pressed speaker before I answered. "Smith."

"What the fuck happened?" The robotic voice, thin and tinny. "Every cop in Brooklyn is looking for you."

Mary leaned closer across the seat back.

"I didn't call them," I said.

"Why're you on speaker phone? Don't fucking tell me you're not, I can hear the echo. Who else is listening?"

My eyes met Mary's. "No one's listening. I'm driving."

"Oh. Driving what?"

"For Christ's sake, I boosted a car! Last thing I need is to get pulled over for being on the goddamn phone! Listen, I didn't call those cops."

"Cops, cops, cops. Yessiree, that place sure was swarming with cops. Maybe I should have said 'no cops.' Oh, wait! I did! Didn't I? *Didn't* I, asshole?"

"They weren't my idea. Someone must have seen me on the fire escape."

"Why so defensive? Oh! I bet you think I'm mad! Well, it was a rule, wasn't it? No cops? You think maybe I killed your girlfriend just now, because of all those the cops? Shot her? Sliced her up? Beat her brains out? Or maybe I did all three, and there was blood everywhere. Everywhere! Or maybe there wasn't any blood, everything was neat and clean because I fed her rat poison on a spoon, like poor little Lei-lei. You think I did that? Do you? Which one do you think?"

Blood everywhere. Or no blood. Lei-lei's agonized face, but not Lei-lei's. "*You*—" All I could get out was that one strangled word.

He laughed. "Oh, relax. God, you're a nervous wreck! I'm just messing with you. Your girlfriend's right here, she's fine. Aren't you, sweetie? I know you didn't call the cops, asshole. I did."

My heart started up again. "I—what—put Lydia on."

"I don't know. That was supposed to be a reward, for doing something right. What you did, you made a big fucking mess. Though I suppose it's true, you did find the place. Hey, did you like my clues?"

"Let me talk to her."

"You didn't answer me."

"They were great. Brilliant. Let me talk to her."

"And fair? They were fair, right? Because I know you like to play fair."

"Put Lydia on or I'm out of here."

"Fuck! Look at that! Swings his dick around even when he's losing."

I clicked off.

Mary straightened in shock. "*What are you—*"

"He'll be back," I said, and the phone rang again.

"Do not fucking do that." The robotic voice froze the air. "Ever."

"Fuck you." I gave back the same ice, though I was feeling the opposite. "I don't talk to Lydia, you can go to hell."

"Hey." His tone turned conciliatory. "Come on, bro, where's your sense of humor? Take everything so seriously, that's what's wrong with you. You gotta lighten up, get in the spirit. I was gonna give her to you, what, you thought I wasn't? Here, honey, it's for you."

A short pause, then Lydia. "Bill?"

Hearing Lydia's voice, Mary bolted upright.

"You okay?" I asked Lydia.

"Yes. I'm still almost completely in the dark, though."

"Me, too. But don't worry. It'll be over soon. I got to Tony, by the way." To let her know I'd understood.

"Good. I'm trying not to get really down here."

"Are you—" I started, but the robot voice returned, a knife in my gut.

"Oooh, princess is getting depressed? Honey, cheer up, your prince is coming. Or he's trying, anyway. He works so hard, you know. Even on shit that's none of his business! So just think how hard he's working on this. But listen, Prince Asshole: now you have to wait. I expected you to be tied up a couple hours. I should've known you'd cheat. Didn't get you anywhere, though. Now I don't have your next clues ready."

"What does that mean, 'next clues'?"

"Come on, asshole, the game, the game!"

"There's more?"

"Of fucking course, there's more! The prize is your girlfriend and you haven't found her yet, have you? So we're still playing. That's okay, right? You're still in? Because if you want to stop, I can always—"

"No. I'm in."

"Sweet. And you still don't know who I am? Do you? Asshole?"

"No. You want to tell me?"

"That's a fucking joke, right? Shit, this is fun!"

"Then tell me something else. You called the cops? Why?"

"Oh, just to screw with you. Minute I knew you found that po' ho, I dropped a dime. How'd you like that, by the way? That was pretty good, right, the girl on the sofa like that? Did you think it was your girlfriend? Admit it, you did, didn't you? That was pretty good. Poor Lei-lei, not nearly as cute as she used to be. I didn't know rat poison twists up your face like that! Must've hurt. Remind me not to go that way."

I pushed away the memory of that room, Lei-lei's face. *Keep him talking.* Make him give something up. "Seems to me calling the cops—"

"Oh, to you, to you, it seems to you! Everything is you! Don't you know there's no 'I' in team? Mostly, asshole, I called them so they'd take you in, make you sweat over some dead chink ho. They had nothing on you—no *evidence,* you follow me?—so they'd cut you loose sooner or later. Probably you even have an alibi for when poor little Lei-lei died. Besides, you're tight with cops, I know you are. They'd just shake your hand, let you go. Or maybe, some trigger-happy ADA would indict you, but you'd make bail. Delay of game, but no real effect."

That was far from the likely outcome, if the cops had taken me in, but I didn't argue with his dreamworld. "You said 'mostly.' What was the rest?"

"Oh, so smart, see how he picks up on a single word! Come on, shitbrain, you're such a freaking genius, figure it out. Maybe you can get bonus points or something. Go on."

"Screw that."

"No, for real. You figure it out, I'll buy your girlfriend a sandwich. Or some chop suey. She must be getting hungry by now. What about it, honey? You feel like you could eat something?"

I couldn't hear Lydia's answer; I couldn't hear much through the surf-roar of my own blood in my ears. When I had control of my voice I said, "All right. If that's a deal."

"Oh, sure, not a problem. Maybe we'll get a pizza, I could use a snack myself. So, what's your theory?"

"Well," I said slowly, "it can't be an accident the girl you killed was Chinese."

"Hey! Hey, good! No, not an accident. Go on."

"That way," I was thinking out loud, "you could be pretty sure I wouldn't tell them about you taking Lydia."

"Because . . . ?"

"Because they find me with a dead Chinese girl, I try to tell them it's all some crazy game because someone kidnapped my Chinese partner, what happens is they start thinking I killed Lydia, too."

"Whoa! Right outta the park. You got it, fuckface. I don't trust you. I said no cops, but you cheat. You might've called them anyway. So now this way, you'll think twice before you go ahead and tell them about us." The metallic voice deepened. "'Look at this, Sergeant Friday. Found this mofo with a dead chink ho, a bag of shit, and a lame kidnap story. Making him play a game! Your mama, buddy. You get off on killing chinks, that's it, right? Now where is she, your girlfriend? What did you do to her? Friday, you got that rubber hose?'" A pause. "No, on second thought, maybe you'd better leave the *po*-lice out of it. Good for you, jerkoff. You get the bonus points and cutie here gets lunch. But I gotta tell you—what you pulled, it was awesome and I didn't see it coming. *You* had to escape! Whaling on cops! What a dickwad. So now it's even better. Now you can't *go* to the cops plus you have to *dodge* them! Screwed the pooch on that one!"

"How do you know what happened? You were watching?"

"Hah! Hahaha! Slip that in, see if I'll give up where I am? Screw you."

"Hope you left that crime scene really, really clean. Because when they find your fingerprints, your footprints—"

"Oh, no, not that CSI shit! Come on, idiot, that was a *bar,* back in the day. Hot! Jumping! Have to be thousands of prints everywhere. And hairs and whatever else they look for except, *except,* they won't be looking. Way expensive, that lab shit, you know? And so-o-o-o many cases, bodies popping up all over New York every day. Poor little Lei-lei was only a hooker—and they already know who killed her! *You,* motherfucker! The way I set it up, you were their best suspect but that's all. You could've made bail. Now—! Fuck, man, you nailed your own ass to the wall."

"You killed that girl to set me up, okay." *Keep him talking.* "But poison? Why like that?"

"Because I wanted to! What do you care? What do you fucking *care?* I know you like to worry about shit no one asked you to, but I'd focus here, if I were you. Listen, nice talking to you, but I gotta go. I need to get set for the second quarter. When I'm ready, I'll give you a ring. From, by the way, a different phone. I got a shitload of phones. So in case you think you can trace me. Haha! Stay out of trouble, big guy." The connection broke off.

I hit redial, but as it had before, the call refused to go through. Lowering the phone, I met Mary's eyes.

"Oh, my God," she said.

6

Then, the explosion.

"*You can't do this alone!*"

"You heard him, Mary. He's goddamn insane!"

"All the more reason."

"He said no cops."

"Every kidnapper who ever did a snatch says no cops! Then they kill the vic when the ransom's paid. You want to find them before that, *we* do it!"

"There's no ransom. It's not about that."

"What is it about?"

"I don't know. But it's personal, it's me. He took her because of me."

Unexpectedly, Mary subsided. She gave me a long look. "And you think you have to save her all by yourself, to make up for it?"

"For God's sake! No!" I shoved my cigarette out the window, shoved that thought away. "But I believe him. If he thinks I brought in cops, he'll kill her."

"You don't think he'll kill her anyway?"

"Not as long as I keep playing."

"And when the game's over?"

"I'll get to her before that." It was a prayer, but I spoke it as fact.

A sigh. "Bill, we're already in. Brooklyn Homicide. *He* brought us in."

"Brooklyn Homicide's looking for *me.* He was right. Who'd believe me now?"

"I'll vouch for you. I heard the call."

"Lydia's friend? You probably helped me kill her, helped me concoct this whole crazy story."

"The clues—"

"Garbage in a plastic bag."

"It may have his prints on it."

"It may have a dozen people's prints on it. So what?"

"If one is someone you know—"

"Then you and I will know who he is. But I'll be at Rikers. He was wrong about how fast I'd be out and you know it. Bail? Never."

"We'd find him."

"And if there aren't prints? If all we have to go on is his next set of clues and I don't get them? Clock runs out, game over. Mary? If it weren't me, if some stranger came to you with a story like this, would you buy it?"

Traffic flowed steadily by. People with a purpose and a way to get there. I watched Mary's face. Lydia's best friend, and also a cop: this was tearing her apart.

"So what are you planning to do?" she asked. "Just keep playing and hope something happens?"

"If that will save Lydia, yes."

"And if the next clues lead to another victim? Are you going to let him just go on killing people, as long as it's not Lydia?"

Sickeningly, I realized I was ready to shout, *YES! Yes, if I have to!* I clenched my throbbing jaw to keep that inside.

"I know," I said softly. "But it may not come to that. He said it would be a while before the new clues. I want to use that time to find the back door. I need to know who he is, what it's about. Give me time, Mary. Please."

"And if I say no? You planning to jump me and run, like you did the two other cops?"

I shook my head.

Mary had been leaning over the seat; now she turned away, looked out through the windshield. After a time, she spoke. "I'm on the four-to-midnight today. I report in at three-thirty. You have until then."

"What if he doesn't—"

"We decide then. *I* decide."

I let out a breath. "Thank you."

I called Linus, whose half-dozen frantic messages, both voice and text, I'd ignored while I argued with Mary. He picked up on half a ring. "Dude! Where are you? That dead girl in Fatima's—tell me it's not Lydia."

"It's not."

"*Damn,* dude! Hey, Trella, it's not! So what's going *on*? That SUV, what was up with that? Calling Aunt Mary—was that a good thing or a bad thing? Did I jam something up?"

"You saved my butt, Linus," I told him. "Now I need to keep low. I need to find a place to work from, then I'll call you."

"My office in Flushing," Linus said. "It's all yours."

"I'm hot, Linus. More ways than one. I don't want to bring that down on you kids."

"What? I'm losing you. Sounded like something about kids."

"Linus—"

"Nope, can't hear a thing. All broken up," he told me, clear as a bell. "Better reception out in Flushing. In my office."

I ran my hand over my face. "All right. Meet us out there."

"Us?"

"Long story. Tell you later. We'll be in Flushing in maybe twenty minutes. Meet us at your place."

"Can't. Or, can, but not twenty minutes. Bus to the subway, even a car service, whatever, it'll take forever from here."

"What happened to your car?"

"Dude! Probably hasn't even made it to the shop yet!"

An automotive blur, screeching brakes, tinkling glass. "That was *you*?"

"Trella. Awesome, huh? We saw them bringing you around in handcuffs. So in case you needed, you know, like a diversion. Trella says buckle up, brace on the dashboard. She stomps the gas! Screech! Whammo! Kaboom! Then, *then,* dude, she jumps out, I move over, by the time the cops get there she's gone! Because, dig, she runs faster than me. Everyone's running toward the crash, she's running the other way, the way you went. So she saw the Escalade. What was up with that?"

"Where are you?"

"A café on Van Brunt."

"Wait outside. We'll be right there."

Mary swung back into Red Hook, where we found Linus and Trella standing obediently at the curb. Trella slipped in the front.

Linus opened the back door, hesitated, made a face, then slid in next to me. "Dude," he whispered. "This is the 'us'?"

Pulling away from the curb, Mary said coldly, "Hello, Linus."

Linus squirmed. "Hi, Aunt Mary."

"You guys are related?" Trella asked.

Mary said, "Only in that Chinese way where a best friend tries to help her best friend keep her jerk cousin straight. And tries. And tries. And tries. Linus, how come you made your friend here call me?"

"Hey, cut me some slack! I was with the cops, explaining how the gas pedal got stuck. Old junker car, you know how it is, officer dude. I thought I was pretty slick, slipping Trella your number in the middle of all that. She called me from around the block, told me about the Escalade. I told them it was my mom."

Mary didn't answer, just tightened her jaw. After a moment Linus shrugged and turned back to me, eyed me critically. "Dude, you don't look so good."

"Thanks. For people who just crashed through a building, you two look great."

"Not *through* it." Trella spoke as though I'd said something crazy. "I just nudged it a little. It was all about the noise. Pounded the horn, squealed the tires. Those huge panes sound killer when they break."

"I had my hands over my head!" Linus grinned. "Waiting for disaster!"

"Chicken," Trella said sweetly. "The hard part was finding an empty store. I didn't want to wreck anybody's stuff." She turned to Mary: "Hi. I'm Trella. Thanks for believing me."

"You told me Kid Screwup back there said to tell me Lydia and Bill were in trouble. Why would I not believe that? But driving like that, risking lives—"

"Whose lives? There was no one around."

"You and him?"

"But that's ours. We can do whatever we want."

"Really? Ask your mom. And interfering with police work. It's a bad road to be going down, Trella."

"Hey, Aunt Mary?" Linus spoke up from the back. "How about you send us to reform school later? We're busy here."

On the rest of the trip to Flushing I replayed for Trella and Linus what had happened since they dropped me off.

"The cops told me," Linus said. "About there was a body. And when you ran off—I saw that. I knew you kicked the shit out of that one cop, but two! Dude, that's awe—" He stopped, glanced at Mary. "Dude, that's really bad."

"I know. I don't recommend it." I went on, gave them Lu, Ming, and Strawman. I played up the pain, played down the rush, but still I saw the glow in Trella's eyes.

"I wonder how he knew," she mused. "To come to Red Hook."

"Maybe the crazy man called him?" Linus suggested. "Like he called the cops."

"Why?" I said. "Lu could've kept me out of circulation for a long time."

"Yeah, like forever."

"Right. Where would the game be then?"

Trella looked over her shoulder. "What about the crazy man? You think *he* was there?"

"I doubt it. If he were, he'd have known about Lu, and if he did he wouldn't have missed his chance to stick it to me. I think he called to find out what was going on."

"What about what he did know? About you escaping?"

"You could get that from a police scanner."

Linus chewed his lip. "I don't know, dude. How'd he know when you found the girl? So he could call the cops? I think maybe he was watching. From where he couldn't follow where you went, but he could see in Fatima's."

I thought about the grime I'd rubbed off Fatima's front window. "Maybe. Listen, Linus, your Verizon guy? Can he find where this call came from, the one I just got? It was from a different phone, but if we're lucky it still could be Verizon."

I expected Mary to erupt, to smack me down for the illegal request. Surprisingly, she said nothing, just kept driving.

Linus, meanwhile, was giving me a look I was coming to know, the one that said he wasn't sure where he'd failed to make himself clear. "Dude? What's the difference if it's Verizon?"

"Well, your guy—"

"Seriously? You think the only place I got someone is at Verizon?"

Linus spent the rest of the ride calling and texting. Trella peered out the window, her gaze moving hungrily over the landscape. Mary drove steadily and spoke to no one.

I didn't speak, either. Something was nagging at me about the lunatic, what he'd said, the way that robotic voice strung words together. I leaned back, closed my eyes. *Goddammit*! I ran through both calls, trying to force it out. Nothing. The son of a bitch was a shadow in the darkness.

I sat up and looked around when I felt the car roll to a stop. Gold ginkgo leaves carpeted the yard of a small brick house. Unlike its neighbors the house had a garage; good for it, because the street was all parked up. The driveway, too; a blue Mailbu stood there. Maybe the Wongs were a two-car family.

Mary swung into the driveway and parked square across the sidewalk. She got out, shut her door and caught me looking over at her. "What?" she demanded.

"Aren't you leaving?"

"Why would I?"

"You said I had until three-thirty."

"I'm giving you the time. If you think I'm going to drive off and let you run around loose until then you're insane."

Linus threw me a commiserating glance.

He led us through the gate, but not to the house: to a side door on the garage. It turned out the Wongs were a one-car family, and the car lived outside. "My office," Linus announced.

Electronic equipment in infinite variety crammed counters and shelves. Monitors, boxes, wires, and blinking lights, all of them from Mars as far as I knew. Plywood covered the windows, and the concrete floor was hidden by vinyl tile, which, near the door, was hidden by a throw rug, which, until we'd come in, had probably been hidden by the large yellow dog now barking and bounding.

"That's Woof." Linus held the door. The dog galloped into the yard and barked at the ginkgo tree. Linus reached into a fridge, offered Cokes. Mary took one, but Trella was grinding beans, filling a Mr. Coffee from a sink in the corner. Linus rolled chairs out to face each other, popped his Coke top and asked, "What now, dude?"

A wave of weariness crashed over me. I sank into a chair, rubbed my face, reached for a cigarette.

"Dude." Linus shook his head. "Not in here. Sorry."

"Oh. The equipment, right."

"Nuh-uh. Trella."

Over her shoulder, Trella grinned and shrugged. "Windows don't open," she said.

"This might help, though." Linus rummaged through a drawer. Trella walked a glass of water over. I wasn't sure why until Linus came up with a bottle of Advil. What a team.

I downed pills. No one spoke. They waited—Mary dubious, Trella glittering, Linus all eager readiness, just like Woof—waited, for me to deliver. I wanted that cigarette badly. "Okay." I rubbed my eyes. "We have a couple of things. Not much, but let's see how far they take us. One, they're in a basement."

"Dude, they are?"

"Lydia said so. 'Almost completely in the dark.' 'Trying not to get really down.' A basement, but not a cellar."

"What's the difference?" Trella leaned back, folded her arms.

"Cellar's underground, basement's partly above ground. 'Not really down.' And, 'almost completely in the dark.' So I'm betting on windows, but dim, maybe onto an areaway. And she said 'still.' So he hasn't moved her."

"So maybe he won't! So if my dudes can GPS the phone—"

"Right."

Linus checked his iPhone, as if there were any possibility he'd missed a message. Nothing.

"All right," I said. "Lei-lei. If we knew exactly when she died, we'd know when this guy was in Red Hook."

"Unless he killed her somewhere else," Trella said.

"Possible but less likely. Two people walking into a building, easier tc go unnoticed than a guy carrying something. Also, if she were already dead, to arrange her on the couch like that he'd have to wait for rigor to pass."

"Why would she go, though?" Linus asked. "Wouldn't she think maybe something was up? She works Manhattan, but this guy takes her all the way to Red Hook, to some closed bar?"

Mary spoke. "He might have had a gun on her."

We all turned to her. The beady-eyed ref, getting into the game?

"Nah," Trella said. "I bet he told her he'd pay double if they could do it in his special place. He probably said he used to own it or something."

I switched my stare to Trella. "Damn! I wonder if he did? Linus, can you—"

"On it, dude." Linus swept his chair across the floor, jabbed a button, grabbed a mouse.

Trella pressed a mug of coffee into my hand. Maybe she made great coffee. Or maybe I just thought so, when really I was so battered and desperate I'd have downed a bucket of mud. I drank greedily, waiting.

" 'K, dudes." Scrolling down his screen, Linus said, "That building's owned by some dude, Louis Spano. Owns the lot next door, too. Since, like, 1954." He whistled. "Sounds kind of ancient to be pulling this shit."

"Maybe he inherited them when he was born."

"He'd still be, like, around fifty-six," Linus said, his point unchanged. "You know him? He hate you?"

"Doesn't ring a bell. Can you find him?"

"Dude." A reprimand.

"And what about the bar itself? Who owned the bar?"

"You don't think it was old man Spano's idea to set up a hookah bar?" Linus didn't wait for my answer. After another few minutes, another Coke for him and more coffee for Trella and me, he said, "Well, big surprise. Old Man Spano rented the place to a woman named Fatima. O'Reilly, though. Fatima O'Reilly. Weird names, I dunno, makes it too easy." He tapped keys, slid the mouse around. "There she is. Sedona, A-Z. Here's her work, here's her cell. If I were you I'd call the landline first. If she's there you'll know she's *there*."

Linus's logic was on the nose. A lot of trained detectives, though, would have called the cell, more likely to be answered. I stole a glance at Mary. She looked reluctantly impressed.

I started to dial the number on the screen but Linus stopped me. He reached into a drawer, pulled out a blister-wrapped cell phone, tore it open, thumbed some buttons, and handed it to me.

"What's this?"

"Dude? It's a phone. Three hundred prepaid minutes. Burn through 'em, throw it away. No using yours anymore except to talk to Mr. Crazy. Me and Trella, too." He tossed a phone to Trella, who swiped it out of the air one-handed. " 'Cause, dig. I may not be the only one with a dude at Verizon. Now give me yours. Your real one." He plugged one end of a three-inch cord into an outlet I didn't even know my phone had, the other end into a matchbook-size device. "To record him." He grinned. "How glad are you that you know me?"

I nodded. "Thanks, Linus."

While Linus went looking for Louis Spano, who didn't have such a weird name and would therefore take longer to find, I called Sedona, A-Z.

"Fatima's." The voice was female; the heavy tone implied I was interrupting. I asked if I'd reached the Fatima O'Reilly who used to own the bar in Red Hook. She blew out an impatient breath. "No, that was the *other* Fatima O'Reilly. What do you think?"

"Can I ask you a few questions?"

"About the murder? You a reporter?"

"You've heard?"

"The New York police called. I don't know anything. Closed that place a year ago. Psycho dumps a body there, has nothing to do with me."

When a subject hands you a cover, you go with it. "I'm doing a story on why gentrification failed in certain neighborhoods. Can you tell me about Fatima's?"

"Tell you what? For all I know it's a crackhouse now. Going down the toilet with the rest of New York."

"Why did it close?"

"Oh, let's see. Because the customers stopped coming! Red Hook was supposed to be the Next Big Thing. Yeah, right. Loyalty doesn't mean shit, the next Next Big Thing comes along."

"But Fatima's was hot for a while."

"Damn right we were. We had a velvet rope. Turned people away! Even out there in the ass end of Brooklyn, I got the A-list." She rattled off names, two or three celebrities and a lot of wannabes. "And we caught on with the Knicks for a while." She snorted. "You should've seen them trying to fold themselves up on the cushions."

As far as I knew, no Knicks or bold-face names had it in for me. "And the rest of the crowd?"

"Club kids. Supermodels. Trust-fund babies playing bohemian. Until they saw something else shiny, then they all ran off that way. Tapas, slow food, some shit. Serves me right for going out on a limb, pioneering in that nowhere neighborhood. The hell with them, with the bar, with New York. Vibe out here is a lot more mellow. Anything else I can do for you, or can I get back to work?"

I hung up, leaving Fatima to her mellow vibe.

"Anything, dude?"

"Not that I could see. Did you find Spano?"

"Check. He lives in a retirement place in Sarasota." Pointedly, he added, "He's eighty-seven."

I called Louis Spano's Florida number, talked to an old man with a shaky voice, no living relatives, and a perfect memory.

"Fatima's?" he quavered. "Lasted longer than I thought. Something like nine years, I'm remembering right. Between you and me, sounded damn boring. Sitting on pillows smoking sissy tobacco with a bunch of bankers. You couldn't pay me."

"Me, either. Though when I talked to Fatima, she said her clientele was celebrities."

He cackled. "That would make it better? Anywho, the paying customers were Gordon Gekkos, believe you me. Any celebrities, I guarantee they were on the arm, to decorate the place. Hey, you wouldn't be interested in the building? I can let you have it cheap."

I thanked him and hung up, reaching for something in the back of my mind. The faint bell was ringing again, but whether it had been struck by Louis Spano or Fatima O'Reilly, or was coming from a totally different place, I wasn't sure. I poured more coffee, tried to focus. The ringtone on Linus's phone—"Call Me"—cut into that. "Yeah," he said. "Uh-huh. Yeah. No shit? Got it. Thanks, dude." He thumbed off. "That was Verizon Dude. The phone Mr. Crazy called you on? It's not Verizon. It's one of these." He tapped a prepaid cell. "But 'cause you were on it, he could trace that tower, and it's the same as before."

"Good, Linus."

"And something else. Mr. Crazy's phone, my guy got interested. He called some guys. The service on that, it's a bundler called SpeedFone. Verizon Dude talked to someone over there." Linus glanced at Mary, who looked exasperated but said nothing. "That phone, Mr. Crazy didn't make any other calls from it except to you and to the cops, like he said. But he got one."

"He did?"

"Went through a tower in Red Hook. Just about when you were in Fatima's."

"Damn. Someone *is* working with him. That's how he knew I was there. Do you have the number?"

"Does the Pope shit in the woods? And dig, dude. That phone that called him, it has a GPS. And it's on."

I'd been set to dial. I stopped, said, "Can you find it?"

"I can't," Linus answered with disarming humility. "But my dude's dude can." Linus swung to the screen again, zooming in on a streetmap. "Union Street. Near Henry. At least, ten minutes ago he was."

"Still in Brooklyn." I grabbed my jacket. "Let's go."

"I don't think so," Mary said.

"Mary! For God's sake! This is it, the break! What did you think, once we found something I'd just sit here?"

"Better than going there." She pointed to the red star on the map. "That's the Seven-six Precinct."

7

I stopped cold. "Shit."

"Shit for real, dude," Linus said softly.

Mary took out her phone.

"Hey!" I said. "What are you—"

She raised a warning hand, turned away. Behind her back Linus mimed grabbing the phone, lifted eyebrows asking me. I shook my head. I didn't doubt Mary would take me in, take this whole thing in if she thought that was the right move. But we had a deal. If she was breaking it, she'd let me know.

"Yo, Patino!" Mary shouted into her phone. Manny Patino, a fellow detective in the Fifth Precinct, a guy I'd met a couple of times over the years. "What? Gee, couldn't you find a louder place to eat? Yeah, okay, that's better. Listen, I need a favor. I'm working something privately, a cousin, you know how it is, I don't want to bring the Job in . . . Well, if it does, I'll be walking it beside you, so I'll buy the doughnuts. Okay, thanks. It's like this: The seven-six has a cell phone over there." She gave him the number. "They had a homicide in Red Hook this morning, it might be they picked it up at the scene. But it also could be just someone's . . . Uh-huh. I need to know. The vic was a pross, Chinese, so maybe some line about Chinatown Vice, you heard—yeah, I know you can, sorry. Oh, come on, you know I'm not a cowboy. Cowgirl, fine, whatever. If it turns out to be more than just this cousin thing I'll bring it in. Yeah. Thanks. This number, anytime. I owe you."

She clicked her phone shut, turned around, eyed us silently, one by one.

"Thanks," I said.

She nodded.

"Aunt Mary?" Linus tiptoed. "You can do that? Work, like, privately? A cop?"

"Of course not!" Mary snapped. Gruffly: "But everyone does. Favors for family, friends. Patino probably thinks my cousin's kid's on the stroll and I'm trying to find her."

"Well, you just about told him that," Trella said.

Mary shrugged, and Trella answered with a tiny smile. Which Mary returned. Linus caught that, glanced quizzically at me.

"I need a cigarette," I said, and stepped outside.

Woof bounded over, wanting to show me his tree, his porch, his rubber ball. I picked up the ball, fingered it. Quivering, he watched me. How would I start the game? What would his move be? I could heave the damn thing over the fence, I reflected. Send it soaring where you can't get at it, dog. It would bounce, roll, come to rest out where you could see it. You'd charge stupidly back and forth inside this fence, never getting any closer. It would be lost to you forever. And you'd never know why.

I cocked my arm. Woof tensed, eager eyes riveted. Spinning, I flung the ball up onto the porch. Woof chased after it, snarfed it up and brought it back to me, dropped it so the game could happen again.

My cigarette was almost gone and Woof was pawing the ball from the roots of a rhododendron when Linus stuck his head out the door. "Dude! News." I crushed out the smoke and strode past Woof, who gave a few hopeful swishes of his tail, then dropped the ball and followed me in.

"The phone was the vic's," Mary said. "Not a cop's." She was trying for neutral but her relief was clear. "Or at least, Crime Scene found it under her on the couch."

"Could it have been put there? One of the first cops on the scene?"

"Bill, you assaulted the first cop on the scene! You see him call anybody before you broke his arm? No other cop went up there until Crime Scene came." With less heat, she went on, "Odd thing about the phone, though. That number it dialed, that was the only number in it."

"And let me guess: when they tried it, it didn't answer."

"No."

"Well, obviously Lei-lei didn't make that call. Someone else had to be in the building. Someone I missed. Goddamn it! How did he get out, though? He couldn't—"

"Dude!" Linus held up a hand. "No way."

"What?"

"I mean, way, it could be, but it doesn't hafta. Coulda been wired."

"Meaning?"

"Simple pressure thing. You move her, shift the weight, it presses the button, some speed dial number. Phone makes the call."

"Wouldn't the cops have found the mechanism?"

"Coulda been her. Stud on her bracelet, something like that."

I thought about that. "So he wasn't watching and he didn't have help. All he had to do was wait for that call."

"Correct," Linus said.

"Though Brooklyn Homicide has a simpler explanation," Mary said. "They think it was you."

"Why the hell would I call someone from an anonymous phone, then stick it under a dead girl's body?"

"They're anxious to ask you."

I sat, rubbed the back of my neck. Woof put a paw on my knee, dropped a rope toy at my feet. I rubbed his neck, too. "Mary?" I said softly. "As long as you're in . . ."

"I'm not in!"

I looked pointedly at her phone, still in her hand. "The time of death. If we knew that . . ."

She flushed, she frowned, but she lifted the phone, jabbed at it, and put it to her ear. I gave Linus a quick glare to stop his embryonic grin.

"Hi, Joanne. Mary Kee, from the Oh-five. Yeah, not so bad, you? Listen, they got the vic from Red Hook on the table yet? No, but I heard, and we had something like it here, cold now, about a year back, that one was rat poison . . . I know, that's what I heard, I was wondering if maybe . . . Yeah, good. No, I'll wait." A silence stretched, all of us looking at Mary, Mary looking at the wall. "Oh, good, thanks. Uh-huh. Uh-huh. What? Son of a— You have? They do? Damn. No, it's a new one on me. Yeah, really, huh? Okay, anything else, I'm here. Thanks." She pocketed her phone, and now looked at us. "Time of death, about midnight last night. Probably at the scene." To me: "I don't suppose you have an airtight alibi? I didn't think so. Preliminary cause of death, brodifacoum, rat poison, final after they run a tox screen. Joanne gave me the vic's identifying scars and tattoos, but personally," she said sardonically, "I'm betting she's a hooker named Lei-lei. Joanne doesn't know her name. But the hooker part, that was her take, too."

"Why?" I asked. "We know that from Lu, but the way she was dressed, you couldn't tell that."

"For the same reason Lu knew how to find you. For what it's worth. She had a GPS."

"That phone? Sure, but how does that—"

"No." Mary touched her hairline behind her ear. "Here."

"What?"

"Joanne's seen it twice before, on Chinese hookers. Most of them are illegals working off passage. They think they're being brought over as seamstresses and nannies. Even mail-order brides. When they find out what they're really here for sometimes they run away. Their pimps hunt them down, cut them or kill them as a lesson to the other girls. That's easier if you can find them. And it cuts down on running away in the first place if they know you can find them."

"So they implant a chip?" Trella gestured at Woof. "As though they were dogs?"

"Even Woof doesn't have that," Linus said uneasily.

"Joanne says the ones they use broadcast for about a year, then they replace them. When girls aren't where they're supposed to be, if the pimp can swing into action before the girl finds someone to remove it, they can't hide."

"So when Lei-lei disappeared," I said, "Lu knew right where to come."

"Dude. That's *so* wack." Linus looked at Trella, who, her back to us, was snapping endless teaspoons of sugar into her coffee.

"It won't take Brooklyn Homicide long to figure out who Lei-lei is," Mary said. "Even if she worked Manhattan. They'll go looking for the blocks she worked, the last guy she went with."

"But that's breaking the rules! Cops!" Linus yelped. "They figure out who he is and go looking for him, he'll think—"

"No," I said. "He was the one who called them. He must have that covered."

Linus's panic faded. "Oh. Duh. Sorry. Right. Probably he just picked her up on some empty street, where no one saw."

I regarded him. " 'Some empty street.' She wasn't dressed to work the street. She was dressed like Lydia."

Trella spun to face us. "He told her to."

I thought back to the Escalade, Lu's snarled words. "Lu said she was valuable. Maybe she was too high-class for the street. A whorehouse. With a mama-san, and upscale clients. If Lu was chasing down her GPS, he was slow about it. She'd been dead half a day by the time he turned up. But say she'd gone off with a client who paid for the whole night and promised to have her back by maybe nine A.M.—"

"Then around eleven's when the mama-san would've called the boss," Mary finished.

"I want to talk to Lu."

"Brooklyn Homicide will turn him up eventually. They'll ask the mama-san who Lei-lei went off with."

"But they'll show her a photo of me. He's a big guy, graying hair. He may even look enough like me, she'll say it was. Especially if she can see that's what the cops want to hear. And if the boss already thinks so."

Mary, after a long, pressed-lip pause, took out her phone. "Hey, Patino. Yeah, me again, sorry. About a whoremonger name of Lu. With two big bad seconds. A bald one called Ming, and a hairy one, Strawman. I know, but you can find him for me, Patino, you're good like that. And as it happens, I have his plate." She flipped her book open, read him the number off the Escalade. "See how helpful? Okay, thanks. Oh, come on, where am I going to get playoff tickets? Yeah, okay, I'll try." She thumbed the phone off.

I started to thank her. She cut me off. "Don't say it. Don't say anything. You're right at the borderline here." She added, "And you need to come up with playoff tickets."

After that, silence. Now it was waiting: for Patino to come through, for the lunatic's next call. Linus popped another Coke. Trella and I shared the rest of the coffee. Woof swept his tail slowly across the floor, then lay down with a sigh.

"Dude." Linus finally spoke. "Can't be we need to just sit here. Got to be something we can do."

I'd been thinking about this. Something did need to be done, I couldn't do it, and it seemed to me pretty safe. Mary wasn't going to like it, but it might not set her off. "It would help to know how this guy got to Lydia, and when. And where. I want to you guys to go to Chinatown, ask around."

Mary frowned, but didn't say anything.

Linus lit up. "For sure!"

I nodded. "Not randomly, Linus. I can't show my face there, and we can't risk cops. But he doesn't know you two. Call Lydia's mother, say you're looking for her and she doesn't answer her phone, does Mrs. Chin know where she is? Ask the ladies at the travel agency she sublets the office from. Tell them"—I looked at the kids, both on their feet—"tell them you were supposed to meet Lydia and this guy and you're late and now you don't know where to go. Ask if they saw her with anyone. Here." I dug in my pocket, took a key off a ring.

"What's that?"

"It's to Lydia's office."

"Dude! You have her key?" Linus exchanged a glance with Trella.

"In case of emergency. I think this qualifies. Listen: no way he could've just grabbed her off the street."

"Totally! She'd have messed him up bad!"

"Or at least, made enough of a scene that someone would've noticed." I looked to Mary.

She nodded. "I see where you're going. Yes, they'd have called me, even off-duty, even if they didn't know it was Lydia. They think they have a kidnapping, they call in all the Chinese-speaking cops. To talk to the witnesses who suddenly forget their English."

"But that didn't happen. So all I can think, she went somewhere to meet this guy, they had an appointment. Maybe he pretended to be a client. So maybe she wrote something down. On her calendar, in her computer. Linus, you can get into her computer, right?"

Linus gave me that look and didn't even bother with the "dude."

"Take a car service," I said. "I'll cover it. And the one in the shop, that, too. And whatever your Verizon guy's costing you."

"Dude, much as I love spending other people's money, a car service won't get here for forever. We'll take my mom's car."

"And the one in the shop's a Lazarus," Trella put in. "Don't worry about it."

"Lazarus?"

"Brought back from the dead already. Twice."

"And Verizon Dude," Linus said. "Don't worry about him, either. He's working off something else he owes me."

Linus glanced at Mary but she made no move to stop them.

They wouldn't be doing anything illegal and there was a small chance they'd turn something up. And they'd be safely out of the way when the lunatic called, which hadn't escaped my attention, either.

Brief cacaphony as three new cell phones rang again and again, each calling each so we'd have the others' numbers. Then Mary went to move her car so Linus and Trella could take off. Just before he left the garage, Linus scooped a few more cell phones from the drawer and stuffed them in his cargo pocket.

Woof was out bounding around the car before Linus and Trella got there. Linus tossed a set of keys to Trella. Woof climbed in, stuck his face into the wind as they rolled.

Back inside, I turned to Mary. "Thanks. For"—I spread my hands—"for all this. I know how hard it is."

"No, you don't! This is a bad tightrope I'm walking. Cops freelancing, it never comes out well. I wonder if I'm really doing Lydia any good. I wonder what she'd tell me."

I said what I knew. "She'd tell you not to do anything that feels wrong. And not to risk your career."

Mary's look was long. "And the fact that you said that, instead of pretending she'd be cheerleading, is one of the few things that could keep me here."

I nodded, stood. "You want coffee?" I headed to the counter to see if I could make coffee as good as Trella's but I didn't get there. My phone rang. Not Linus's prepaid. Mine.

"Smith," I said as calmly as I could.

"No shit?" That robot voice, that laugh.

Heart racing, I nodded to Mary. She jumped up, came over and leaned close. I couldn't risk putting him on speaker again.

"So, how's everything? Found ourselves a safe hidey-hole, did we?"

"Let me talk to Lydia."

"Um, what? Sorry, but fuck you. That's for when you do something right. Say, after you decipher your next clues. Well, unless you don't."

"When we started this bullshit you said the clues would lead to Lydia."

"God, you're impatient! They will, they will. Just not right away."

"You planning on leaving bodies all over New York first? That's not what I agreed to."

"Oh. Really?" He gave it a few seconds, as though he were thinking. "Well, I guess I must not give a shit what you agreed to."

"What kind of a game is it where you keep changing the rules?"

"Oh, listen to you complain! I'm not changing the rules. I just didn't tell you all the rules. Come on, don't you like surprises?"

"No."

"Too bad. I wouldn't go whining to the refs, though: the no-cops rule, that's still in effect. Now, you want to keep playing? Or should we just call it off? It's a big country. I could grab my sneakers, find another game. After I clean up around here, I mean. You know: throw out the trash."

"No. No, go ahead."

"You sure? I don't want you to feel like you're being forced into anything."

"I said go ahead!"

"Hey, calm down! You can't play well when you're out of control, you know. So speaking of trash, your next clues are in a can on Eighty-eighth and Lex. Right there on the corner. And it needs to be you, my friend. Anyone else makes a withdrawal there instead of a deposit, I'm not gonna like that. And you might want to hurry. Sanitation comes by at one."

"I'm not close. I might not make it."

"Hmm. I wonder what happens then? Oh, I remember! Your girlfriend gets whacked! Have a nice day." And he was gone.

The air around me was fiery, red-streaked. I couldn't breathe, couldn't move.

"Bill!" Mary's voice brought me back. "You get it taped?"

I lowered the phone, released my vise-grip on the counter. "I'll kill that motherfucker."

"Great. Later." Mary grabbed her jacket. "Let's go."

8

Mary raced that car through Queens. She wasn't the natural driver Trella was, but she was motivated. The hard braking and whiplash starts told me she was used to letting sirens and flashing lights cut her a path, but we couldn't risk picking up an escort, some bright-eyed radio car looking for a commendation for helping a detective in a hurry. So Mary pushed it, but, as Trella had, under the radar. We did fine most of the way, roaring over the bridge, through Harlem, down Second Avenue. Then at Ninety-sixth we hit traffic, a snarl-up like a wall. Mary slammed the horn, but everyone was doing that. So she clicked the siren on. Other drivers turned to look. She slapped the flashing gumball onto the dash. One or two cars halfheartedly tried to move; but when we made no progress, they gave that up, joined the herd again.

"Damn you!" Mary yelled to all of them, to no one. "Pull over! *Let me through!*"

Lots of noise, no movement. We sat, stuck, eight blocks north and two long ones west of where I needed to be. "Arrest them all," I said, and got out.

I'm not young, but I'm not ready for the rocking chair. But I'd been through the sledgehammer-Ming treatment not so long ago. And I smoke. Ninety-Sixth and Second, that's Carnegie Hill. Absolutely nothing got me up to Lexington but fear and adrenaline. Gasping when I hit the avenue, I turned south, more slogging than running, my heart outpounding my leaden feet. I slid around pedestrians, cut off a cab whose driver honked and cursed. I'd covered three blocks, wheezing like an accordion, when I saw, a few streets ahead at Eighty-ninth, a humpbacked Sanitation truck waiting for a man in green to empty a trash can into its hopper. He did, it started to grind, he dropped the empty can back on its corner and pounded the truck's side to signal the driver. The truck rolled on. The garbageman followed, sauntering down the sidewalk.

Heading for the next trash can, the one at Eighty-eighth.

My trash can.

Where I got the burst from I will never know. I was flying. I was the Flash, Superman, Lightning Boy. My feet barely touched the ground until Eighty-eighth Street, where I leapt across space and brought down one of New York's Strongest.

He was hefting a trash can, not a situation a coach ever covered. My tackle was bad: I hit him off center, grabbed more shirt than shoulder. But it worked. I laid the poor guy flat, heard his groan and then a faint, "What the hell?" He said it again when I yanked the plastic bag from the can he'd been manhandling and ran off.

Bill Smith, Reverse Santa, charging through New York with a stolen bag of garbage. Lydia would laugh herself silly. Except garbage was goddamn heavy and it goddamn stank, I hadn't drawn a breath in what felt like a month, and it was stop or die.

Ahead: Eighty-sixth Street, a subway station. A wheezing guy with a battered face and a smelly plastic bag, who'd notice? I staggered down the stairs, swiped my card through, and leaned on a steel column, hoovering up air until a train came. I got on, ignoring the curled lips and cold looks, rode three stops, got off outside Bloomingdale's and called Mary.

"Where the hell are you? What did you do?"

"I got the bag."

"Mount Sinai just sent an ambulance to Eighty-eighth and Lex."

"He's not really hurt."

"Who?"

"The garbageman. I had to fight him for it."

I waited in the shadows of Fifty-eighth Street, trying to look homeless but harmless. As soon as I got my breath back I lit a cigarette. Even I knew that was wrong. A guy who can't do ten blocks through the city, he might think about quitting.

It was the best smoke I'd ever had.

Mary popped the trunk as she pulled up. I slung the bag in, slammed it, climbed in beside her. "We have to look through it right away."

"No, I thought we'd just drive around with it for a while. Damn it, can't you do anything without attacking a city employee? You know the penalty for assaulting a sanitation worker is the same as for a cop?"

"Ought to be more. Cops, it comes with the territory. That guy, you should've seen his face."

"And he's seen yours."

I shrugged. How much more wanted could I get? "Where are we going?"

"How many options do you have left?"

She maneuvered us down the FDR and off onto Fourteenth Street. As we waited at a light her phone rang. "Text," she said, thumbing buttons. "Phone number for your buddy Lu." She rattled it off; I wrote it down. "And," she muttered, "the seats Patino likes at playoff games." A few blocks later she headed the car into an underground garage. We grabbed the bag, rode the elevator to three, unlocked a door at the end of the hall.

We were in Mary's apartment. Small, neat, lots of light. Comfortable furniture, photos on the walls. Her family, her boyfriend, her friends. Lydia.

Mary spread a sheet on the wooden floor. I dumped out the bag. The loudest smell was dog shit, with old coffee a strong second. Brown stains leached along the sheet away from the mound in the center. Mary tossed me rubber gloves from her sink, found a pair of ski gloves for herself. We waded in, sorted, trying to find an order, a way to understand.

A pizza crust nestling on a Blimpie's wrapper; a pretzel tangled in an exhausted bouquet. Crumpled paper frothing everywhere, and baggies of scooped poop. Full and empty plastic grocery bags: D'Agostino, Gristedes. I moved half a sandwich, a yogurt container dripping gunk. I lifted the sports section of yesterday's *Post,* soggy with God knew what, and stopped.

"Mary."

She looked up.

I nodded at a tied-up grocery bag. Orange, thin, the kind cut-price stores give you. The kind you get in Chinatown.

The kind I'd found on my door.

I extracted it, dumped it out on the edge of the sheet. "This is it."

Mary didn't argue. The contents—a fragment of a bicycle wheel, a jar of honey, a Lord & Taylor bag, a Bruce Lee biography, and a horseshoe-patterned silk scarf—were too random and too clean to be garbage. The bag hadn't been used, the honey was unopened. The book wasn't new but it was in good shape.

"All right," Mary said, not sounding any more upbeat now than before. "What does it mean?"

"I don't know."

We stood staring at this collection of unrelated junk, this fragmented garbage Rosetta Stone. I tried to clear my head, let the things in front of me float back and forth, nudge against each other, turn and bump and show new angles. I got lots of things—bike/fast/go/tire/bee/sweet/hive/sting/shop/department store/Fifth Avenue/fight/read/kung fu/life story/horses/accessory/silk/keep warm—but none of it amounted to more than noise and glare. Mary didn't seem to be doing any better.

It was almost a relief when my phone rang.

"Linus?"

"Dude, this ain't happening." Linus sounded discouraged, a strange note for him. "Nobody here knows anything, not Mrs. Chin, no one. The Golden Adventure ladies say Lydia didn't come in yet today. Nothing in her computer or on her desk or anything. Should we, like, ask up and down the block? At the noodle shop and like that?"

"No. It was a long shot anyway. Come up here. We need those fresh eyes again. We got more clues."

"Dude! You did? You didn't call right away?"

"We had to race into Manhattan, he didn't give us much time."

"Race where?"

"To the Upper East Side. But we're not there now, we're at Mary's. You know where she lives?"

"We're on the way." Low mood gone, Linus was back in gear. "And check it out: send me pictures."

“What?”

“Cell phone pictures. We can look while we drive.”

“I don’t know how—”

“Not that el cheapo phone I gave you, it won’t do it. But probably Aunt Mary’s does.”

Mary’s did and she knew how. She sent them to Linus while he asked, “Where did he leave them? On another door?”

“In a trash can. We had to dig through the rest of the garbage to find them.”

“You sure what you have is them?”

“Yes. But we don’t know what they mean.”

“’K, here they come.” A short silence; then: “Wow! Dude! Gross-arama! Hey, Trella, check this out! Godzilla puked in Aunt Mary’s living room!”

9

Fifteen long, unproductive minutes later, a buzzer growled and Linus's voice came squawking from the speaker. Another thirty seconds and in they came.

"Shit!" Linus said. "It smells like it looks!"

Mary had thrown wide her windows, and it was cold enough that I'd zipped my jacket, but Linus was still right. We all stood together, silent, on the shore of the reeking garbage sea. Silent except for Woof. Trella held his leash and the dog was frantic, wagging, whining, straining to get into the mess and roll around. Linus crouched beside him, rubbed his ears. "This stuff at the edge here? This is it?"

"Yes."

"Nasty. Could make me want to never eat honey again. Or ride a bike. Hey, that the Bruce Lee book? Wow, it is! Hey, I read that."

"You did?" Trella asked.

"Man, I read everything about Bruce Lee! Had his picture on my wall, big poster. I was gonna *be* Bruce Lee. A serious badass mofo, just like him." He ignored Mary's snort. "I went to kung fu school for a year."

"Couldn't take the discipline?" Mary asked. "Master whacking you with a stick, all that?"

"Cut me some slack, Aunt Mary. I was digging it. My folks made me stop."

"Their mistake."

"No shit."

"Linus?" I asked. "What is it about Bruce Lee? About that book? Why would this guy include it?"

Linus shook his head.

"Could be it's not this book," Trella said. "Just, *a* book. Or maybe, something about the author."

"If Bruce Lee and the dead girl and Lydia weren't all Chinese, I'd buy that," I said. "But the coincidence is too big. Linus? What can you tell us?"

"Dude." Linus looked a little desperate, but he frowned in concentration, and said, "All I know, I was heavy into Bruce. I wanted to do everything just like him. You know, get up at five in the morning to practice, meditate all the time, that stuff. My folks thought it was, like, weird, but they were all, okay, whatever, with lifting weights, and when I started drinking protein shakes, and stopped eating bread."

"Bruce Lee didn't eat bread?" I didn't see how that could turn into a clue, but it was unusual, it was specific.

"Wheat. Thought it was bad for you. My mom said that was stupid, but she gave me rice and told my dad it was a phase and he should leave me alone. But when I told them I didn't believe in God anymore, that was the end of Bruce. Of course," he reflected, "it probably didn't help that I karate-chopped the coffee table in half."

"I didn't know that about you." Trella looked impressed. "You were that good?"

Linus shrugged modestly. "It was a pretty dinky table."

"Wait," I said. "Go back." I swept my eyes over our clues, rested on the shopping bag, "Lord & Taylor" in brown script flowing along its side. "You stopped believing in God? Because of Bruce Lee?"

"Check. Talk about getting grounded! My dad's an elder, Chinese Presbyterian church out where we live. I had to mow the lawn there all summer. See, the there-is-no-God thing, it's, like, the only bad thing about Bruce. But it's really bad, you know? He made a big deal about it. Anyone into martial arts, they all know. That was the thing about the curse, when he died so quick? Everyone said the triads got him. But you ask my mom, God got him. She didn't want God to get me, so it was bye-bye Bruce."

"A really bad thing about a hero," I said slowly. "That sounds like our guy, focusing on that." I pointed to the shopping bag. "There is no God," I said. "No Lord?"

Linus and Mary followed my finger. Trella's glowing eyes were fixed on me. "No Lord," she repeated. "Just a Taylor?"

Mary pointed to the length of silk, asked, "To sew up a scarf?"

"No! No!" I said. "God*damn*! Honey: bee! Tire rim: spoke! A bespoke tailor!"

"Wow! Yes!" said Trella.

"What?" said Mary.

"Dude?" Linus stood. "Dude*s*?" Looking from me to Trella. "Um, what are you talking about?"

I said, "Custom clothes. When they're very high end. That's who makes them. That's what you call him, a bespoke tailor."

"Like Old Man Wu at the laundry?" Linus was skeptical.

"No," Trella said. "Like my uncle Luigi."

"Luigi's cool," Linus admitted.

Mary was frowning at the trash. "I don't know."

"Yes," I said. "*Yes!* Look: the first clue, Fatima's. A bar that was hot, in its time. Fatima said she got the A-list but Spano said it was all money people. Bespoke clothes, it's a big status thing for money people."

Linus, for his part, was also unconvinced, but willing to follow along. "But where, dude? Suppose you're right, that's four of these things. The where must be what the scarf is for."

A long, still moment.

Mary said, "Silk."

Linus said, "Horse stuff."

Trella said, "Hermès."

Mary asked, "Wasn't there once a Silk Stocking District?"

I asked, "Then why isn't it a stocking?"

Linus asked, "Where do they keep the horses? To ride in Central Park?"

I said, "Maybe a carousel horse?"

Mary said, "The carousel has a canopy. Is it silk?"

Trella said, "Guys! *Hermès!*"

"Wait." I held up my hand to the others. "Trella? What about Hermès?"

"That's what it is. A Hermès pattern. Very ritzy. All the Park Avenue ladies wear them."

"You think it's about Park Avenue?" Linus asked.

"Or Canal Street," Mary said. "Big business there, Hermès knockoffs."

Trella shook her head. "This one's real."

"How do you know?"

"The colors are subtle. From expensive dyes. The knockoffs are coarser and gaudier." Trella fingered the fabric, nodded to herself, found the tiny label sewn into the hem. "Yes. Real."

Linus stared at her.

"They sell real ones at some of the department stores," Mary said.

"Yes. But they have two boutiques, too. Just Hermès. Downtown, and on the Upper East Side."

Linus had his iPhone out. He swiped his finger along the screen. "Madison at Sixty-first, and fifteen Broad. Trella, how do you *know* that shit about dyes and stuff?"

I said, "Linus, look for—"

"High-end custom tailors, I know, dude, I know." More swiping, more jabbing. Silence in a room so tense it seemed to vibrate. Woof whined. I'd have grabbed the phone from Linus and done it myself if I'd known how.

Then a whoop. "Dudes! There's a custom tailor on Sixty-second. At Madison, on the corner." He punched some numbers, lifted the iPhone to his ear, lowered it again. "And the phone's disconnected."

The room's voltage soared. Woof yapped, sensing it. Something was happening. We were about to move.

Mary squashed that. "I'm going. You're all staying here."

"A cop?" I couldn't believe it. "Are you crazy?"

"What I *should* be doing is sending a CS team! You don't think *you're* going?"

"I'm the one he wants."

"Last time he set you up!"

"Dude? Aunt Mary's right."

"Thank you, Linus," Mary said acidly.

"Mary, we had a deal."

"I'm not going to stand here arguing. You're staying. That's a direct order. Whatever I find, if it's not a crime scene I'll decide what to do then. If it is, and I expect it will be—"

"Mary, goddammit! If he sees a cop—"

"What cop? I'm a real estate agent."

That stopped me. It stopped the kids, too. Mary disappeared into her bedroom and came out ninety seconds later with her braid pinned into a bun, her jeans exchanged for a wool skirt, her shoes for heeled leather boots. She left her jacket, grabbed a wool coat, turned and pointed a finger at the rest of us. "Do not leave this room."

"When you get there, how are you going to get in?"

She leveled a cold stare. "You think you're the only one here who can pick a lock?"

"Actually," Linus said, "I think I'm the only one here who can't."

Mary strode across the room, turned once more to glower over her shoulder, then slammed the door behind her.

I lit a cigarette, counted the seconds. I didn't like this plan and I couldn't stay here, whatever Mary said. High-heeled boots or not, she looked like a cop to me. I just needed to give her time to get in the car and vanish around the corner.

"Dude," Linus said quietly. "You think Mr. Crazy really killed someone else? Just to mess with you?"

It wasn't hard to tell what answer he wanted. "Maybe not. Maybe this time he left something else, not a body, for me to find."

"You're just saying that to make me feel better."

"You're right."

"So he's, like, going around picking random people to kill?" Woof, uneasy at Linus's tone, lifted a paw and whined. "Like you could be walking down the street, and—"

"Linus!" I stared. "Wait! You're a genius! No, of course he's not. That wouldn't make a good game." I dug out the scrap of paper from the car, dialed the number on it.

10

Two rings, and that cold Midwestern voice. "This is Lu."

"And this is Bill Smith. You know, the guy who didn't kill Lei-lei?"

"Well, shit. You out already, or is this your one phone call? And how the fuck did you get this number?"

"Shut up and listen. You missing any girls?"

"What?"

"That's what happened to Lei-lei, right? She went off with a john and she never came back? So you followed her GPS?"

"She went off with *you*. And how—"

"Anyone else missing?"

Warily: "Not that I know about. What the hell's going on?"

"Call around and ask. There's a lunatic out there kidnapping Chinese hookers."

"Oh, right, the lunatic! You still trying to sell me that bullshit?"

"Hey, I'm not in your car getting stomped on by Ming anymore. Why would I call to sell you anything? This guy's kidnapping Chinese hookers and he's got one on Sixty-second Street. Corner of Madison. A custom tailor shop. Closed. You may have to break in, but I'm sure Ming and Strawman can take care of that."

"How the fuck do you know?"

"He's leaving me clues. He thinks this is a game."

"Why?"

"He hates me."

"He's not alone."

"He says if I keep following the clues I'll find my partner."

"What does this have to do with *my* girls?"

"My partner's Chinese. A woman. He's playing with me."

"Your partner— Wait, a Chinese girl private eye? Not what's-her-name, Chin, Lydia Chin?"

"You know her?" A spark flared in my chest, but any hope that the better angel of Chinese solidarity might change Lu's attitude was squelched right away.

"She's a pain in the ass around Chinatown, of course I know her. That's all I need in this shit—her, too."

I went back to business: "Look, Lu, check out the tailor shop. Only thing, when you find your girl, if there's anything else there, I want it."

"Anything like what?"

"An orange plastic bag." Whatever Lu had to say to that, I didn't want to hear it. I hung up, grabbed my jacket, told Linus and Trella, "I'm going up there."

Linus reached the door before I did, pulled it open. "We." Woof bounded into the hall.

I stopped. "'We,' nothing."

"What are you going to do?" Trella asked. "Take a cab?"

"And plus, dude, no way we're hanging here in Stinkville."

"If Mary finds out—"

"What? We're not, like under arrest or anything. She can't make us stay here."

"She'll be mad as hell."

"She's been mad as hell since I was five. I don't remember why."

I looked at them. "All right. But I drive."

They exchanged glances, then Trella nodded. Linus shrugged.

"Where are you parked?" I said when we hit the street. The air was crisp and cold and car exhaust had never smelled so good.

"Bus stop, two blocks."

We were halfway to the car when my phone rang.

"Smith."

"A girl named Angelique. Where you said, Sixty-second Street." It was Lu, not sounding any friendlier just because I'd been right. "She doesn't answer her page."

"Same whorehouse as Lei-lei?"

"'*Whorehouse*'? Fucking asshole. No, a different crib."

"But a high-class girl?"

"That's all I run, cocksucker."

"Yeah, fine. You on the way?"

"I'm almost there. I swear, if this is some setup, Fatboy Cho or somebody—"

"Yeah, that's a hell of a setup, Sixty-second and Madison in the middle of the day."

"Maybe the cops are waiting."

"For what, Ming to kick down a door so they can hang a B&E on his fat ass? They don't sit around with kidnap victims waiting to see who shows. I'm telling you, they don't know she's there."

"But you do. Why aren't you calling them? Instead of me?"

"The lunatic you don't believe in? He said no cops or he'll kill Lydia. This Angelique—how long has she been gone?"

He grunted. "Her mama-san says she left early last night."

"And she hadn't been missed yet? A little careless, looks like to me."

"The john was taking her to a party. With friends. He paid very, very well. That kind of thing can run long. Listen, you son of a bitch, I still don't get why you're calling me. If this is a game and you're supposed to find that Chin bitch by finding my girls, why don't you just go up there and find her?"

"Can't risk it. That cop, the one who stopped you, she let me go—"

"Why?"

"Christ, why do you think? I bought her off!" Linus, eavesdropping, looked at me in mock shock. "But I'm still on the top of every cop's list, for murder and assault. Show my face in Midtown, I'm completely fucked."

"So I'm supposed to break into some closed store? Help you out?"

"Why not? Someone sees you, you say she didn't answer her phone, you were worried about her. As a friend."

"And me finding her, your lunatic's good with that?"

"I'll deal with him."

"Or I could just cut my losses. Write Angelique off."

"He'll keep doing it. Angelique won't be the last."

"You threatening me?"

"Christ, Lu, how stupid are you? Forget it. Hell with the lunatic, I'll send the cops, they'll find her, she'll get deported, screw you. Or maybe she hates the idea of going back so much, she'll roll on you and your operation. If they give enough of a shit to offer her that deal. Or are you too small time?"

A moment. Then: "You and me, Smith, we're not done yet." He hung up.

Half a block later, Linus, Trella, Woof, and I reached the car. Parking in a bus stop is risky business. They really do tow. But through the windshield I could see a bright orange card on the dash. EMERGENCY TELECOMMUNICATIONS REPAIR. KEEPING NEW YORK CONNECTED. It had a New York City seal in the right corner, New York State seal in the left.

"That works?" I asked Linus.

"Has that Homeland Security smell, know what I mean?"

Trella pressed the unlock button on the keytab, then flipped me the keys over the hood. She, Linus, and Woof had scooted inside before I got my door open.

"You don't trust me?" I said, buckling in. "You think I'd drive off and leave you?"

"Dude." Linus grinned.

Trella beside me, Linus and Woof in back, I started the engine and peeled out, cutting off a bus.

New York traffic lights are timed. If you're not a cop car with a light bar and siren, the best idea is to keep it to twenty-eight mph. Any slower, any faster, you get caught behind a red. I learned that long ago and that was the speed I drove at all the way uptown.

With my jaw clamped, and fingers almost tight enough to crush the wheel.

Once we were rolling steadily I unhooked one hand, took out my phone, dialed Mary.

"Bill? What?" Her peremptory voice was fuzzed by traffic noise.

"You're going to have company at the tailor shop. That pimp, Lu? He's on the way."

"What are you talking about? How do you know?"

"He called me. He's missing another girl."

"And she's there?"

"Apparently."

"You didn't tell him to stay the hell away?"

"He'd listen to me? Besides, it's good. Whatever happens, better him than you. It'll throw the lunatic off his game, and you won't get made."

"He'll think you sent him."

"If I have to I'll tell him about the GPSs. And I told Lu if there's an orange bag in there, I want it."

"You think the clues are there?"

"No, I think it's the same as before: I'm supposed to find a dead Chinese woman, then get more clues. But just in case."

"So I'm supposed to let Lu and his boys stomp all over a crime scene?"

"Do what you have to do. But if our guy's rattled he might make a mistake."

"Or decide this whole game was a mistake."

That was a risk. When all roads lead down, you go with the least steep. "Watch for Lu," I said, and clicked off.

From the back, Linus said, "That was pretty slick."

"It's true."

"Sorta. You didn't say you called him first. You also didn't say we were on the way."

"She didn't ask."

"Hah! But dig, dude. You also also didn't tell Lu his girl was dead."

"He wouldn't go if he knew."

"And the place might be wired again, like last time. Cops might come anyway, whatever Aunt Mary does."

"They might."

"That's slick, too."

"Linus? He's a pimp who puts GPS chips in his girls."

"And besides, his guy beat the crap out of you."

"You think this is personal?"

"It would be with me."

I lit a cigarette. Trella rolled her window down. "It would be with me, too, any other time," I said. "Right now, everything's about Lydia. All I care about is buying time, and the guy calling me again."

"Dude?" Linus asked. "You really think we can find her? Lydia?"

"We have to."

After about a hundred years we hit Sixty-first Street. I swung over and pulled into a bus stop on Madison.

"You guys stay in the car until we know what's going on." I got out and Trella slid into the driver's seat.

"Where are you going?" Linus demanded.

"I want the lunatic to know I got here."

"Well, don't go over that way, dude. There's Aunt Mary's car, with Aunt Mary in it."

"And up there," I said, "there's Lu's."

The Escalade idled in a no standing zone two blocks away. No one got out, and no giant Chinese men were icebreaking through the pedestrian river. Lu must have beat us by a lot; Ming and Strawman must already be inside. I was about to slam the door and leave when I heard the pulse of a distant siren.

"Dude, it *was* wired! Here come the cops," said Linus.

Trella and I agreed.

We were all wrong.

When the siren wailed around the corner, it wasn't coming from a cop car. It was an ambulance.

11

The ambulance sped past us, setting Woof howling, and pulled up at the closed tailor shop on the far corner. I squinted to read the tattered awning: BUCKINGHAM HABERDASHER. The window, in chipped gold leaf, added, CUSTOM AND BESPOKE GENTLEMEN'S CLOTHING. REWEAVING. REPAIRS. ALTERATIONS. The door's glass was smashed and sprinkled on the sidewalk. Like iron filings to a magnet, people had started to collect around the scene. A break-in and an ambulance, your classic New York sideshow. A few folks who had somewhere to go—a dog walker, a chubby woman, three guys in business suits—pushed impatiently through, but the corner was growing thick with people who didn't.

That worked for me, because they hid me from the Escalade. I left the car, crossed the street, broke through the crowd. I couldn't risk staying here long, where cops were sure to show, but if the lunatic was here I wanted him to see me. Probably he wasn't. Probably he was safe in his basement, wherever he had Lydia locked up, listening to his police scanner. But maybe he had a closed-circuit camera. Or X-ray vision.

Something moved inside the dusty storefront. The EMTs

wheeled a gurney from the ambulance but they didn't get inside. Strawman burst out the door, held it open for Ming, who followed, his sport coat swathed around a small Asian woman he carried in his arms. My heart lurched: but again, not Lydia. No, not Lydia. Ming laid her down on the gurney and the EMTs buzzed around, fitting a mask to her face and a drip to her arm. They covered her with a blanket, rolled the gurney into the ambulance, and took off. Their siren, dwindling in the distance, crossed paths with more sirens rushing our way.

I stood stunned on the sidewalk. This girl was alive. That had never entered my mind.

The best way to fight the lunatic for time, doing what he wanted while I tried to outsmart him, how to use her—his second victim—to help me: all that I'd been frantically working on. That she was alive, that she could be saved, and the flip side, that while we were screwing around with disguises and cleverness she could have run out of time: that never occurred to me.

The approaching sirens turned out to be cops, two cars. *Fade back into the shadows, Smith, you're a wanted man. SON OF A BITCH!* I wanted to shove my fist through a wall. But a voice in my head said, *Later. Lydia.*

I was trapped playing games with a lunatic, for Lydia.

I'd almost let a girl die, as part of his game.

I'd told Linus it wasn't about me.

That had better be true.

I retreated to a Starbucks across the street, fueled up on a coffee the size of a popcorn bucket, watched a cop who'd just arrived hold a long discussion with Ming and Strawman. Strawman showed him the same granite disinterest he'd shown me. Ming waved his concrete-block hands around. Neither looked once toward Lu's black Escalade.

Finally Ming tapped behind his ear, at what would have been his hairline if he'd had hair. From his belt he unclipped a handheld device, showed it to the detective. The GPS thing was a new one on this cop, too. I could see that in the stare, the recovery shrug. The detective spoke to two uniforms, and Ming and Strawman were loaded into the back of a radio car.

Two blocks uptown, Lu's Escalade pulled out, blended into traffic.

This was Manhattan, not Brooklyn. This wasn't a homicide, at least not yet. Ming and Strawman would be out in an hour. A B&E into an empty building to save a life, what judge wouldn't laugh that out of court, creepy GPS notwithstanding? But it wouldn't be long before the NYPD connected this to the dead girl in Red Hook. And connected them both to Lu. What would happen then? The lunatic can't have thought he could scatter bodies around—similar bodies, a pattern of bodies—just for me, and the cops would stay out of it. I gave it two hours, maybe a shade over or under—depending on whether Angelique lived, and woke up, and talked—before detectives were pounding on the door of her whorehouse. Her crib. Another five minutes until they hit the street again, armed with her mama-san's description of the man Angelique went off with.

The same description Brooklyn Homicide, with the help of Chinatown Vice, would have gotten from Lei-lei's mama-san.

The description Lydia had encoded in that first phone call.

Which also fit me.

I looked up the street. Mary, who'd found a legit parking place, hadn't left her car. The detective entered the tailor shop and the crowd began to drift apart.

I wondered which of my phones would ring first.

The new one.

Lu.

"Motherfucker. You're dead, motherfucker."

"Are you crazy? You think I did that?"

"Did what, dead man? Tried to kill my girl? Or set me up? Fucking cops, you said there wouldn't be any fucking cops!"

"Back off. One: the guy who killed Lei-lei was responsible for this, too. And two, who called 911 for an ambulance? You, right? Ming, Strawman? What the hell did you think would happen?"

"Where are you?"

"I was watching. Now I'm on the move."

"You get your kicks like that, watching? I'll kill you."

"You'd be wasting your time. And the lunatic would still be going after your girls. This—Angelique? Was she poisoned, same as Lei-lei?"

"Like you don't know."

"Humor me."

"Sick fuck. You want to hear it? She was on the roof. Tied, gagged. In a baby-doll nightie."

Shit. "It was cold last night."

"Cold today. She wasn't even shivering anymore. That what you were looking to do? Freeze my girl to death?"

"Christ, you sound like you care."

"Sweet kid, Angelique. A favorite of mine. That why you picked her?"

"God almighty, you trip over that ego when you walk? I don't give a shit about you, your girls, your operation. All I want is my partner back."

"From the lunatic who kills Chinese girls."

"That's right. Who left the orange plastic bag on the roof with Angelique."

"Oh, right. The imaginary bag, left by the imaginary lunatic."

"It wasn't there?" No surprise. I'd just been hoping.

"Nothing was there except my girl, freezing to death. Don't ever stop looking over your shoulder, motherfucker."

"If I were you I'd focus on keeping an eye on your other girls. Until I get this lunatic, maybe you don't want to let them out of the house."

"How am I supposed to make a living?"

"Oh, there's the Lu I know. See you around, amigo. I have to find my partner."

He paused. "If there really is a lunatic, don't you think when you find her, she'll be dead, too?"

"I hope not," I said. And again: "I hope not."

I called Trella, told her to drive around to the other side of the block where Mary was less likely to spot her.

"Where are you?"

"In Starbucks, waiting for the cops to clear off."

I drank my coffee. Something was scratching at the back of my brain. I tried to stop thinking, to give it room. Angelique, in a nightie, left to die in the cold. Lei-lei, poisoned. Same pimp, different cribs. Brilliant clues, great game. Frozen, poisoned. Poisoned, frozen.

I'd just about finished the coffee when my phone finally rang. Not the new one, mine.

"You can't really be that stupid?" Under the mechanical monotone, an earthquake rage. "You can't really think you can call the cops and I won't mind? Just because last time *I* called the cops?"

"I didn't. I didn't even get there first."

"What I hear, you didn't get there at all."

"You hear wrong. I'm here. Why don't you come up, see for yourself? Your sources obviously suck."

"If you're there, who're the rice-eating gorillas? That my sucky sources told me about?"

"They work for the girl's pimp. They called the ambulance, the dispatcher must've called the cops."

"Oh, you're dogging it, man, you're not even trying. How did they know where to go? You told them! You called!" He was petulant, an angry child.

"You stupid shit. They have GPSs."

"The gorillas?"

"The girls."

"In her phone? I trashed it, moron. Next?"

"Not in her phone." I had to tell him, but I didn't have to tell him the truth. "In her shoe."

"In her fucking shoe? What the hell for?"

"Jesus, why do you think? In case they need help, like they run across a nutjob like you. A girl disappears, her pimp can find her."

A pause. "You are fucking kidding me."

"I'm not in a funny mood."

He suddenly was, though. He cracked up, howled like an electronic hurricane. "You are fucking *kidding*! Chips for the chippies!

Holy fucking dumb-ass shit! I never thought of that. Hey." Theatrically suspicious: "You wouldn't be making this up?"

"You should've done your research."

"Well, shit. Well, fuck. So you didn't get to find her, my frozen fortune cookie?"

"No."

"Goddamn, that sure does butter my nuts. I thought you'd enjoy that one. But you saw her, right? You were there? When they brought the body out?"

I'd been fishing when I said "sources." What happened in Red Hook he could've gotten off a police scanner, and I thought he might be using one now. But then he'd know Angelique was alive. He had eyes, reporting in. Someone who'd been stationed here waiting for me had seen Ming and Strawman break into the tailor shop, had split before they brought Angelique out. Before they could see the EMTs treating a live girl, not processing a body. Split so he wouldn't be seen? Or because he assumed, as I had, that she was dead, and, having made his report—it was gorillas, not me—he was done?

"Yes," I said, "I saw her. And I didn't enjoy it."

"Okay, you caught me. I *really* thought you'd hate it and be seriously pissed off."

"I am."

"Dynamite! Then I guess it doesn't matter who found her. Too bad about her, though. Angelique, she was everything Lei-lei said she was, back when me and Lei-lei were partying. Now why don't you go take a snooze, big boy? You wanna be in shape when the third quarter starts! It's gonna be nonstop action!"

"Let me talk to Lydia."

"Why? You didn't find Angelique, the pimp's gorillas did. The

Pimp's Gorillas, hey, we ought to make that flick! Kick-ass, fucking kick-ass!"

I could hear it: he was high. Soaring, racing. Coke, probably. That's what the wildness was about, the difference from before. Jesus, you headcase, do another line. Stoned could be bad, unbalanced, could make you more dangerous. But if that's where you are, stay there. Don't come down. No black depression, no life's-not-worth-living. Yours isn't, won't be when I find you. But not yet.

"I solved your goddamn clues," I said. "I got there. Without a GPS."

"Hmm. Hmm, hmm, hmm. You know, you're right. And you, Smith, when you're right, you're right. And when you're not, you still fucking *think* you're right! But hey. Okay. Yo, sweetheart, you busy? He wants to talk to you."

A few endless seconds. Then, "Bill?"

"You okay?"

"Yes, baby, I'm all right."

Baby?

"You sound low, but not as low as you could be." To let her know I'd gotten it about the basement.

"It's not just me. Anyone would have a hard time staying sunny for long in a place like this."

And before I could answer, the robotic sneer: "Aww, she's depressed again. You better speed it up there, Prince Asshole."

"Tell me where to come, I'll be there in a flash. You and I can have it out. Isn't it about time for that?"

"Oh! Oh, no, not yet. We're only at halftime. Aren't you enjoying the game?"

"No."

"Yeah, see, it's a pain in the ass when you lose, isn't it? Especially, when you do everything right and you lose anyhow. Any-fucking-how. Which you're gonna do, by the way, bro. Gotta admit you did okay so far, but I just have this feeling you're not gonna make it in time. See, time, ti-yi-yi-yime, it's not on your side, no it ain't! Wow, would you look at that, you've just about burned up six of your twelve hours!"

I caught myself glancing at my watch. Why? I knew he was right. I'd felt every second draining away.

"Oh, and the clues get harder now," he said. "Did I say that? Second half is always tougher, if the game's good. Me personally, I wouldn't lay odds on you. But maybe I'm wrong! We have to play to the end to see. Now, go plug that phone in. You don't want it running out of juice. And hey, by the way, you still don't know who I am, do you?"

"No." But if I kept him going, gloating, sticking it to me, maybe he'd give something away. "I'm working on it, though. Like, for one thing, I get the feeling you don't like cops very much."

"That mighty brain, check it out! Here's a hint: I don't like cops very much."

"Does that have to do with me?"

"No shit, Sherlock."

"Did I jam you up?"

"Did you ever."

"I helped put you away?"

"*Bingo-o-o-o!* Bonus points this round! Yes, you cocksucker. Yes, you put me away."

"When?"

"Back in the day."

"Where?"

"What's this, twenty questions? Inside, idiot."

"Yeah, I gathered that. Upstate?"

"What's the difference? Upstate, downstate, some fucking other state? Four different bings, you really need to know. But it don't mean shit! Inside it doesn't matter where you live because you *don't* live! That's the joke! Big, big joke! They have capital crimes they execute you for, and then they have ones they let you stay living for. But *it's not living*! You're a zombie! The living dead! You do what they tell you, eat what they tell you, piss when they tell you, you don't get a fucking choice about anything! They feed you shit that's not food, you wear shit that's not clothes—starting with that fucking orange jumpsuit, *jumpsuit,* Jesus in the Christmas tree, you should've seen me in that! Ohhh, you *did,* didn't you? What did you think?"

"I don't remember."

"I can't believe this. You don't remember. You were so happy when they stuffed me into it! All these years, I've been comforting myself that no matter how fucking miserable I was, at least Smith was happy. At least I'd made someone happy. And you don't even remember! I went to prison, you went to lunch. You bastard. You cocksucking, shit-eating dog."

"I think you should tell me. I think we should get together and you should tell me to my face exactly what a motherfucker I am."

"Nice try, asshole. Listen, that's about it for this phone. In case you're tracing it or something. Just not quite long enough, right? Hah! See, I got it timed, bro. Talk to you later."

And silence.

And I knew.

12

Boiling crimson rage blew me to my feet. That sneer, that vicious joy, that petty cleverness. *Bastard! Kevin Cavanaugh, you sorry-ass, motherfucking BASTARD!*

Simultaneously: *Smith, you stupid, stupid fool!*

How could I not have known? How could I have missed it? If I'd had a brain, if I'd come to it sooner—Jesus Christ, what was wrong with me? All morning, cocking around with fucking clues, Lydia locked up with Kevin Cavanaugh in some goddamn basement. *I'll kill him, I'll kill that son of a bitch!* I looked wildly around, as though I'd find him here. Smirking over coffee. Sneering through the window. There! That fat slob on the corner— No. Wrong. No. No.

Get a grip. Get a goddamn grip. All right: You're the stupidest most broke-down motherfucker who ever lived. Congratulations. You going to beat yourself up, or you going to try to save Lydia's life? You didn't see what you should've seen. But you see it now.

I had to have a cigarette. I pushed outside, stayed in the shadows, kept the gawkers between me and the cops. I lit my smoke, tried to think: what to do, which way to go?

As I watched, one path was cut off.

The detective, leaving the tailor shop, spotted Mary in her car. With an inquisitive grin he knocked on the window, and she got out. They stood and spoke in the attitude of old friends.

Another long draw on the cigarette and I pulled out my phone.

"Dude! What's *happening*? I almost was gonna call you, but Trella said I couldn't!"

"Where are you guys?"

"Sixty-third and Second. Miles from the action!"

"Stay there."

Forcing myself to the sidewalk's slow pace so I could stay invisible, I moved around the corner, headed east. I made another call.

"Me again," I said to Lu.

"Jesus, you son of a bitch!" Lu exploded. "You're just too stupid to live, aren't you? What the fuck do you want?"

"There's another girl. Maybe two more." I was thinking, third and fourth quarters. The time clock to run them down, and a goal in each: a girl's life. Different from what he'd laid out to me when we started, but what did I expect? Consistency, reasonableness, rules?

Kevin Cavanaugh was a psycho.

Probably these girls were dead already, as Lei-lei was, as Angelique was supposed to be.

But maybe not.

I said, "The lunatic called me."

"That lunatic shit again! Motherfucker, I don't know who you are or why you decided to fuck with me, but it was a bad mistake."

"They'd be from different houses—different cribs—from Lei-lei and Angelique. They're missing since sometime last night."

"Oh, and they're stuffed in orange plastic bags, I bet. Just tell me where they are, tell me now."

"I don't know where or which girls. Their GPSs—"

"Fuck you, motherfucker, don't play with me!"

"I'm not. You can—"

"I fucking can't and you fucking know it! Ming has the tracker, on his way to jail, where you put him!" After that outburst Lu calmed down. "You, motherfucker, are in a deep and steaming pile. Tell me, and if the girls are alive, it won't be so bad when I find you. I'll kill you straight out. Instead of what I'm planning now."

"Call around. By the time you find out which girls are missing Ming and Strawman will be out."

"And then send them to wherever the girls are, so they can get busted again? I don't fucking think so."

"No. When you find the girls, tell me where. I'll send someone in."

"No. Tell me where *you* are, and I'll come kill you."

"Hell of an offer." I hung up.

I'd reached the corner I was headed for, spotted the Malibu at a hydrant, Trella behind the wheel. I slid in back. Woof greeted me like he'd known me all his life and missed me almost as long.

Linus turned from the shotgun seat. "Wow, dude! You look like you saw a ghost."

"Heard from one. Trella, head up to the Bronx. There's a bar I know."

"That's the next place?" Linus asked. "Mr. Crazy said so?"

"No. But we need to go someplace I can think. Where I won't be made."

Trella eased the car into traffic. "If that's what you want, I can take care of that, doesn't have to be the Bronx."

"I—" *You what, Smith? You really need the Bronx? Or you just need to call the shots? So far today, who's been right more often, these kids or you?* "Yeah, okay." I leaned back. Woof flopped his entire sixty pounds onto my lap. "If you're sure it's safe."

Trella grinned. "It's safe."

"Dude, what—" Linus began, but "Bad Boys" chirped from his iPhone. "Aunt Mary," he gulped. "Do I answer it?"

"You'd better. I want to know what she's up to."

Linus put the phone to his ear. "Hey, Aunt Mary, what's going on?" he said noncommitally. His face furrowed. "Hey, no, don't, I can't—" He listened hard, nodding, mumbled, "Umm-hmm, umm-hmm." Hunching over, finger in his other ear, he mumbled some more things I couldn't make out. When he clicked off he slumped against the seat. "Damn! I wish she wouldn't do that."

"Do what?"

"Talk to me in Chinese."

Trella laughed.

I said, "I thought you went to Chinese school."

"Yeah, I can recite Wang Wei if you need it. And my calligraphy's great."

"So you don't know what she was telling you?"

Linus flushed. "I do, sorta. She said, I think she said, her cover got blown."

"I saw that. The detective at the tailor shop."

"Yeah. She knows him. She gave him a story, she was tailing Ming and Strawman because of some friend's kid she thinks went to work for Lu. He was, like, all sympathetic. He said working for Lu is risky, girl of Lu's got killed last night, too, could be some guy has it in for Lu. They have a suspect but they didn't find him yet. I guess that's you, huh?"

"I guess. What else?"

"He said Aunt Mary should come back to the precinct with him, she can question Ming and Strawman about the friend's kid. She couldn't think of how to say no. She told him she was calling the friend about maybe she got a lead."

So much for when they'd make the connection. "That's it?"

"I think she told me the tailor-shop girl isn't dead. Is that true, or did I get it messed up?"

"No, it's true."

"Cool! And she wanted to know if the crazy man called."

"What did you say?"

"Dude, I can hardly say my name! I told her no."

"Good. But he did."

"He *did*? He called you? Dude—!"

"I'll tell you. But first go on. Tell me what else Mary said."

"Well, what she said, *I think* she said, 'You guys stay put until I call you.'"

"Did you tell her we'd already split?"

"Why would I?"

"And besides," Trella grinned, "even if you wanted to, what you would've told her was she should go wash her yak."

"What*ever*! Dude, the crazy man! Did you record him? Did you talk to Lydia again? Is she okay?"

I passed Linus the phone. "I pressed the button the way you showed me, but I don't know if it worked. I did talk to Lydia. But guys? I know who he is."

"Shit!" Linus yelped. "Oh, shit, dude, that's awesome! Who?"

Trella said nothing, but in the rearview I could see her eyes glow. Woof pawed and whined.

"His name's Kevin Cavanaugh. I knew him a long time ago."

"And pissed him off big."

"Yes. I did."

"Who is he? Where do we find him?" Linus was fiddling with the recorder.

"I don't know. That's why I need to think."

Linus flicked a glance at Trella, then back to me. "Can we play the tape? While you think?"

That wasn't likely to help me think and I didn't want to hear that voice again. But maybe they could pick up on something I'd missed. "Go ahead."

Linus blinked as the metallic monotone sliced into the car. Trella steadily drove. My muscles twitched, burning to dive through the phone, strangle the mockery out of that voice. Linus leaned in when Lydia spoke. When the replay was done, he pressed the button, handed me the phone as if he wanted to be rid of it. "Shit," he breathed. "How wack is that freak?"

I didn't answer.

We'd hit East Harlem. These streets, solid Italian a few generations back, are Latino now. All that's left of the Italians are a few restaurants. One's famous, the others you have to know. Trella knew. She pulled in at a row of tattered storefronts. We left Woof in the car and walked a quick half block.

"Dude?" Linus looked troubled. "Now that Mr. Crazy knows about the GPSs, even if he thinks it's the shoes, don't you think, if he already put more girls someplace, he could just say screw it and leave them there and start again? I mean, with, like, just random girls, so they won't have them?"

"I'm counting on him being too impressed with his own cleverness to want to do that. What I'm hoping, actually, is he'll go back and take their shoes. If he has to improvise, do anything that's not already planned out, there's a chance he'll make a mistake."

"What if the other two girls, they're not Lu's?"

"Then what did I lose by telling him? But I bet they are. Lei-lei told him about Angelique. He probably asked Angelique who else was good, and then asked that one the same question. It's a pattern. He likes that, patterns."

Trella pulled open a door beside a shop window where ELAINE AND LORENA's drifted like steam out of a painted soup cauldron. Her entrance stirred a buzz of long-time-no-sees from waiters and customers alike. Even Linus got a beaming kiss from the woman at the register, whose eyes glittered like Trella's. "Elaine," Trella said. "Lorena's in the kitchen." They spoke in Italian, Elaine shooing us to a back table.

"So dude," Linus said, sitting. The garlicky air awoke a hunger I hadn't known I felt. "This Cavanaugh freak. What's his beef? How do we find him?"

"What you said at the beginning: he's been in prison. Can you search for Kevin Cavanaughs, the five boroughs, New Jersey, Long Island, Westchester?"

"Who is he?" Trella asked as Linus brought out his iPhone. "What did he do?"

"He killed a girl."

We hadn't ordered, but food arrived: bread, olives, cheese, sausages, soup. I was starving, Trella was hungry, and Linus was a teenage boy, so nothing lasted long.

"And you nailed him? Long time ago?" Linus spoke without looking up from what absorbed him: the phone and the food.

"Ten years."

Another minute passed; then, "Dude." Linus swept his bowl with a crust, eyes on the phone. "Two. One in Yonkers, he's eighteen. One in Bellport, Kevin's his middle name, and he's sixty-three."

I hadn't expected that to work, but it had to be tried.

"If he's out of prison," Trella said, "he's done, or he's on parole?"

"Parole. It was a fifteen-year bid." I'd done the math. "First time he was eligible would've been eight months ago."

"So doesn't he have to report somewhere?"

"Yes, and they'd have an address. But the Corrections computer—Linus, you can't get at that, can you?"

Linus shook his head. "Beyond me, dude. Aunt Mary could."

"Can't risk it. There'd be cops everywhere, soon as they have an ID."

"You don't think she'd give you the address and not—" He stopped. "No, me either."

I ran my hand over my face. Exhausted, burned out, battered, and no way to stop. "Dude—" Linus began, but Trella shook her head. Linus clammed up and focused on his plate.

I took two bites in silence, then threw down my fork and pulled out both phones, mine to find the number, the new one to dial. I didn't like this idea, but I didn't have a better one, and the clock was ticking. Six hours gone, halftime probably winding down. Kevin would call soon, send me into frantic action. If knowing more than he thought I did was going to do me any good, I had to move on it now.

Four rings; then, "You've got Hal Ross." It grated right away, that cynical rasp: you've got him, but you probably didn't want him, it's a mistake.

"Hey, Hal. Bill Smith."

"Well, fuck me," Hal said, long and slow. "Bill effing Smith. What's this, a Jiminy Cricket moment? You checking up on me?

'Yo, Hal, good buddy, screwed anything up lately? Need your ass burned, can I help?' "

"I don't have time for it, Hal. Kevin's out."

A drawn breath. "The hell you say."

"Much worse. He kidnapped my partner. If I don't find her, he'll kill her."

"What the—" He stopped, a long, wobbly pause.

Jesus, Hal, be sober. On the wagon, in the gutter, it's your life, I don't give a shit; but right now, I need you sober. "He's on parole," I said. "I need his address. You still have connections on the Job?"

"He came for you." Wonderment filled Hal's voice, but edged with something tighter: I might have said, envy.

"Can you do it?" I leaned on each word.

"Shit, Smith. You gotta have better hooks into the Job than ol' Hal. This a pity fuck?"

"Jesus Christ! *Did you hear me?* We're talking about my partner's life." A long silence. Resigned, I added, "I'm hot. Kevin set me up, the NYPD's looking for me. I can't call anyone else."

"Ah, okay." The relief of understanding. "You *can't* call anyone else. *That's* when you call Hal."

"Yeah, and sounds like it was a mistake."

"He set you up how?"

"What the hell's the difference? Forget it. Thanks a lot."

"Nah, hold your water. There's a guy I could try. Where are you?"

"You can call this number."

"And you're sure it's me you want? Because if I find that cocksucker, I might really kill him this time."

"I don't want you, but you're my only option. And *do not* go near him. Find the address, call me. That's it."

"'Yeah, Hal, don't fuck this up, too.' That what you mean?"

"I mean, my partner's all that matters. Not you or me proving anything. You get me? Find that address."

I thumbed off to see both kids staring.

"Dude," Linus said. "It totally sounds like you don't like that guy."

I shook my head as the waiter clinked a double espresso down by my elbow, gave Trella a single and Linus a Coke. "Hal Ross. Ex-cop." I tried the coffee, bitter and rich.

"He knows Kevin?" Trella asked.

"Dude." Linus looked up. "He on Kevin's hate list? Is he gonna try to get him some way, too?"

"Should be the opposite. He ought to be grateful. What Kevin did should've been good for more than ten and parole. Hal screwed it up and the DA had to go to a plea deal. That's how I know Kevin, Hal and I played basketball with him and a friend of his, ten years ago. Listen, Linus, try that guy, Kevin's friend. Jim White."

"Oh, wow, dude. You couldn't make it more generic?"

"You said weird names were too easy."

"Yeah, well, you better give me a clue, or you'll get more Jim Whites than you can use."

"He used to live in the Village. He'd be mid-thirties. Ten years ago, worked on Wall Street, a brokerage, something." I tried to think back, shook my head. "Sorry, that's all."

Poking the iPhone, Linus said, "If you don't like this Hal guy how come you and him played ball?"

"I liked him then. I'll tell you about it. But first I want to go over what Lydia gave us."

They exchanged glances. Trella, I could see, was with me: let's move on, let's *do*. Linus wanted the story, the facts, the data. I wanted to find the tiny signposts to our next step.

"Dude," said Linus, "she gave us something? She only said like three words."

And I had them all memorized. "Look: 'Hard to stay sunny for long in a place like this.' Remember, we said a basement with an areaway, windows? I think that means they actually catch some sun. Briefly. So likely, not on the north side of a street. South, or possibly west."

Trella asked, "Why not east?"

"I'm thinking she gave me everything she had each time we talked. If she saw sun in the morning she'd have told me sooner. So midday, south or west, maybe surrounded by buildings not hugely tall. Or tall, but a slot, alley, something, between the two opposite. And she said, 'It's not just me.' I think maybe she was telling me he hadn't left. That she hadn't been alone."

"Makes sense, dude. Because he didn't know the tailor shop girl's not dead."

"Linus, when you're through with that, can you check if that call came from the same tower? I'll bet it did, but I want to be sure."

"No problem."

"And something else. But I don't know what it means. She called me 'baby.'"

"She doesn't usually?" Trella asked.

Linus, swallowing Coke, said, "It would be kinda like you calling me 'baby.'"

"Oh. Yeah, then it means something else." She thought. "Maybe a storefront she can see? Maternity clothes?"

"Toys? A preschool?"

"A gynecologist?"

"Linus, after you—"

"I can do it." Trella took out her own iPhone. "I'm not as good as he is, but I can handle this."

We ate in silence, the kids working the phones, me willing Hal to call. Then Linus sat back. "'K, dude. Found you five Jim Whites in the financial biz. Actually, I found another eleven, but with how old they are and when they got to New York, I exed those ones out."

"Give me their numbers. And after you check on the phone tower, here's something else. Kevin had a fiancée. On the Upper East Side. Megan something, I can't remember, but it had something to do with beer."

"Seriously?"

"You find it, I'll know it's her."

He rolled his eyes. "Why not? But dude. If this freak Kevin is working with somebody, it could be him. White. The old friend."

"I know."

"So you don't want him to know you're onto him, right?"

"Right." I dialed the first Jim White's office. "I'm an old friend and client of his," I told the secretary in my best British accent, subtle, underplayed. "We've been out of touch for a number of years, but I've just come into some money, and I thought, well, old Jim did quite nicely on my behalf back in the nineties." That got me through to his assistant, and the next two Jim Whites' assistants, and the first two Jim Whites. It was their voices I wanted to hear, their pitch and cadence. But one rang of the south, maybe Texas; and if the other hadn't been born Tomacz Witrovicz or Witrovski or Weitz, I'd eat my hat. I called the third number, listening, in my head, to the minutes ticking away.

I was met with a brief pause, then told Mr. White wasn't available but his assistant could help me. I got transferred to a harried-sounding young man and gave my spiel.

"Oh," he said. "I'm sorry."

"Is he not taking new clients? I'm sure he'll want to talk to me. It's been a long time, but it was a special friendship, you see."

"Mr. White is unavailable." The young man spoke with an odd tone, part bristle, part confusion.

"You're not saying you're unable to get in touch with him?" That was the one thing I knew about all this new technology: there was no such thing as *He's away, I can't reach him* anymore. But if this was the right Jim, maybe he was ducking calls from strangers, in case they turned out to be me.

"I'm sorry," the assistant said again.

"I really must—"

"No, you don't understand." His voice got higher, faster. "Mr. White passed away."

"He— When?"

"Over the weekend."

"I didn't know he'd been ill." I was suddenly, icily sure this was the right Jim, and he hadn't been ill.

"No, he . . . he had an accident."

"This is a shock. What happened?"

An audible swallow. "He drowned."

"Where?" I was playing stunned, which wasn't a stretch. "He'd gone on holiday? To the beach?"

"No. He has a lap pool in the basement of his brownstone."

"A lap pool? But those are quite shallow. I'm sorry, I don't see how this is possible. Old Jim, he was a good swimmer, as I recall. I mean, I imagine you knew him much better than I, so perhaps this makes sense to you, but as for me—"

"That's what I thought, too." As I'd hoped, the assistant's words came in a confiding rush to match my own. "You're right, he *was* a strong swimmer. When they told me, I said, 'He can't have just drowned in a *lap pool.*' He must have had a heart attack or something. Or . . . something . . ." He trailed secretively off.

"Or been high?" I dropped my voice. "Old Jim and I were known to hit the slopes, back in the day." The slopes: snow, cocaine. "Perhaps he'd been partying?" *With his old friend Kevin?*

"Exactly!" he whispered. "I thought that! Lately he'd looked terrible. Haggard and tired. That look you can get when, you know, something's taking it out of you." He sniffed with knowledge and disapproval. "But they said no. He has one of those wave machines, you know? They said the current was just too strong, he had it set too high. It must have knocked him down, he got disoriented and couldn't fight his way out."

"Can that happen, with those machines?"

"They say it can. But really. These last few weeks! I spent a lot of time covering for him, I can tell you."

"I'm sure you did. That's a shame, it's work for which one never gets recognition. Did they find anything of the sort?"

"Not a thing! But drowning in a lap pool because the current's too high? I plain don't believe it."

"No," I said slowly. "Neither do I." I clicked off. "Shit."

Again, wide eyes across the table.

"Dude? What's the story?"

"This one, this Jim White. Find me everything you can on him."

"He's the one? Did you talk to him?"

I paused. "Linus? He's dead."

13

Linus and I were back in the car, me driving. We were heading downtown to see Jim White's widow. Trella was in a black sedan on her way across town.

Jim's widow had been an easy find. "That Jim White," Linus said from across the table in Elaine and Lorena's, "he worked at Chase, wife's name is Nicole, lives at eleven Perry Street. Before that, three-oh-three-A West Twelfth. Ten years ago he worked for Star Advantage Capital Management. That him?"

"Star Advantage. Shit. Yes, that's him."

"You think Kevin, you think he killed him?"

"Yes, I do."

"Why?"

"He was prepared to testify at Kevin's trial. It didn't come to that, because of the plea. But Kevin was livid. Said Jim was helping me sell him down the river."

Megan, Kevin's ex, had been harder. Together, we'd run through every beer we knew, Linus checking the whole country in case she'd left New York. "Dude," he'd report. "Found six Megan Millers the right age but none of them lived on the Upper East Side ten years ago. And one Megan Coors, but she's sixty-two."

"No, those aren't right. Dammit! Why the *hell* can't I think of it?"

After a couple of exchanges like that Linus had thumbed toward the window. "How about you go to the bodega across there, take a look? Maybe if you see a bunch of different cans."

"Not cans. Kevin wouldn't drink from a can. Only imported bottles, or microbrews on tap."

"But this isn't Kevin's beer," Trella objected. "It's his fiancée's name."

"I know. But I have the idea it matters." I closed my eyes. We're all in a bar, hot and sweaty, a round of whatever's on tap except not Kevin, he orders some goddamn pretentious microbrew, frosted glass or he won't drink it, no, not a glass, a mug, an iced mug, got to have a handle so the thing stays cold—"*Stine*!" I opened my eyes. "Goddamn son of a bitch, her name was Stine."

"Yes! Beer stein!" Linus pumped his fist, started swiping and poking.

"No," I said. "The English way." I spelled it for him.

"Hah!" he said. "This is your brain on 'charades.'" He finished off his Coke while he waited for something, swiped and poked again. "Megan Stine! Dudes! Megan Collings now. Married five years ago. Ulp, ditched that guy, too. About a year."

"Still in New York?"

"Damn skippy! On the Upper West Side. So. Where first, this Jim guy or her?"

"Not that easy," I said. "I met Megan a couple of times. She might remember me. Especially since Kevin might have been to see her, warned her I might show. I need to think a minute, who I can call."

"Like, another PI?"

Another PI. If this were another case, that would be Lydia.

"Yes. But most of them are ex-cops, and this may not be the time—"

Trella jumped on it: "I'll go."

"No way," I said. "It's too dangerous."

"Dangerous how? Crazy Kevin's downtown, with Lydia."

"We don't know that."

"Lydia said he hadn't left. Why would he leave now? Anyway he might not have been in touch with the fiancée at all."

"Then what's the point?"

"Your idea. It's a stone. We have to turn it over."

She was right about that, but: "I can't let you."

"Um, excuse me, you can't stop me. Wait. Just listen. I'll go over there. Talk to the neighbors, not her. I'm a jealous girlfriend, I think my man's two-timing me with this Megan. Has anyone been hanging around her lately? I'll describe him. If I get a hit I'll call you. Then you can tell me what to do."

That final line got a grin and a "Yeah, right," from Linus.

"It's good," I admitted. "But you're not going."

Trella's eyes flashed. She stood and strode away. I jumped up, thinking—what? I could grab the car keys, peel out in Linus's mother's car, leave both kids in the dust? But Trella stopped by the door. She leaned over a table, had a short conversation with a young guy in a suit jacket and open white shirt. He shrugged and nodded. She spun around to face me. "I'm going," she announced. "But not alone. My cousin, Joey."

"Yo," said Joey, hooded eyes on me. The two other men at his table were also watching me. I got the feeling that behind me, the entire restaurant had taken an interest.

After a long moment, I nodded back.

Trella handed over the keys and climbed into Joey's black town car. Linus and I walked to the Malibu, Woof pawing the glass at the sight of us. "So dude, this Kevin Crazy Man," said Linus. "What did you do to him?"

"I'm surprised Trella left without the whole story."

"Yo, in case you hadn't noticed, she's not so into talking. Action Jackson, that's more her thing."

"Could get her in trouble."

"Dude! I'm a geek, all I do is stare at a screen, I'm always in trouble anyhow."

"Is Joey her real cousin?"

"Italians, they're all related, worse than Chinese."

While Woof scarfed down salami Linus had brought him, I drove downtown, filling Linus in on what this was all about.

"Like I said, we used to play basketball, years ago. Smug young shits, Kevin and Jim. First time Hal and I showed up at the playground, it was, 'Bring it on, Grandpa.' I had ten years on them, Hal had a few more, they thought we were geezers. So we whupped their asses."

"They played bad?"

"It was more than that. Kevin hated to lose. So much, he'd mess up his own head. Throw elbows, make dirty fouls. Out-and-out cheat. It was easy to piss him off and make him lose it. Then if you just stayed cool, you were golden."

"Didn't it piss him off worse when you won?"

"Way worse. Then he'd pull out the excuses. Sun was in his eyes. He was hungover. Jim wasn't pulling his weight. More than once, Kevin slammed down the ball and stomped off the court cursing out everyone in sight."

"But you kept playing."

"If they were going to come back, so were we. It got so every Saturday it was a blood feud."

Linus shook his head. "Playing games with people you hate. Doesn't sound like fun to me."

"Kevin wasn't in it for fun. He was in it to win."

Linus gave me a look I couldn't read. After a moment he said, "So, what got him to jail? That he blames you for?"

I lit a cigarette, chucked the match out the window. "Sometimes, after a game, they'd go for Chinese food, or a beer. Kevin and Jim. Mostly I didn't go: I had a short fuse for Kevin's bullshit. Everything was a game with him. Work, women, everything. Who played the 'eighty-four Superbowl, what's in my pocket. They were all games, but the same as basketball: if he lost he was furious. Stare like he wanted to kill you with his eyes. Sometimes he'd explode. I didn't usually need a beer that badly."

"The times you did go, did you win those games, too?"

"I wouldn't play. Only basketball, nothing else. It pissed him off.

"Sometimes Hal would go with them, though. One weekend, after I split, they turned it into a bar crawl. In one place, late that night, Kevin hit on a girl. Hal said later he knew it was trouble, but by then he could barely walk, was too far gone to do anything. The next morning the girl was found beaten to death in Central Park."

"Shit, dude."

"Kevin was arrested. We thought that was it, but when Hal and I went up to the playground the next week, there he was. Crowing. '*Fucking cops, fucking bitch. Yeah, I picked her up, what the fuck, you saw her, Hal, she was hot, right? The park, that was her idea, what is it with women, disgusting, like some fucking jungle. Yeah, we did it rough, how she liked it. Mostly they like it rough, whatever they say. What do you mean, then what? I kissed her off and went home! Hadda save some for Megan, you know? She must've picked up some other asshole later, for more.* Hours *I sat in that shithouse telling those cops that, over and over. Fuck, Hal, you work with those cocksuckers, place like that, no wonder you're an alky. Let's play ball.'* "

I paused, seeing Kevin's face that day, hearing his sneer.

"Hal blew up. Jumped on him, suddenly they're pounding each other. Jim and I had to separate them. I told Hal to get out, go home. Thought he might pull the gun from his gym bag and shoot Kevin and me, too. When he left, I apologized to Kevin, grabbed some kid from the sidelines, asked if he wanted to play."

"Dude, you *did? Apologized?*"

"And played badly. We lost. Kevin was strutting, God, he was all that and a bag of chips. I suggested a beer."

"Oh." Linus grinned. "I see it coming."

"I kept buying rounds, egging him on. I said I believed he hadn't killed that girl because he'd never have been able to get over on the cops if he did."

"And he bragged and told you he did?"

"No. He wasn't that drunk and he's not that stupid. But he got louder, more full of himself. The cops, the bitch, the cops, the bitch. I listened. Then later, I went looking. Turned some things up. Nothing the cops wouldn't have found if they'd kept at him. But I wasn't sure they would.

"One of the things I heard while he was ranting was a gap between when he and the girl left the bar and when he got home. The cops heard it, too, but they couldn't squeeze anything from it. He claimed he'd stopped for one more, too drunk to remember where.

"I thought, if I were Kevin, what would I have done? Obviously, play a game. 'Outsmart the Cops.' What would that involve? I'd ditch my clothes, wash off before I got home. Not near where I lived, and not near where I killed her. But not someplace random. Kevin didn't have the imagination for that. Someplace he knew.

"Where we played ball, the playground, that was the Village. He didn't live there and it's far from Central Park. So midnight, I went there. Talked to the bums on the benches. Found one who'd seen a big, soft guy scrub off at the spigot, middle of the night, week before. He couldn't ID Kevin's picture, but it was enough. Once the cops knew what to look for, they found it. The cabbie who drove him down Third, another who took him crosstown. Clever, see, changing cabs? A clerk in the all-night CVS remembered him buying a T-shirt and running shorts. The clincher was the bum who'd dug a pair of sweats out of the Dumpster. He didn't want to give them up, but when he did, they were Kevin's. And they had the girl's blood on them.

"When Kevin found out where the new evidence came from, he went ballistic. Swore he'd kill me. I wasn't worried. Evidence they had, they should've been able to put him inside for decades."

"So why's he out?"

"He made bail, and when the trial started his lawyer went to work punching holes in the DA's case, in the cops, in me. It wouldn't have paid off. The jury would've nailed Kevin to the wall. But Hal got all liquored up one afternoon, after a particularly bad day in court. It had never quit gnawing at him, that he hadn't saved that girl, hadn't stopped her from going off with Kevin. He went up to Kevin's place. Why Kevin let him in I don't know. Probably so he could crow about how he was winning. Probably he mocked Hal, or maybe Hal didn't need that. In the end Hal did what he went there to do: he beat the crap out of Kevin, left him lying in a pool of blood.

"And then," I tossed my cigarette butt out the window, "then he called me. 'Hey, pal, I killed that little prick!' Shit, he was so happy. Thought I'd be happy. I called 911. It was touch and go but Kevin pulled through.

"Kevin's lawyer was all over it. Instant plea or they'd sue the NYPD, the city, everyone in sight. Got Kevin a soft deal, and Hal was allowed to retire, full pension, no charges."

"Sounds lucky."

"For Kevin. Hal saw it another way. If Kevin had died he might have gotten away with it. No one saw him there, no one knew it was him. Except me. He blames me for calling 911, ending his career."

Linus thought for a while, then shook his head. "Dude, I don't get it. About Kevin Crazy Man. Even with the R2-D2 voice, seems so obvious it was him."

I'd been kicking myself about that, over and over. "It's been a lot of years. And Lydia's description threw me off."

"If it's not how he looks how do you know it's him?"

"A few things. Some of those phrases sounded so familiar: 'grab my sneakers, find another game.' Before, he told me to lighten up. Kevin was always saying that. Meaning don't get riled when he got over on you. The crowd at Fatima's, bankers chasing the A-list. Bespoke clothing. Ways to prove you'd made it: that was Kevin."

"But the difference?"

"When I knew him his hair was dark. Longish, wavy. But ten years in prison, time enough to get a jailhouse buzz. To go gray. Back then he was flabby, too. Big soft spare tire. But years pumping iron, that could do it."

"Yeah, dude, but still. How come it took you this long?"

I felt a burn creep up my face. "Like I said, I haven't thought about him since then."

That wasn't enough for Linus. He turned to me and waited for the rest.

"What I did," I said slowly, "nailing him after he thought he'd won, to him that was the biggest, worst thing that ever happened. To me . . ."

"Dude," Linus nodded. "I get you. To you, it was a game."

"I said I didn't play his other games. But I did. I played 'I Won't Play.' It pissed him off and that made me happy. Nailing him wasn't about justice. It was about outsmarting the smug shit, like on the court. When I did, I got a rush. And then, over. Like any game: the only thing while it's on, meaningless when it's done."

A long pause. "You whupped his ass," Linus said.

"I'm just like him."

"Oh, dude. Oh, what bullshit."

I didn't answer. I wished I had another cigarette, a beer, a thousand miles between me and everyone else in the world.

"Dude," Linus said. "Whatever. That was then, this is now."

Meaning: don't get lost in the videotape. This game's still on.

"The girl Kevin killed, back then," I said. "Marly Lin. From LA. But her parents, from Taiwan."

Silence, until Linus finally said it. "A chink ho."

14

We were close enough to our destination that I was looking for a place to park when Linus spoke again. "Dude? Okay if I ask you something?"

After the last few hours, how could it not be? "Go ahead."

"Well, just, you and cousin Lydia. I mean, what's that?"

I didn't know what I'd been expecting, but that wasn't it. When I didn't respond right away he went on. "See, dig, I know Lydia's mom's not into it. A bunch of the older folks don't like it. But there's people on your side, too."

"What are you saying? Your family discusses this?"

"Dude! A Chinese family? You think? Seriously, a couple of Lydia's brothers think you're cool. And some of the cousins. Like, you know, me."

I shook my head, not even sure where to start. "The brothers and the cousins . . . It's what Lydia thinks that matters, Linus."

"Oh. But I thought—you mean she—but, dude—" After a moment: "I didn't know that. I totally dig. It's the same as—" He stopped again, and flushed. "As, you know, Trella and me."

I glanced over. "Is that what you think?"

He nodded. "She's, like, not so into me."

I spotted a parking space, started pulling in. "I could be wrong," I said. "I'm bad at this. But from where I am, that's not what I'm seeing."

Linus didn't answer. He just stared at me.

"You ready?" I asked Linus as we got out of the car, Woof watching from the rear window.

"I dunno, dude. Trella's better at this stuff than me."

"Trella's not here. I need you, Linus."

"Dude!" A bright grin. "This morning you were all, like, *go away*."

"When this is over, ask Lydia. She'll tell you I'm usually wrong."

I pressed the bell at Jim White's brownstone. The door opened, not far. The bony woman who peered out had straggly blond hair and a fading bruise on her cheekbone. "Yes?"

"Mrs. White? Greg Bowen. Alliance Casualty." I offered her a card from my wallet, one of a small cluster I keep around. "This is Linus Wong." Linus offered her a bored nod. "We're sorry for your loss. We need to ask you some questions."

Nicole White's frown swept us. "What kind of questions?"

"Your late husband had a million-dollar life insurance policy with us."

"He—Jim did? He was with MetLife. And," a soft, bitter laugh, "it wasn't that much."

"This was paid by his employer. Automatic at Chase for executives above a certain level. Standard in the industry."

Nicole White stood digesting that. I might've expected her to perk up—no matter how fresh the loss, a million unexpected dollars should catch a widow's interest—but she actually seemed to deflate. "So. It didn't cost Jim anything."

"No."

"That makes more sense. As long as he didn't have to spend money on me."

I said, "Maybe you'd be more comfortable indoors?"

For the first time she seemed to notice the cold leaking through her sweater. A brief hesitation, then she stood aside and let us in. I was more comfortable off the street, too, though that had nothing to do with the weather.

Jim White, I could see, had spent this last decade being good to himself. A brownstone on a trendy street. Gleaming wood floors, oversize leather furniture. On the kitchen counter, an espresso machine the size of a small car. Watching his wife, though, I got the feeling he'd been less good to her. Her pallor and sunken eyes could be shock, sleeplessness, the dull ache of loss. But the bruise on her cheek, and another on her wrist, melded with her skittish and defeated air to tell a longer story. Well, I'd known Jim. Not hard to believe he'd knocked his wife around.

"The police made me go over it a hundred times. I really don't want to go through it again." Nicole White spoke listlessly, as though she were used to what she wanted not mattering. Sitting, she pulled a Salem from a pack. I leaned to light it. Instinctively she shied away. Then she saw the flame, met my eyes, leaned in. "Jim wouldn't let me smoke in the house. I guess I can do what I want now, huh?" She swiped at a tear. He beat her up, ordered her around, cowed and frightened her, still she cries over him. People are staggering, but rarely surprising.

"Thing is," Linus spoke with an air of impatience, "there's a problem. With the policy."

Nicole White regarded him as though she wasn't sure what he was. "What kind of problem?"

"Cocaine. Cops found it in your husband's system."

She looked from him to me. "No. I thought they didn't."

"Not enough to be a legal concern," I said soothingly. "But it raises issues with the policy."

"What kind of issues?"

Linus said maliciously, "We might not have to pay."

Now, a spark. "Why?"

"There's a clause. If he was stoned, drunk. 'Impaired,' dig? Ask me, I wouldn't have come, I'd have told Alliance go ahead and fight it, but I'm just a junior investigator. Big boss here insisted." Linus rolled his eyes. "It's like this. Three years ago they had a case. Before me, you dig? Policyholder wrapped her car around a tree. Blood alcohol miles above the legal limit. We don't pay, right? Wrong. Because check out this bullshit, pardon my French. Seems she was a regular at the ER. Walked into lots of doors, haha. That night they were at a bar, her and her husband, him buying beers and making her drink. She was scared to say no."

I watched Jim's widow while Linus talked. Hunched over, she dragged at her Salem.

"The husband was in the car beside her, didn't get a scratch. His lawyer—his!—said because she was drinking involuntarily, she wasn't responsible, so we better pay. Serious crap, right? But the jury bought it. He wasn't the beneficiary, the kids were, and they all came to court, very sad.

"So now, things like your husband, we gotta pay unless we can prove, one, the drugs contributed to the accident, and second, the insured took them voluntarily. So: how long had your husband been snorting cocaine?"

"I— He wasn't. He didn't." Nicole White blinked.

"Linus," I said, "you're not being fair. I've spoken to you about this before. Mrs. White has a right to the whole story." I gave him a senior frown and took it up. "We talked to someone at your husband's office. He said Mr. White had run into a man he used to know. Someone he was afraid of. I told the company, if he was afraid of this guy, maybe he was afraid to say no when the guy brought out the cocaine. I said we had to speak to you, we couldn't just reject the claim out of hand."

Linus muttered, "Couldn't, my ass."

"Linus, you know as well—"

Nicole White found her voice. "Who is this someone he used to know?"

"A man called Kevin Cavanaugh."

"Kevin?" The widow blanched. "My God, I forgot all about Kevin. That was years ago. He's out of jail?"

"A few months now. When did your husband first see him after he got out?"

"I don't think he did. I don't think he knew that. You mean this might be Kevin's fault?"

"If he was here," I said. "If he coerced your husband into taking drugs, we'll have to pay."

Linus stuck in, "Yeah, well, we'll have to talk to him first. Get his side."

"I . . . I suppose it's possible."

"Where do we find him?"

"Kevin? I have no idea."

"We will need to speak to him," I confirmed apologetically. "Before we can pay."

Wildly, she laughed. "Wouldn't that be just like Jim! A million dollars and I can't get at it because he didn't tell me he'd seen Kevin. Goddamn liar!" Suddenly she was crying. "Maybe he saw

Kevin. It wouldn't be the first time he'd seen someone and not told me. That bastard. That bastard! He said he loved *me*. How could he?"

Linus and I exchanged glances. "I'm afraid I don't follow you," I said.

"Maybe *she* gave him the cocaine. Honey, I'm working late. Party time! Then I wouldn't get paid, would I? But could they put her in jail?"

"Who are we talking about?"

"Jim's mistress. His whore! His piece on the side." Her words poured out. "He thought I was stupid. Sometimes he wasn't so smart, either. He should've told the agent, don't call my house, whatever you do."

"Agent?"

"Some stupid real estate agent. The paperwork needed a signature. I asked what the hell she was talking about. She hemmed and hawed, oops, her mistake, forget it. Her mistake! No, Jim's. But he was like that sometimes. Sloppy. What an idiot." Another roughly smeared tear.

"What paperwork? What was it for?"

Now the tears flowed, shining her cheeks. She didn't bother to wipe them away. "He rented her an apartment."

Linus threw me a look of alarm. I was right there with him. If Jim was having an affair, maybe that explained his distraction, his exhaustion. Maybe his death was an accident, maybe Kevin had nothing to do with it and maybe we'd just wasted half an hour we could have used to actually do Lydia some good.

The widow sniffled and ignored us. I was about to thank her and get us out of there when my new phone rang. Trella, reporting in?

As it turned out, no.

"Where the hell are you guys?" Mary whispered fiercely.

Why lie? "In the Village."

"Get the hell out of wherever it is. Cops on the way. *Move!*"

She clicked off. On the way, how close?

And how come?

The car was around the block, couldn't risk it. I stood. "I'm sorry if we've upset you," I told the widow. "If we could just see the basement? The pool itself. Then we'll go."

After a blink Nicole White nodded, led us to a door by the kitchen. She unbolted it, flicked on a light and started down the stairs. I held Linus back. When she was halfway down I slammed it shut, threw the bolt.

"*Dude!* What—"

"Come on. Don't argue."

I raced up the stairs to the second floor, then the third, Linus behind me. We could hear Nicole White shouting and pounding on the basement door. *Sorry, lady, but the cops will be here soon.* From the third floor a tight spiral staircase led to the roof. "Stay here," I told Linus.

"Dude, I'm going where you're going."

"*Stay there!* Just wait!"

"WTF?" But he stopped.

At the top I slid the door's heavy bolts, stepped onto a teak deck. The view over the rooftops was good; I saw a police car turn the corner. I ducked down, took off my watch, wrenched at the band. My arms shook with effort until a link finally broke. I tossed the watch onto the next roof. It skidded amd skittered, came to rest where you could see it. I swept back down.

"Dude—"

"Quiet."

Pounding rose from three stories below, now the basement door syncopated with the front, the widow's screams with "Police, open up!"

I pulled open a closet, told Linus, "Get in." Eyes wide, he pressed into a mass of hanging clothes, me beside him. "Cell phone off," I whispered. "Don't move."

Frozen in the dark, we heard the cops kick in the front door. A bedlam of men's shouts tumbled over the thin wire of Nicole White's panic. Very fast footsteps thumped up the stairs. I felt Linus tense, grabbed his arm to steady him. The footsteps went on up the iron spiral to the door I'd left swinging. A yell: "Here, that way!" After heart-thudding eons the footsteps came down again, along with the voice of a cop on a cell phone or radio. ". . . the roofs, probably down the back somewhere. Do the whole street, they could be in a backyard, try to break into . . ."

We couldn't hear after that, except for the occasional rising word, and the front door opening and closing. I gave it fifteen minutes—fifteen estimated minutes, chances were I'd never see that watch again, but it had served its decoy purpose—then eased the closet open. I stepped without noise to the top of the stairs, listened. No sound at all. If the widow was still here, she was alone. If it were me, I might've gone off to stay with friends; it had been a rough day.

She hadn't, though. She was sitting in the living room, staring and smoking, and when Linus and I clattered down she screamed to wake the dead. We tore out the battered front door and around the block, dove into the car. Woof caught the excitement, wagged and whined madly. I drove, joining the traffic stream on Hudson at the same pace as everyone else. I prayed Nicole White hadn't had the wit to follow us, hadn't seen the car. It was the best I could do.

"Dude," Linus said weakly. "I told you Trella's better at this stuff than me. I just about wet my pants."

"You don't think she would have?"

"Are you kidding? She'd have *loved* it. Dig: I have like a billion questions. How'd you know they were coming? How'd they know to come? Where to now? But first you gotta stop and let me take a piss."

I pulled over, idled at a bus stop while Linus charged into a diner. I considered driving off and leaving him. This was trouble too deep for a kid. But I couldn't do without him, the only secret weapon I had. Lydia would've told me to do it anyway, drive off. She'd have said, *Linus is my little cousin, you shouldn't have brought him in in the first place!* Well, she'd have to yell at me later. It would be music.

I wondered if I had another weapon, too, though. I wondered if I still had Mary. I dialed her number from the prepaid phone. No answer. I had just left a message, basically "Thanks" and "Call me" when Linus came back.

"Brought you coffee."

"How'd you know?"

"Uh-huh." He passed me the cup from a paper bag, popped open a Coke for himself. "So, dude, how—"

"Mary," I said.

"Aunt Mary? That was *her* who called?"

"She said the cops were coming and to get out."

"Wow." He guzzled some Coke. "Wow. We coulda got arrested and she saved us? That's, like, weird." He shook his head. "But dude. How did they know? They followed us? They following us now?" He twisted in his seat, looked out the back in alarm.

"No. They'd have stopped us already."

"So then—"

"I think Kevin set it up somehow."

"But that means—"

My phone rang. The one Kevin used.

"Well, if it ain't that lying, cheating son of a bitch. Hell are you trying to do, asshole, get this game called on account of you're a big fat liar?" No more robot: the real Kevin Cavanaugh sneer.

"What are you talking about?"

"Hmm. You playing innocent, or you playing stupid? 'Ooh, let me guess, did I jam you up, when was that, I don't remember?' Motherfucker! You know exactly who I am."

"I only just figured it out. After you hung up on me last time. I'd've let you know if you'd given me a way."

"Yeah, I'm sure. You'd never have kept quiet so you could try to get over on me. Not squeaky-clean Luke Skywalker. But don't worry, I don't really give a shit. It actually took you a lot longer than I thought it would. Maybe you're slipping. Gee, that would be too bad for Princess Leia here, wouldn't it? So, now you know, how's it feel, Lukey boy? All warm and fuzzy, like your high school reunion?"

"Yeah. I can't wait to see you in person, get reacquainted. How about it?"

"God, that one-track mind. No. Next?"

"Did you kill Jim?"

"Jim was a worse asshole than you, you know. You, at least I never thought you were my friend."

"Let me talk to Lydia."

"No fucking way, fucking José."

"The deal—"

"Deal, deal, deal! You cheat and you lecture me about the deal?"

"You just said you didn't care."

"I don't care you know who I am. I do kind of care that there were cops all over Perry Street."

"That crap is getting tired, Kevin. You called them."

"Hah! Okay, maybe you're not slipping. But I didn't exactly call them. Streaming video with an address stamp."

"You have a camera at Jim's?"

"Webcam. Had. They took it with them. You know all that Nicole bitch ever does is sit and smoke and cry? Bo-o-o-ring. Nice house, though. I could've had one like that, you didn't fuck me up."

"Why—"

"*Because. You. Cheat!* I thought you might turn up there sooner or later, and not tell me about it."

"If you keep calling the cops on me we'll never finish the game."

"I thought you didn't like this game."

"The one I'd like would be where you and I play face to face."

"Ohhhh. Well, if you do real good at this one, maybe we can play that later. And that camera was supposed to be just so if you showed your ugly face, I'd know you knew, you know? I wouldn't have dropped that dime, but you pissed me off."

"How?"

"Nya-nya, wouldn't you like to know? No, okay, I'll tell you. It was that fat fucking alky Hal Ross over my place bothering my neighbors. Out there in fucking Queens where they fucking sent me, those nice people don't like to be reminded about all the dangerous felons in the halfway fucking house."

Hal! *Shit, you goddamn idiot!* "I didn't send him."

"Oh! It just occurred to him, now I've been out eight months, two weeks and four days but who's counting, to drop by, see how I'm doing? Your drinking buddy?"

"We're not buddies."

"No, I know, you jammed him up, too. See, that's *your* favorite game, am I right? Jamming people up? Shit, why am I even playing with you? What a motherfucking bastard. And you know, this being on the outside ain't all it's cracked up to be. Life is *not* good, Smith, you know that?"

A raggedy split in his voice. My heart jolted. "What's wrong?" I asked. "Starting to dawn on you I'm winning?"

"The fuck you are!"

"Gee, seems to me—"

"Yeah, well, whatever it seems to you, you're wrong. Damn, asshole, you're fielding a whole roster of benchwarmers, I'm still way ahead."

"I don't think so."

"Oh, fuck your mama, do I care what you think? Though why you'd bring in Ross, that limpdick, I don't know, but that's up to you. Useless, though, I'll tell you that for free. Me and your girlfriend, we're not out there. That place is way clean. Nothing to find."

My needle had worked. He'd steadied, was back in the game. My pulse started to slow. "Let me talk to Lydia."

"Shit, I could've sworn I said no already. But here's what I want to know. Who's that cute chink boy toy you had with you at Jim and Nicole's? He listening right now, that why I'm on speaker? Hi, Chop Suey."

Linus raised an eyebrow, pointed at the phone; I shook my head.

"He's not here. I'm back in the car."

"You know, speakerphone's not the right app for this. What you should do, you should get yourself one of those cool earpieces.

Big deal private eye, oughta have the right equipment. Any street vendor—"

"Jesus, Kevin!"

"Yeah, you don't like people telling you what to do, do you? Me, either. Ten years, I hadda listen. Ten fucking years, assholes who couldn't find their own dicks with both hands and a map, telling me where to go, when to talk, when to shut up, when to shit. Now I get to tell you. Much better. Much, much better."

"To my face. Come tell me to my face."

"Oh, stuff it. Answer my question."

"What—"

"Chop Suey! Who was he?"

"Borrowed from a friend. I didn't want to go see Nicole alone."

"Scared?"

"Sure, Kevin."

"Borrowed from who?"

"Charlie Chan, for God's sake! You don't really think I'm going to tell you?"

"Well, you don't really think I care? Just, I worry you've gone nancy on me. If it's not Chinese girls for you anymore, if it's Chinese boys, then you might not care as much about your girlfriend here as I thought you did. You might not be trying all that hard. Chinese girls! Fuck you, anyway. Wasn't enough for you to jam me up like that, you had to take up with a slant just to stick it to me."

I was momentarily wordless. "You think me and Lydia, that's all about *you*?"

"You gonna tell me you ever had a Chinese girlfriend before you fried my ass for that Oriental chick? But I gotta admit, you're right. They're a turn-on, aren't they? Lei-lei, and Angelique, and all their little friends. Get me awfully hot. Remind me of that cunt in the park, I guess. Your girlfriend's not so bad herself, really. Long as she keeps her mouth shut. Well, gotta go."

"Dammit, let me talk to her!"

"What, your girlfriend? Umm, let's see. No."

"If I don't know she's okay—"

"Christ Jesus, the bitch is fine! Didn't I say I wouldn't mess with her unless you stopped playing? You gonna stop playing?"

"No."

"Then relax, Max. I'll keep my hands to myself. Though she really is awful cute, so that's getting harder and harder. Or maybe that's not what's getting harder."

"*Kevin, you bastard—*"

"See? Shit happens and you can't do shit about it, man, that's rough. Isn't it? Just think about what could be happening here, you locked out, can't get at us. I could be doing any shit to her I want. Kinda like the opposite. Kinda like when you're inside and there's all kinds of shit going on in the world and you can't get at it. Pretty fucking painful, right? You know, up there where I was, where *you* put me, you know I had friends with country houses right up near there? Fucking country *estates*! I mean, they *were* my friends, they *used to be* my friends. But inside, I guess I was invisible. Superpowers! Hey, I had superpowers! Invisible Man! They'd come up, swim in their pools, ski on their slopes, have their perfect kids with their perfect birthdays, their perfect little family life. I was just down the road, breathing the same fucking air, but I was invisible! Wow! How wild is that?"

"It's wild, Kevin."

"'It's wild, Kevin.' God, I hate you."

"Let me speak to—"

"*No!* Knock that shit off, okay? Listen, fuckface, at least I'm giving you a chance. More than you ever gave me. You keep playing, I'm a gentleman. Besides, I need her. Your girlfriend. She's taking care of something else for me."

"What are you talking about?"

"Guess what?" A pause. "I'm not gonna tell you! Listen, there was a little delay with your next clues. Those shoes you mentioned? Hadda deal with that. But it's cleared up now. Just hold tight, I'll get back to you."

"Let me—" But no. Just silence. Empty silence.

15

"Dude," Linus said when I slammed my hand on the steering wheel. "Pull out. Drive."

"Where the fuck should I drive?"

"Doesn't matter. Cop comes to give us a ticket for standing here, we're toast."

"Maybe we're toast anyway."

"I am so not hearing that."

"Fucking Hal! I'll kill that bastard."

Linus blinked. "He's not the bad guy."

"Who the fuck told him to go up there? One fucking thing I asked for, he can't get it right!"

"If Mr. Crazy knows he went," Linus said equitably, "he'd have known if you went, too. And like he said, they're not there and there's nothing to find."

"I might've found something." I threw the car into gear and pulled out, fighting myself not to accelerate as though I were trying to leave the planet. A sudden icy thought sliced its way through my anger. "Linus. Call Trella. He may have a camera somewhere up there, too."

Linus's eyes flew wide. "Shit, dude!" He pressed speed dial. "Trell? Where are you? You okay? Yeah, listen, the ex's apartment. You get near it? Because there might be a camera, Mr. Crazy might've seen you— Oh. No shit?" I could feel him relax. "Hey. Way cool. Yeah, but he's driving. I'll put him on speaker." He pressed the button. "She wants to talk to you."

"Trella? Everything all right?"

"Here, sure. But what did he mean? Why would there be a camera?"

"There was one at Jim White's. Kevin thought I might show up."

"He— But that means he knows you know who he is."

"He does. I talked to him."

Her words raced. "Are there more clues? Is Lydia okay?"

"No more clues yet. And he wouldn't let me talk to her."

"Oh. Damn." After a moment: "Bill, if he saw you, does that mean he's seen Linus?"

"Yes."

"Oh," she said again, sounding wary. Hearing the unease in her voice, Linus flushed and grinned.

"Well, you don't have to worry about me," she went on. "Unless he's got one on the streetlight or something."

"You didn't get inside? Talk to the neighbors?"

"Didn't get in. But talked to a neighbor. And I saw her. Megan."

"Oh God, Trella, did you—"

"Of course I didn't."

Of course. "Sorry. How did you know it was her?"

"The neighbor. Joey and I were in the car, scoping things out before I started ringing doorbells, when out comes this older lady, with a dog. Just what I needed. I hopped out, oohed and aahed about the dog, then got shy, asked the lady if I could ask her something. Gave her my sad boyfriend story. She was all sympathy, said I didn't have to worry. She hasn't seen Megan with a man since Megan's husband, that Collings guy, ditched her while she was pregnant. Megan doesn't have very much good to say about men. About anything, in fact, except her kid. Always short-tempered and bitter, says the lady, the kid's the only thing that can make her smile. Always complaining: the weather, the smell, the apartment. I said, 'What's wrong with the apartment?' More to keep the lady talking than anything else. She said, 'Oh, Megan's *always* complaining about the apartment.' The noise, the smell from the Chinese restaurant next door—Megan especially hates that because it reminds her of her ex-boyfriend, he was crazy for Chinese food. And the apartment's a fourth-floor walkup, and she had to admit, the lady did, it *was* hard, with a six-month-old, and the stairs are too narrow for the stroller, see, there it is in the hallway and she carries the baby. And there was the one that got away, that made it worse. The husband, I said, was he the one that got away? Or the ex-boyfriend? No, no, she says, the *apartment*. The ex-boyfriend, before the ex-husband, did I know about him? He went to prison, for murder! Oh, my God, I said. And then I said, My God, don't tell me he's been around, that guy? The lady said, No, no, that's not what she meant. Megan wouldn't give him the time of day, if he ever got out of jail. He was a lying, cheating— Well, Megan uses bad language, the lady doesn't like to repeat it. But Megan's always saying she wishes she'd married him. *Why?* I say. Because, the lady says, he was buying a condo. The deal fell through when he went to jail, of course. Megan still curses him out over it, all these years later. One good thing she might have gotten from him, and he screwed it up. Just like a man. So the lady tells me I shouldn't worry about my boyfriend. Chances are, anyone interested in a nice girl like me wouldn't be attracted to Megan.

"I'm about to say 'Have a nice walk' so she and the dog can go and I can talk to other people in the building, when the lady says, 'Oh, look, here she is!' She gives me a wink, like we have a secret, and says, 'Megan, darling, how are you?' This dumpy woman coming up the sidewalk glares at her, says, 'Oh, just fine!' and shoves past us, stomps in the door and up the stairs. 'You see, dear?' the lady says. 'You have nothing to worry about.'

"The thing is, I don't think Megan even looked at me, but probably I'd better not go into the building now just in case. But I'm waiting in the car with Joey, so if she comes out and goes away again, I can try some more neighbors. Maybe the lady's wrong and Kevin's been here."

"Sounds like Megan would slam his fingers in the door if he showed up," Linus said.

"But he might not know that," I said. "He has enough ego, he might assume she'd want to see him. I don't think there's much chance, but Trella, go ahead and give it some more time. But if you do spot him, anyone answering that description—"

"Call right away and don't let him see me. Something like that?"

"Yeah," I said. "Something like that."

Linus took his phone off speaker, brought Trella up to speed on what had happened to us. I drove, thought, came up with nothing. Linus was animated, a lot of "Dudess!" and "It was awesome!" I wove through traffic, listening to the clock ticking in my head. Hearing Kevin sneer. Seeing the wasted face of Hal Ross, that stupid, stupid son of a bitch. A cab cut me off and I smashed the horn, slammed on the brakes. Linus, thrown forward in his seatbelt, looked at me, said to Trella, "Gotta go," and lowered the phone. He said, "Dude. Do not flip out."

"*Goddamn son of a bitch!*" I pounded the steering wheel. "All I want is to kill that bastard. Get my hands on him—"

"Dude? Here." From the bag Linus pulled a second Coke. "Drink this."

"I still have this."

"Coffee's terrible when it's cold. And this has sugar in it. Caffeine works a lot better with sugar. Caffeine and sugar. Two of the essential food groups."

He was trying to distract me, jolly me along. I wanted to punch him. I also wanted him to stop breaking my heart.

He popped the can and I took it. I drank, a long swallow. He watched warily. I must not have looked quite ready to be human yet, because he chattered on. "See, what they need to do, they need to invent one with pizza in it."

"Sounds revolting." I was trying.

"No, for real, then it could take care of all your needs, right in that one can."

A bell. A faint bell, in my mind.

"And maybe another one with fries. What else would you need? Well, maybe if it kept you warm, too. Then you could—"

It was all I could do not to slam the brake, pile up traffic behind us. "Son of a bitch!"

"*Dude!* I'm telling you, you gotta not—"

"Say it again."

"Say what?"

"Pizza in the Coke. Everything you need. Linus! Goddamn, that's it! That's Kevin's pattern!"

A stare. "Um, what?"

"How he chooses how to kill. And where." *Poisoned, frozen. Frozen, poisoned. Drowned. Goddamn, Smith, how stupid are you?* "The necessities of life. Water. Food. Clothing. He said, in prison you have no life. Cons are the living dead. You get no choice, have to do what they tell you. You get food that's not food, clothes that aren't clothes. He's killing people with what he was deprived of. Jim, water in his fancy lap pool, in the house Kevin should've had. Lei-lei, poisoned food. In a bar he used to go to. Angelique, clothing—or, lack of—at his tailor shop."

"Oh, dude, wow! Oh, awesome, yeah!" Linus bounced in excitement. Woof, in the back, felt the crackle in the air, sat up and whined. "So," Linus said, confidently waiting. "What's next?"

How the hell did I know? "Shelter. Air." *Oh, goddamn!* "Shelter! Linus, the apartment!"

"Um, what apartment? The one he didn't buy for Megan?"

"No! The one Jim rented."

"Oh!" he breathed. "Oh! You think? Dude! But . . ."

"He used a real estate agent. Remember, Nicole said the agent called her?"

"Yeah. Yeah." Linus was nodding, poking at the iPhone. "So we think, downtown, we think, the last few months, we think, Jim White on the lease."

"And we think, loft. If it's not the same building as the one Kevin was going to buy in, it's a building like it. Call Trella. Both of you work on it. Find real estate agents who handle downtown. High end."

"Damn, dude. There's gonna be a lot of those. And a lot of Jim Whites. Take forever. Be better if Kevin did buy it. Then we could just look up the real estate records."

"Yeah, it would be nice if it were easy, wouldn't it? But he didn't!"

"Dude?" Linus shot me a cautious glance. "You remembering not to flip out?"

I pulled out a cigarette. "I'm sorry."

"You don't need to be sorry. You just need to not flip out."

I looked over at him. "You know that's exactly what Lydia would've said?"

He shrugged. "Seriously, dude. I'm doing what I can here but Robin doesn't save the day. Batman does."

I took a long pull on the smoke, wishing wildly, suddenly, that I'd just wake up. I'd promise to learn all the lessons that could be learned from this nightmare, to be the man I should've always been, if this could just end.

Nothing, not a single thing, changed. Another long pull, then, "Okay. Call Trella. First thing, have her call Nicole White. See if Nicole remembers who the real estate agent was, maybe even where the apartment is."

"You're kidding me. You think she'll tell? Instead of just scream and hang up?"

"No, but if there were a miracle and she did it would be the fastest way. If not, then between you, call every agent you can find. You're investigating Jim White's death, you're looking for an apartment he rented recently."

"We're cops?"

"No. You say that, it's a crime."

Linus grinned. "Oh, as opposed to what?"

I did my best to smile back. "You're investigators, don't use any other word. If they push it, say you work for the insurance company."

"Like before."

"Right. Linus?"

"Yeah?"

"You were good. Before."

A hissed "Yes!" A fist pump. Then a call to Trella, an explanation, and back to the iPhone.

I drove aimlessly around the Village, keeping away from Perry Street and from the Sixth Precinct. Linus made calls, got nowhere, but he was right: It would take a while. Not, I hoped, forever.

I was trying to calm down enough to call Hal Ross, burn his ass for stupidity, get Kevin's address from him, and cut him loose. I wasn't sure whether to go to wherever it was Kevin had been living. Chances were he really hadn't left anything around to give a hint about where he was now. But I was thinking this: how positive are any of us of anything? Now that he knew I knew who he was, could find out where he'd been staying, might he not go back just in case? Check the place, do one last sweep? If he did, I'd have to be the world's luckiest guy to find him there. If I were, none of this would be happening, so that was out. But even if he'd been and gone already, maybe someone saw something. Which way he went, what he was driving. What the hell else did I have?

So I took out the phone. And it rang as I did. Hal, calling me.

"Hey, buddy."

I'd have kept my cool, maybe, except for the casualness of that. I blew up: "You stupid fucking bastard!"

"Hey! What the—"

"Kevin knows you were there! Surprise, that's all I had, and you blasted it for me!" I knew that wasn't true when I heard myself say it. Kevin's webcam would have spotted me with Nicole whether or not Hal had played cowboy. In fact, the rational part of me—getting shouted down by the fury, trying to make itself heard—pointed out that Hal's screwup might have done me a favor. If

Kevin had kept quiet once he saw me, I'd have gone on thinking I was getting over on him when I wasn't. The rational part almost scored a point, but Hal was playing to the other part.

"Oh, fuck you, Charlie! I was a cop, remember? I get info, I check it out!"

"This isn't your case!"

"No, I got no cases anymore. I just sit on my pension all day. I used to work, but, you know, shit happens."

"I don't care, Hal. I don't care, okay? Your tough life, it doesn't mean shit to me. My partner, that's all that matters."

"Well, your partner's not at Kevin's halfway house. Nothing is. Bed, desk, closet with two shirts and a pair of pants, looked like from Goodwill. If Kevin was ever in that room, you can't tell by looking."

"Give me the address and go to hell."

"I don't think that's what you want."

"You're fucking wrong."

"I'm fucking right."

"Don't try—"

"Kevin called me."

Briefly, I was wordless. "What?"

"Yeah. He said, as long as I was in, I might as well be in. Two assholes are better than one. Besides, he said, he owed me a favor. Since he could see I wanted to play, he put me on your team."

"I don't want you."

"You do. He told me where to find something you do want."

"What the—"

"And I found it."

My heart stopped. "What? You found what?"

"Not your partner, if that's what you're thinking. A plastic bag. He said you'd know."

16

Hal lived in what was now Chelsea. Thirty years ago, when he moved in, it had been Hell's Kitchen. The apartment was a dump; it had been that when he moved in, too. He was waiting when Linus, Woof, and I clattered up the stairs.

"What the fuck's that?"

"It's a dog. You have the bag?"

"Keep it away from me." Hal might've gained weight since I saw him last, or he might just be sagging more, his flesh sodden with liquor and years. He moved to his kitchen table, a grimy Formica thing on wobbling metal legs. "Here," he grunted. "What is this shit?" On one corner of the table, an orange plastic bag. Scattered around, miscellaneous trash: paint chips, a Cub Scout badge, lengths of straw, the chopped-off front half of a Knicks jersey from some seasons back.

"Clues," I said.

"Clues to what?"

"Kevin's playing a game."

"Fucking asshole never changes, huh?"

"Assholes don't." I fingered the jersey.

"What are we supposed to do with this shit?"

"Figure out what it means."

"What does it mean?"

"Jesus, Hal! If I knew that I wouldn't be standing here."

"Dude." Linus pointed to the jersey. "Twenty-one. You think maybe that's an address? Or the street?"

Hal turned as though he'd just noticed Linus. "Who the hell are you?"

Linus gave me a quick glance, in case I wanted this to go one way or another. "Friend of mine," I said.

"He got a name?"

"Linus," said Linus.

"You're shitting me. Like in Peanuts?"

"No," Linus said evenly. "Like in Pauling."

Hal scowled. Either he'd never heard of Linus Pauling, or booze had bleached the name from his memory bank.

I picked up the badge. "This has a number, too. Pack forty-one."

"So do all these. Different colors of green. With kind of stupid names. 'Emerald Night.' 'Mist o' Morn.' "

"Maybe it's the names, though."

Hal tilted his head. "What about the straw? Each one of those got a number, maybe a little tiny name engraved on it?"

"Shut up, Hal. Where did you find these?"

"Fuck you."

"*Where?*"

After a second: "On my doorknob." He went to his fridge, pulled out a Bud.

"What are you doing?"

"Fuck is it to you? You want one?"

"Dude," Linus said, in a transparent effort to distract me. Whether he was afraid I was about to punch Hal's lights out, or take him up on his offer, I didn't know. "Did Mr. Crazy used to be a Cub Scout? This was his troop or whatever?"

Hal said, "It shoulda been me."

I looked up. "What?"

He popped the beer. "I shoulda put that mutt away. He should be coming after me."

"Well, you didn't."

"Yeah. And you did, big hero."

"Drop it, Hal."

"She didn't want to go with him. The Lin girl. Did you know that?"

"You said it before."

"She told him she was saving herself for her husband. What the hell did she tell him that shit for?"

"Hal."

"Can't tell that shit to Kevin. Guy like that? And hammered like he was that night. He talked about it when he called just now. Like we were reminiscing. 'Remember, old buddy? How I took that chink chick on her maiden voyage, and Smith tried to nail me to the wall but you did me a big fucking favor, Ross, old buddy?' I did *you* a big fucking favor, Smith, not hanging up on the son of a bitch!"

"Hal, put a cork in it."

"I shoulda stopped him." He slugged down half the beer. "Fucker. Fucker!"

"Doesn't matter now. This right here, this is important."

"Yeah, important," he muttered. "Because you, you're a big hero. Me, I'm just a drunk loser. That what you mean?"

"Shut the fuck up and let us think!"

Woof barked, echoing my shout.

Linus said, "Dude."

And Hal shut up.

But I wasn't thinking. I didn't think anything, except I was sick of this bullshit. Women dead and dying because Kevin hated me. Lydia's life, the prize in a game. Clues and cleverness. Hal drunk and wrecked. It was beyond insane, way past horrifying. I wanted to just leave, walk away, run, go far, far, far. And I couldn't. I couldn't get out.

"Dude. Dude! Your phone's ringing."

I started, came back. It was. What the hell was I doing, spacing out in Hal Ross's rancid kitchen, staring at trash? The ring was Trella's. "What's up?"

"I found it."

"You— Wait, you found what?"

"Six-seventy-two West Street."

"The apartment?

"Nicole White told me."

"Just like that?"

"She'd do anything to catch you guys. She didn't even ask why I wanted it."

"Catch us?" It took me a second. "Jesus, Trella, did you say you were a cop?"

"Oops."

"I told you—"

"He rented it under his own name. Didn't even try to hide it. She started to cry. Okay, meet you there."

"No. You and Joey keep doing what you're doing."

"Sitting here, waiting for Kevin? He's not going to show. You know it. She hates him. You're just trying to keep me out of trouble. I can't just sit here. It's driving me bananas."

"Trella—"

"I'll meet you there."

"No." I rubbed my eyes. "You're right. But don't come here. You and Joey head downtown, see if you can spot anywhere that might be likely based on what Lydia told us, in the area of the cell tower Kevin's calls come through. Basement, areaway that catches some sun—"

"Baby stuff nearby. Got it. Cool."

"Thanks." I clicked off, said to Linus, "Let's go."

"She told you where?"

"West Street. Close to Jim's." I swept up the trash and the bag.

"I'm coming," Hal said.

"Not a chance. Have a good life." Linus, Woof, and I exploded out of there.

While I rocketed the car south Linus checked his iPhone. "Six-seventy-two, that's not any of those numbers. Maybe they add up to that? 'K, anyway, I got the map. Yo, Six-seventy-two West Street, it's right around the corner from Perry Street. If that Jim White dude was renting it for a girlfriend it sure would be convenient."

"He wasn't. I'm sure. He was doing what Kevin told him."

"Lotta good it did him, huh?" Linus muttered.

I glanced over. This had been a hell of a heavy day for these kids, and it was far from over. "Linus? How're you holding up?"

He shrugged. "Don't worry about me, dude. Just about Lydia."

Silence for a few blocks.

"What about all this stuff?" Linus lifted the plastic bag.

"I don't know. We can figure it out later."

"Yeah, but . . ."

"But what?"

"Well, what if it's to somewhere else?"

"It's not."

"You sure?"

"I'm sure." Or close enough to sure. We didn't have time for sure.

More silence, unconvinced around the edges. Then a yip from Linus, still working the iPhone: "Dude! Six-seventy-two West, right here, Jim White, nine-C. And dig: it has a name. Greenwich Gardens. All those paint chips, they're green! You think—"

"I do. I do! Because: Straw, broom: witch."

"Green witch! Damn! Yes! And the Cub Scout thing, maybe it's a gardening badge? No. No, dude. It's not."

"Doesn't have to be. Den. Cub Scouts hang around in dens."

"They do?"

"You were never one?"

"You serious? Okay, but the shirt?"

"The shirt?"

"Knicks. Number twenty-one."

"That's Wilson Chandler's number. No, wait—that shirt's from years ago. Probably ten years, the season Kevin went in. That would have been . . . Charlie Ward! Damn, it's Charlie Ward's jersey."

"Uh, so? We're not looking for Ward-den. Are we?"

"No. Though that would be Kevin's kind of joke. Prison, you know? But guard-den. Charlie Ward was a guard. Plus," I added, "the Knicks play at the Garden."

"Dude." Linus peered into the plastic bag, closed it up. "I can see why none of you could stand this Kevin freak."

"You got that right."

A few blocks later I said, "We need to make a stop." I pulled up at a hardware store, raced in, found what I needed, out. Back behind the wheel I told Linus, "When we get there, jump out, see if you can find the super's phone number. It's usually on a plate by the door. Be fast, I'd rather no one sees you."

He didn't ask why I wanted that, but he did ask, "Why am I getting out?"

"You won't be able to see it from the street."

"Why aren't I checking the Web site?"

"What Web site?"

"The building Web site. Where I was on before. How I know it's called Greenwich Gardens. Your building doesn't have one? Or maybe it's not big enough." That wouldn't be the reason, but I didn't say so. "Mostly they do. Tenants chat, complain, hook up, check out what's going on . . ." He trailed off, consulting the iPhone, leaving me to my ignorance. "Got it." He held the phone where I could read it.

"Good. But you're going to call."

"I am? What am I gonna say?"

"You're Jim White. You're sending a contractor in to take measurements, check out some details. You didn't give him a key because you don't like to hand out your keys, you never know. You want the super to let him in." I handed him my wallet. "There's a contractor's card in there somewhere, see if you can find it."

He thumbed through a stack of business cards. "Bill Reinka? Rose City Contracting? You wanna be him?"

"Sure."

"The super, you think he'll buy it?"

"If you're good. Like before."

Linus frowned out the window for a few seconds, an actor running his lines. Then he dialed. "Yo, Laslo. Jim White, I'm the new guy in nine-C? Yeah, what I mean, I'm not there right now, but here's the deal . . ." He was good. Laslo must have balked, because Linus apologized for bending building rules, said he was sorry and he wouldn't do it again but he'd appreciate it if Laslo would help him out here so the work could be done soon, he wanted it wrapped up before *Christmas* and once it's this cold in October you know *Christmas* must be just around the corner.

"Okay, dude," he told me, lowering the phone. "You're in."

A few more minutes, we were there. A gleaming glass loft building by the Hudson, just Kevin's style: vulgar and ostentatious, lording it over smaller, quieter neighbors.

I drove past and pulled around the corner. I got out, my new steel tape hooked to my jeans, new clipboard in hand, and leaned back in the window. "Stay nearby, but be invisible."

Linus shook his head. "Not one of my superpowers, but I'll try."

The doorman in the marble lobby summoned Laslo, a stocky mustached guy who shook my hand gruffly, examined my business card officiously, and led me to the elevator wearily.

"This guy White," he said in a heavy Slavic accent, as we rose. "He don't live here yet, ya?"

"I don't know. I'm just doing some work in the apartment."

"Hope he don't give me no trouble. Don't even move in, already lending his place out."

"He is?"

"Ya." He poked my arm. "Hey, maybe he ain't planning to move in? Maybe he thinks it's okay he rents it by the day?"

"I don't know. Is he doing that?"

"Don't know what he's doing. But that guy, some friend of his."

"What guy? What about him?"

"Came yesterday. With his girlfriend." Laslo snorted. "I'm tell you, that's the kind of girlfriend got a meter on her ass. Anyway, came back, just now. Doorman tell me he forgot something."

Time stopped. "He's here now?"

Laslo gave me an odd look. "Hey, you okay? You know this guy?"

"No. Is he here now?"

Laslo shook his head. "Nah, don't worry, he don't get in your way. He left before. Half an hour, maybe."

Half an hour. Kevin had been here and we'd missed him. *Goddamn it!* "That guy—he has a key?"

"Sure. Ask me, if I was owner, I give you a key, not him. You honest hardworking Joe. That guy, shithead. But no one ask me." He pulled a jingling ring from his belt, unlocked 9C, stood there. "You need anything else?"

I didn't, but he clearly did. I pulled a ten from my pocket and handed it over. "Ya," he said, another honest hardworking Joe, and plodded back down the hall.

I opened the door he'd unlocked for me, stopped just inside to survey the apartment. I searched the high ceilings, the corners, the shadows, looking for a camera, found none. In fact I found nothing. Totally, totally empty. Stainless steel and granite kitchen, empty. Living room, full-height glass meeting polished wood floors, empty. Bedroom, three strides inside showing me every expensive square inch, empty. Bathroom, showercurtainless and empty. Hall closet and alcove closet, standing open, empty. No furniture. No drapes. No rugs. No sign I wasn't the first person ever to walk in here. Were we wrong? Jim White had really rented this smug aerie for some squeeze he was planning on keeping, Kevin Cavanaugh had nothing to do with it, and I was wasting time I could be using trying to accurately read the new clues, which would lead us to an entirely different place?

But yesterday a shithead and his metered girlfriend came up here. Today, the shithead came back. Right after I told Kevin about the GPSs in the shoes.

The kitchen cabinets were standing open, too, dishless and bare, and the broom closet. The only place I couldn't see, because of the position of the center island, was the cabinet under the sink.

I stepped around the island.

Unlike every other door in the place, the cabinet door was shut. I crouched, pulled it open.

Jesus.

My first instinct: don't move. My second: move fast. I yanked out my phone, called Linus.

"Dude, what's up?"

"Call Laslo. Empty the building. Call 911. Tell them there's a bomb up here."

"Why am I saying that?"

"Because there's a bomb up here."

I thumbed off, looked from the device with the wires and tubes to the cabinet's other cache: an unconscious Asian woman bound up in more duct tape than I'd ever seen.

Was the bomb attached to her somehow? I played my penlight in there. No, no connection. My taking her out of the cabinet wouldn't be what set it off. What would? I didn't know and didn't have time to guess. Whatever it was, it could be any second. And I had another a problem anyway: once again, the cops were on the way.

And this time, I had called them.

Fire alarm bells in the halls began to shriek. Doors slammed, voices yelled. I could hear, in the distance and approaching, a sound I'd heard enough of today to last me a lifetime: sirens. I had to cut this woman loose from the pipe she was bound to and get us both out of here.

Unless she was already dead. But no: I put the back of my hand to her nose, could feel, very faintly, her breath. So faintly that I took precious seconds to peel the tape from her mouth. I was remembering myself in Lu's car: she could be slowly strangling, dying right here.

As the tape came off she stirred, groaned. Then her eyes flew wide. "No," I said. "I'm not going to hurt you." She tried to scream but she didn't have the breath. She writhed, wriggled as best she could in the miles of tape cocooning her. I slipped out my pocketknife.

She froze, eyes welling up. "Please. Mister. Okay, I be quiet. Okay."

She flinched as I reached over. I sliced through the tape at the pipe. She dropped forward and I caught her. She was tiny, I realized, and very young. If she was Lu's, he probably got a lot for her. I lifted her out of the cabinet. The tape had her hog-tied, that wriggle the only movement she could make, but she didn't make it. She stayed completely limp. Except for the trembling.

"It's all right," I said. "He's gone. What's your name?"

"Name Junie," she whispered, very fast, giving me whatever I wanted.

As I spoke I was working my knife into a gap in the tape, freeing her wrists from her ankles so I could sling her over my shoulder in a fireman's carry. I did my best not to nick her; she whimpered when I did but didn't scream and didn't try to stop me. Whether she understood I was helping her, or she was just terrified, I didn't know.

She let me pick her up, envelop her in my jacket, shoulder her. I threw the door open, headed for the stairwell. The piercing alarm still screeched in the corridor but it was empty and so were the stairs. Little Junie and I were the last out.

Eight flights later I burst into the empty lobby. I raced outside and up the cleared sidewalk inside the bomb squad's perimeter. A cop jerked a barricade aside to let me through. "Ambulance up the street!" I shouted to him, and I ran. He nodded, turned his attention back to the building. As the bomb squad robot rolled out of the truck I think someone might have yelled after me. I have a faint memory, a voice shouting my name just before the blast.

It was a deafening wild roar, thunderous, rolling. Following instantly, the concussive pound, much more frightening, a punch deep inside you from all sides at once. It staggered me, sent little Junie flying. She hit the sidewalk and started to wail. I dove to cover her, arms over my head as debris rained around us. Glass crashed and tinkled, car alarms honked and screeched, people yelled and screamed. A man and his dog crouched behind thin shrubbery, the dog barking like mad. A heavy-set woman froze on the sidewalk, eyes and mouth wide. Under it all the explosion's echoes bounced off building walls, slowly died down. I twisted, looked upward. 9C's grand windows were nothing but glittering glass daggers. Cracks spiderwebbed two or three floors above and below. As I watched, a large shard let go, tumbled to the street and burst into diamonds on asphalt littered with them. The cops were springing into action, yelling orders. A fire truck screeched around the corner from the highway. I jumped to my feet and scooped Junie up. She was still bawling. I ran up the block and bellowed, "Get in the car!" at Linus, who'd come around the corner and was gaping at the damage, at the street, at me.

He outran me, had the car started by the time I tumbled with my cargo into the backseat. "Call the dog!" I said. "Get him up front." Woof was barking, climbing, and slobbering all over me and the poor kid in my arms. Linus ordered Woof to the front, a clumsy maneuver, and peeled out of there.

"Fuck, dude! Fuck! What was that?"

"Go to St. Vincent's. Seventh and Greenwich. That was Kevin."

"What was— I don't—"

"I think his timing was off."

Another siren howled in the distance, growing closer, aiming for where we'd come from.

"It was supposed to happen when you were in there? Blow you all to shit? End the game? Why?"

"No. I think it was supposed to happen when I first got here. Before I went up. So I could see it." I pulled Woof's blanket off the seat, wrapped Junie in that, took my jacket back. Junie's wailing had subsided to shuddering sobs.

"I don't—"

"Shelter, Linus. He was going to kill her with the building."

St. Vincent's Hospital was a short ride. I held the girl close, made soothing noises. A couple of times I spoke her name, tried to ask a question, but she didn't respond at all.

I told Linus what he'd have to do at the hospital: settle Junie on the nearest chair like a concerned relative, then run like hell. He nodded silently. When he pulled up at the ER entrance we both got out. I handed Junie to him, the blanket hiding the tape. Sunglassed and baseball capped, he carried her in. I was behind the wheel, Woof in the backseat again by the time he scooted out seconds later. "Let's go, dude!"

And we were gone.

17

"Dude." Linus leaned against the headrest as I drove crosstown, away from the wreckage. "Dude, this shit is wack. *Way* wack. I mean, shit. I mean, dude. I mean . . ."

"I know what you mean."

Weakly, he asked, "What now?"

"I think we wait. Kevin will call soon. But first, can you send a text message?"

"Why couldn't I?"

"To Mary. Tell her to call me. Tell her I have a peace offering."

"You do? And how come I'm texting and not calling?"

"Because you're on videotape with me at Nicole's, and she's a cop. It would put her in a bad position to pick up the phone at the precinct and find it's you. This way she can go somewhere else to make the call if she wants to."

"Smooth," he said, thumbing buttons. "But that's not videotape. It's a webstream."

Just as he finished, my phone rang. Kevin, of course. I didn't use the speaker, just lifted the phone to my ear.

"Hey-hey, asshole! You were fast on that one, bro. My clues weren't so good?"

"Oh, they were great. I'm just getting used to you, is all."

"And lard-ass Ross? He was a big help, I'll bet. Like he always is."

"Yeah, he was terrific."

"Did you like it? The big ka-boom?"

"Did you really think I would?"

"No, I hoped you wouldn't. Did you see her?"

"Who?"

"Junie, stupido. Or pieces of her, anyway."

Which meant I was right: it was supposed to happen as soon as I got there. So I could see it. It also meant another thing: he didn't know it hadn't. I poured on surprise: "You had a girl up there?"

"You bet your fucking ass I did! A hottie, too. A little young for me, but she was a friend of Angelique's so I asked for her. Angelique was right, she was good. Too bad she won't get any older. She'd probably have been great."

"You're a sick fuck."

"You think?

"Let me talk to Lydia."

Shifting into a slow singsong, he said, "You didn't answer me."

"Do I think you're a sick fuck? I sure as hell do."

"Very funny. Not that question. Did you?"

"Did I what?"

"See her!"

"Who? The girl? No."

"You didn't?" He sounded disappointed. "No arms and legs flying?"

"Jesus Christ, I don't know what I saw! Boom, crash, and I got the hell out of there. Did you expect me to stick around?"

"You don't have to get sarcastic."

"Let me speak to Lydia. Then tell me where the next damn clues are. I want to get this over with."

"You know, I'm really sorry you're not enjoying yourself. I think it's because you're such a stiff. That stick up your ass, that righteousness thing. You should loosen up, have a little fun."

I spoke through clenched teeth. "The next goddamn clues."

He sighed. "I'm beginning to think you have a problem. ADHD or something. Maybe you should get tested. Wouldn't be so bad. You could get some good drugs."

"The—"

"Oh, shut the fuck up. Your next clues will be where your last clues were."

"What are you talking about?" Then it dawned: "Hal?"

"I had something else in mind, but this is better. Gotta be flexible with your game plan, you know."

"You're bringing him in? That's a big risk. You saw what happened before."

"Excuse me, but which one of us brought him in? I just gave him a rest-of-the-season contract. And besides, that was fun, before. Watching that alky pretend to be a cop."

"He *was* a cop. He threw it all away on you."

"It's *my* fault? I *asked* him to crack my skull against the floor? Anyway, I'm a forgiving kind of guy. He wants to play, he's on your team, bro. He'll be calling soon. Now, you want to talk to your girlfriend or not? Because I'm kind of busy here."

"Put her on."

"Well, I don't know. You don't sound that into it. Maybe if you say 'please.'"

Rage seared me under the skin. A cab pulled out; I slammed the brake, threw Linus forward. He looked over in alarm. I took a breath, managed to croak, "Please."

"Please what?"

"Please let me talk to Lydia."

"God, that sounds silly, coming from you. You don't say that often, huh? Mostly you just do whatever the fuck you want, right?"

"Game's over, Kevin. See you."

"Bullshit."

"I don't talk to Lydia, I don't play. Five, four, three, two—"

"All right, all right, God, you just can *not* have a little fun, can you? Here, honey, you better sweet-talk him, he's cranky."

A wait, short but endless. Then: "Bill?"

Relief like a breaking wave. "You okay?"

"I'm beginning to feel . . . I don't know, beaten down."

My blood surged again. "Has that bastard touched you?"

"No, no. It's more abstract, more at a distance. It stops and starts. But I feel it."

"Hang on. I'll be there soon."

She started to answer but didn't get to finish. Kevin came on, said, "Aw, a little wear and tear on the princess? Could be she's not holding up so well, asshole. You better get a move on."

"How can I until—"

"You can't. Hahaha! Good one! Just sit tight. Lard-ass'll call. Oh, unless *he's* tight. Then you're screwed, aren't you? What a damn shame."

Then cold, empty silence.

I stomped the gas, ran a light, swerved around a cab. Why? I don't know. Where was I going? Anywhere, anywhere that wasn't here.

"Dude. Dude!" Linus shouted. "You keep driving like that, we're gonna get pulled over."

"What?" I looked around, found us all the way on the Lower East Side. I slowed to the pace of the traffic around us. "That bastard! I'll kill him. I swear I'll kill him!"

"Yeah, well, that's not news. The clues, dude. What did he say about the clues?"

"Hal will have them."

"Hal? That same guy?"

"We're supposed to wait for his call. Fat chance. I—" Linus's iPhone interrupted me, playing "Bad Boys."

"It's Aunt Mary, dude. Pull over."

That was good advice. I slipped to the curb next to a hydrant and he handed me the phone.

"Mary? It's Bill."

"Where the hell are you? What's going on? Why did that text come from Linus, not you?"

"Because you calling Lydia's cousin would seem natural. Not like you calling a fugitive. Unless you fingered Linus, too, from the webstream."

"No," she said reluctantly. "Sunglasses, odd angle, could've been anyone." God bless you, Aunt Mary. "But you have to come in. This is bigger than you now."

"It's been bigger than me from the beginning. It's about Lydia. That's why I can't come in."

"The Department knows Lydia's missing. Not from me. Patino figured it out."

"Shit! How?"

"He connected up you, the dead Chinese woman in Red Hook and Lu's other hooker at the tailor shop. He started out walking on eggshells around me, because he had it worked out the way we thought: that you'd gone off the deep end, killed Lydia, then started on other Chinese women. I had to tell him the truth."

"All of it?"

"You mean, the part about me helping you after you were wanted? And losing track of you after you skipped out from my place? No, I'd like to keep this job. I told him Lydia's been kidnapped and you were doing everything the kidnapper told you, trying to find her."

"Did he buy it?"

"Patino did." Said cautiously.

"Meaning the NYPD's still looking for me, right?"

"Of course they are! And every second you don't come in makes it worse."

"I'm not coming in. Stop. That's it, Mary, that's all. I called to say I have a peace offering. There's a girl at St. Vincent's, another of Lu's hookers. See if you can get to her before Lu does, maybe she can tell you something." *About Kevin,* I almost added. But I bit that off: the NYPD didn't have his name yet.

"What girl?"

"She's supposed to be dead. The lunatic doesn't know she's not. He doesn't know the tailor shop girl's not, either. I'd like it to stay that way."

"Why are you giving me this?"

"St. Vincent's will have called the cops already anyway."

"Bill—"

"I'll call again."

I clicked off, gave Linus back his phone, then made the call I'd been thinking about when Mary called us.

"You've got Hal Ross." Autopilot, slurred.

"It's Smith."

"Oh. Oh, I'm supposed to care?"

"Listen to me. Kevin's going to leave you another set of clues. Another bag. I don't know if it's going to be him or he's sending someone else, but I want—"

"You want. Who gives a rat's ass what you want?" In the background, clinking, talk, the fuzzy sounds of a sportscaster. He was in a bar. Not home, not where the clues were headed.

"Hal—"

"Anyway it doesn't matter. That chickenshit isn't coming and he isn't sending anyone."

"Yes, he is."

"No, genius, he is not."

"Yes—"

"*Listen to me!*" Hal roared. "He already called."

"He— What?"

"He told me you'd be calling and I should wait until you did. There, happy now?"

"When?"

"Few minutes ago."

I wondered if Hal was sober enough to know a few minutes from a few hours. "Why didn't you call me right away?"

"Hello? Because he said to wait."

"And you listened to him?"

"Do I have this wrong, or isn't this the guy who's got your partner someplace? Who's blowing shit up? Maybe you don't want to piss him off. Maybe he's got my cell phone tapped and he'd know when I called you. 'Hi, Kevin, how're you doing, you fucking asshole?' "

"You could've gone out. To a pay phone." Unless you were too drunk to move. "And how do you know he's blowing shit up? He told you about that?"

"I saw it."

"You were there?" A voice, calling my name, just before the blast. "How the hell did you know where to go?"

" 'West Street. Close to Jim's.' Someone said that in my kitchen. I wonder who?"

"You got there fast."

"After you, though. I was outside trying to figure out what the hell to do next when you came out and the place went blammo."

"So you saw?"

"Yeah. Yeah, I saw. So when fucking Kevin says wait for you to call, I think it's a good idea to wait. Okay with you?" He raised his voice. "Okay with you, too, fucking Kevin?"

"He told me you'd call me."

Hal brayed. "And he told me you'd call me. Asshole. Funny game."

"All right. What did he say when he called?"

"Oh, you care?"

"Yes, I care!"

A pause. "Okay, now, pay attention. You paying attention?"

"Yes!"

"I wrote it down because it made no fucking sense. But he said it twice the same way. He said he knows you like old fart music, so I'm supposed to tell you, 'Hurry, get on, now it's coming, and I have a broken dream, so lay down your sword and six-gun.' " He stopped.

"That's it?"

"Yeah. Pile of bullshit, huh? But that's what he said."

"No plastic bag?"

"Yeah, it came through the phone and I pulled it outta my ear. What do you think?"

"Say it again."

He blew a raspberry, but he repeated it. "'Hurry, get on, now it's coming, and I have a broken dream, so lay down your sword and six-gun.' What the hell is that?"

"I don't know. Where are you?"

"In a bar up Hudson Street. First place I found. Needed something to steady my nerves."

"And how are they, Hal? Your nerves?"

"Fuck you. When you figure out what this hurry shit means, you're going to tell me, right?"

"If Kevin calls again, you're going to tell me, right?"

And that was how we left it.

"So, dude?" Linus asked. "No bag? I heard that."

"Song lyrics." I made a quick right, headed west, to the highway.

"Where are we going?"

"Harlem."

18

I ran through Kevin's gibberish as Linus and I raced uptown. Woof had his face out the back window, sampling the breeze.

"Dude. That sword and six-gun thing, it sounds kinda like 'lay down my sword and shield,' from church. But the other stuff . . ." He shook his head.

"No," I said. "It's good for us. Kevin was improvising because he wanted to use Hal. So I think it's pretty straightforward. 'Hurry, get on, now it's coming,' that's from 'Take the A Train.'" Linus looked at me blankly. "Billy Strayhorn," I told him. "The song's about how you get to Harlem."

Linus knit his brow. "Oh. Well, the sword and six-gun, if it was sword and shield, the next line of that is down by the riverside. You think? The riverside in Harlem, that's where we're going?"

"Yes."

"But where? Harlem, that's a big riverside. Both rivers. And the six-gun? That doesn't belong at all."

"No, that's it, the six-gun: the wild west. So, the West Side: the Hudson."

"The Hudson. Okay, that's still a long—"

"A hundred and twenty-fifth street. Martin Luther King Boulevard."

"I have a dream!"

"A broken dream. 'Boulevard of Broken Dreams.' Just in case."

"'Boulevard of Broken Dreams!' Oh, dude! I know that one! Green Day!" He launched into a tune and a set of lyrics I barely recognized.

"Sort of," I said, and kept driving.

Getting off at 125th Street, I paralleled the chain-link fence, searching for a way onto the broad apron of cracked concrete west of the highway. At a broken gate sagging on twisted hinges I swung in, skirted a rusted front-loader and a flat-tired, old-style garbage truck. There was no sign anyone but us had been here in years. In New York's tougher days the waterfront was all like this: ragged, abandoned, adrift between bare-knuckled past and gentrified future. Once, a shadowed cove on a no-man's coast—rusting steel, collapsed piers, sun glinting off debris-locked oil slicks, saltwater scent folded into the stench of floating garbage—would have been easy to find. But not now. Whatever Kevin had planned here, he must have looked long and hard for a piece of the harbor as desolate as this.

I wasn't sure how much weight the piers under the asphalt could bear, here where everything was crumbling, so I parked a distance from the edge and Linus and I got out. At first we saw nothing, no sign this was the place Kevin meant. Slowly, we walked closer to the water's edge.

"Oh, shit," Linus whispered, standing next to me on the potholed concrete. He stared ahead, toward a half-sunken wharf. "Shit. What the hell is that, in the water there?" He started forward.

"Don't move." I grabbed his arm. "We don't know how it's wired."

He froze. I squinted at the contraption bobbing in the shadowed water about fifty feet from shore. Now we could see why Kevin had chosen a place so deserted, so derelict: he needed to be sure he wouldn't be interrupted during the time it took to construct the device we were staring at, and then to place the prize on it. He needed somewhere he could leave a young Asian woman bound and gagged on a floating scale, and be sure no one would notice.

"It's a seesaw," I said. "We do this wrong, she drops in the water." I stepped carefully forward, looking for trip wires, switches, buttons, something that would make our mistake before we began. I found nothing, got to the edge, took my sunglasses off, stared across the water to examine Kevin's insane device.

An empty oil drum, fixed out there to the rotting wharf so it wouldn't float away, supported a wide plywood platform. Fastened beneath the platform, two smaller barrels, one on each side, floated on the water's surface, keeping the seesaw balanced. That worked while the tide was high. But now it was going out. Once the tide fell below a certain level, the small barrels wouldn't be supported by water anymore. Then the seesaw would tip. The young woman, clearly heavier than whatever was on the other end, would slide right in.

"It's all right," I called to the trussed-up woman, looking at her huge and panicked eyes. "You'll be all right. Just don't move." Whether she heard me, whether she spoke English, whether she was out of her mind with terror, I couldn't tell. But she didn't move. She must have not moved for hours. At the beginning she must have been made to understand that if she moved, she'd drown.

And that someone would be coming to save her.

"Dude," Linus said. "We have to do something."

That was for sure. The solution seemed easy, if unpleasant as all hell: swim out and get her. But this was Kevin. I took another minute to scan the water.

"Son of a bitch."

"Dude, what?" Linus came up beside me.

A length of chicken wire fencing stretched through the water perpendicular to the seesaw's platform, toward us. It was staple-gunned, as far as I could see, to a row of rotting pilings. Flimsy, but enough of a barrier to keep you from making it from one side of the seesaw to the other if you were in the water. I pointed to the other end of the platform, the one the woman wasn't on. Resting there, set to slide into the water the instant the woman's weight was gone, was an orange plastic bag.

"Holy shit!" Linus exploded. "But dude. I thought this was the fourth quarter. Isn't that what Mr. Crazy said? That's what he said! There's more clues? That's wack! Shit, dude, that's lame! The freak—"

"Linus? Are you remembering not to flip out?" I spoke quietly, steadily. "We need to do this."

He swallowed. "Yeah. Yeah, okay, you're right. But that freak! I tell you right now, dude, you don't kill him when we find him, I'm gonna do it myself."

"You'll have to take a number." I took off my jacket, my shirt, dropped them on the concrete. "All right. The good part is, he didn't know there'd be two of us. So what we're going to do, we're going to swim out there. One on each side of the fence. I grab her, you grab the bag, at the same time." I crouched, unlaced my shoes. "You up for it?"

"Dude?" he answered in what may have been the saddest voice I'd ever heard. "I can't swim."

That stopped me, one shoe off. *CAN'T SWIM? Who the hell can't swim? What kind of goddamn stupid— Hey.* I forced myself calm. *Dude. Are you remembering not to flip out?* I took off my other shoe and stood.

"Dig, dude, I'm sorry. For real, I'm sorry."

"It's okay. It's okay. Let me think."

I thought. Nothing happened. The tide slipped lower and the woman begged with her eyes.

"That's what he wants, isn't it?" Linus said, not really a question. "That freak. Whatever's in the bag, it's probably just enough, you take it off, in she goes. He wants you to get the bag, and let her drown."

"Make her drown. He wants me to kill her."

"But dude, water? He used water already."

"Not water. That's secondary. Choice. What would kill her would be choice."

Another minute, during which no brilliant idea occurred to me. I said, "I have to get her. Any second, that thing's going to tilt."

"The bag."

"I know. Maybe it'll float long enough—"

"You know it won't."

"Then it won't."

"Then what about Lydia?"

"*Jesus Christ, you think I'm not thinking that?*" He flinched; I brought my voice back under control. "Linus, what the hell else can I do?" I crouched at the edge, ready to slip into the slimy water.

"Wait! Dude, wait!"

I turned, about to tell him that I'd dive under for the bag, or it would get caught on some floating debris, or we'd get around needing it the way we'd gotten around Kevin's clues about Jim's apartment, or some other bullshit more for myself than for him; and that he shouldn't even consider something crazy like jumping in and trying anyway, because I couldn't save both of them. But he wasn't beside me. He'd raced to the car, and now he was running back. With the dog. "Woof!" Linus shouted. "Woof can swim!"

"Yeah," I said. "Great. But he can't—"

"He can!" Like a banner, Linus waved the plastic bag we'd brought from Hal's. It was empty, and he knelt, scooped up a chunk of broken concrete, dropped it in, tied the bag. "We're gonna do, like, a split-second precision elite military rescue operation. Like Navy SEALs."

He explained what he had in mind. It was nuts. But I had nothing in mind.

So we tried it.

Step one: me in the water.

I tried to brace for the shock of the cold but it hit me like a hammer. Pulling in short, shivering breaths, I breaststroked through debris-clogged murk. I made slow progress, probing the water as I had the land for trip wires and traps. Styrofoam cups and water-polished wood circled me, along with other, less identifiable junk; but though some scraps clung to my skin, as though they wanted to be rescued, too, nothing seemed to be designed to hold me back. I reached the woman on the seesaw's end, spoke to her gently, examined her as carefully as I could without touching her or the device to make sure she wasn't bound to the plywood in any way. Her pleading eyes grew even bigger and behind the duct-tape gag she made tiny wordless sounds, but she remained as still as stone. I could imagine Kevin placing her here, smiling and explaining that someone would come to save her and all she had to do was not to move at all until he did. And I could imagine what he'd expected her to feel when I swam for the bag on the other end instead.

And what he'd expected me to feel as she sank.

Treading water, I turned to the shore, signaled Linus. He waved back, picked up a jagged wooden slat, held it for Woof. Woof bounded and barked. Linus flung the slat into the water. Without a second's hesitation the dog jumped. I held my breath: submerged wreckage was a danger here, which was why I'd gone in so carefully. "Yeah, but you explain that to a dog," Linus had said. "Jumping in, that's part of chasing it. Dude, he'll do fine."

He did. Swimming straight for the stick, he grabbed it and paddled back. He heaved himself on shore, shook off, and wagged madly. Linus spent a few moments telling him how wonderful he was, then showed him the plastic bag, cocked his arm back to throw it. Now the game was established; Woof jiggled in anticipation at the water's edge. Linus made a switch, threw a lump of concrete instead. The dog took off. When he got to where it had splashed in and sunk—right at the seesaw—he circled, searching for his plastic bag. Linus called his name. The dog looked up, and Linus lobbed the weighted plastic bag. At the second it hit the water, I grabbed the terrifed woman from the seesaw. I was holding her, keeping her head out of the water, sidestroking to shore; I didn't see the critical moment. But I heard splashing, shouting, Linus yelling to Woof that he was a good dog, that he should bring it here. By the time I got near the concrete apron, Woof was already out and bounding around, shaking himself, barking for me to get out of the water so he could show me his orange plastic bag.

"Dude! Dude!" Linus was practically bounding, too. "How great was that! What a dog! Awesome! Superdog! Get him a cape, he's gonna save the world!"

"He did it?"

"Of course he did it! What a genius!"

That was actually backward, because the whole plan revolved around the dog's inability to tell one plastic bag from another. But Linus's joy was justified and I didn't interfere.

"Help me here," I said, handing the woman in my arms up to him. She was looking wildly from me to him to the dog. He bent and took her, then put her down on the concrete as I pulled myself out. Woof came over to sniff her, and then me, as well he might. She, I, and Woof himself were all soaked and stinking. Now that Linus had held the woman and hugged the dog he was no model of germ-free sanitation, either. I bent and gently removed the duct tape from the woman's mouth, something I was getting good at. "Shush," I whispered, and she made not a sound even when her lips were free. I took out my knife to cut through the tape on her wrists and ankles. She sat up woozily.

"Take her to the car," I said to Linus, heading toward Woof who was once again standing with pride over his prize.

"Back to St. Vincent's?"

Good question. I was about to tell him, no, St. Luke's this time, it's closer and they don't know us there. But I stopped, frozen. Linus froze, too. Woof didn't. He jumped around, barking either in welcome or warning, because he didn't know whether the black SUV slamming on its brakes two inches from Linus's car was friend or foe. I did, though. I leaned and grabbed his collar before he had a chance to go charging over and try to defend us from Ming, Strawman, and Lu.

19

"Well." Lu stood planted on the broken concrete, flanked by his mountainous minders. "Look at this. It's Dead Man. I thought you had nothing to do with it, motherfucker. Wasn't it supposed to be a lunatic kidnapping my girls? Strawman, go get her."

Strawman's pistol glinted when he tucked it into his belt. Ming's was enough, anyway. Strawman crossed the concrete and picked up the dripping woman. Her eyes had glazed over and she didn't seem to notice. Her head lolled against Strawman's giant chest. Linus, though his mouth was open, had enough sense to stay silent.

"It is a lunatic," I said.

"Oh! This punk here, that's him? Have to admit, he looks a little crazy."

"Not him."

"Oh, so, what, the dog?"

Ming, who'd moved the gun to point at Linus, now shifted it to Woof. Linus stepped in front of the dog. Ming chuckled.

"Hold him," I said quietly, passing Woof's collar to Linus. "And don't move again."

"You got a death wish, I guess," Lu said conversationally. "It was your idea for me to check out the girls' GPSs. It seems there's one at St. Vincent's, too, I'll go get her later. They say she's okay, just dehydrated, bruised up, hysterical but they have her on meds. What the fuck did you do to her?"

"I saved her life."

"After you beat the crap out of her or something? I mean, what?"

"It wasn't me. Tell Ming to put the gun down."

"No. He just got it back and he's enjoying it. He and Strawman just got out of jail, or we'd have been here sooner. Because Ming had the tracker, so we had to wait before we could follow your helpful advice. You, kid. Take your fucking dog and get out of here. I ever see you again, you're dead, too."

Linus didn't move.

"Go," I said. "It'll be all right."

"The fuck it will," Lu said. "But go!"

"No." Linus found his voice, though it squeaked. "You're wrong. We saved her."

Lu shrugged. "Well, it's all the same to me. This is a good spot." He looked around approvingly like a man who'd been searching for a place to picnic.

"Linus, get the hell out of here!" I said.

"Too late," said Lu.

Ming waved the gun, trying to herd us closer to the water. Woof began to growl. "Lu—" I said, but someone else was speaking to Lu, too.

The woman in Strawman's arms had lifted her head. A light had come back into her eyes and she was croaking out raspy Chinese, coughing as she talked. Lu answered and they went back and forth. She shook her head emphatically, spat a machine-gun round of words as her voice got stronger. I glanced at Linus. He shrugged. "Fujianese. Even if I spoke good Chinese I wouldn't understand that."

Lu said to Strawman, "Take her to the car." He turned to us with a smile, but it wasn't a smile I liked. "Well. I'll be a son of a bitch. Jasmine says it wasn't you after all. She says you saved her life."

Ming gave his boss a look of confused disappointment. But he didn't lower the gun, and Lu kept smiling.

"She says a completely different cocksucker came to her crib," Lu went on. "Paid for an all-night party. He asked for her particularly because Junie recommended her. Junie's the girl at St. Vincent's," he added helpfully. "I'm sure, since it wasn't you, you didn't know that."

"I did know that. She told me her name when I saved her life."

"So let me see if I've got this straight. A lunatic's running around kidnapping my girls so you can save them?"

"I told you that this morning."

"I still don't get it. It's like a scavenger hunt? You two are playing a game with my property? You think that's okay?"

"I think it sucks."

"You do? But you're doing it."

"I also told you he has my partner. Remember, the clues? The plastic bags?" I pointed at Woof's treasure.

Lu pursed his lips, gave an exaggerated nod. "That's one of them? The clue bags? You mean they're real?"

"The whole thing's real."

"No. The whole thing's bullshit even if it's real. What the fuck does your partner, your lunatic, your clues, any of this crap have to do with me and my girls?"

My answer was cut off by a shout from Strawman, the first sound I'd ever heard him make. We all turned. Flashing red and blue lights, about six blocks east, but headed down the hill and right this way.

"Shit!" spat Lu. He spoke some quick Chinese to Strawman. "You." He pointed at me. "Get in the car."

A stonier rock and a harder place, I couldn't imagine. But Lu might be on the verge of believing me. The NYPD was a whole different story. If I stalled until they got here, I'd be safe from Lu but I'd be in lockup and Lydia would be out of luck.

"Let the kid go," I said.

"Get in the fucking car!"

Well, he could hardly shoot Linus with the cops about to swoop down. I said to Linus, "Stay on it," wondering if that would be possible without me. He nodded, biting his lip, and I got in the Escalade.

Not back on the floor, as it turned out, and not on the seat. Strawman put Jasmine down outside the car, made sure she could stand, if shakily, on her own feet, and lifted up the backseat bench. He grunted me to the empty space under it. It wasn't lost on me, as I crawled in and he dropped the seat into place, that the compartment was the right size for a body.

For about five minutes I knew nothing except the stink from the river water soaking me and the heat from the cooling driveshaft, for which I was ridiculously grateful. Then three thuds as three doors closed, some squeaks as weight dropped onto the seat over me, and a jostle as the car started to move.

The driveshaft became a less agreeable companion now. I had to keep shifting as it heated up, and I had some argument with the Escalade's suspension, too. I wondered where we were going. I wondered what Lu had said to the cops. I wondered where Lydia was, and how she was doing. I hoped Linus and Woof were okay, and that Linus had remembered to pick up my jacket, because he'd need my phone when Kevin called again. I didn't know whether Kevin would speak to him. But if anyone could think of some way to make that happen, it would be Linus.

And what other choice was there?

I was twisting repeatedly, breathing deeply, trying not to panic and just about at the end of my talent for that when the car stopped. Doors clicked open, springs squeaked, and finally the seat lifted up. "Jesus, you stink worse than Jasmine," Ming growled. "Get out."

He held a gun in his hand, not pointed at me but discreetly by his side. He clamped on to my arm as I climbed from the hold. He might have been helping me out of the car if he and I had both been different people. As it was he propelled me onto the sidewalk, and then, elbowing aside tourists and little old ladies, to a nondescript apartment building's shadowed doorway. We were on the south side of Bayard, the heart of Chinatown. I tried to pull away. Ming yanked me closer.

"I can slam you over the head and carry you in," he said quietly. "Or you can walk in. Mr. Lu wants to talk to you and that's not a question."

A small plaque by a buzzer read CHINATOWN ASSOCIATION FOR ANCIENT ARTS. Ming shoved me through the front door. At the end of a short hallway a door opened. The middle-aged, heavily made-up Chinese woman who held it wrinkled her nose when I got within sniffing distance. I couldn't argue. She stood aside for us, and when I entered I saw, surprisingly, a staircase running along the rear wall. Left and right from the entry foyer ran two smaller hallways, with doors opening off them. The entire first and second floors had been transformed into one huge duplex. No way this was legal, and I wondered how much it was costing Lu to get the city to ignore it.

Ming steered me left, into a cliché Chinese parlor: bamboo birdcages, fringed upholstery, crimson silk wallpaper. I could see the open door of an identical one across the hall. Lu lounged on the sofa, and Strawman in the easy chair.

"One of your cribs?" I asked Lu. "A little gaudy, don't you think?"

"Not my taste, either," he shrugged. "But the clients like it. Go take a shower."

"What?"

"You think I'd let you sit here like you are? You know how much this shit cost? Mama-san will show you."

The woman with the wrinkling nose gave me a cold bow.

"The hell with that," I said. "I don't have time for this, Lu."

"Yes, you do. Your lunatic already called."

"What the— He called? Goddammit!" Now I spotted what I should've seen before, my jacket and shirt, my shoes, and the plastic bag on the table next to Lu. And my phone in his hand. I started forward but Ming clamped on to me again. I said, "Tell this son of a bitch to let go or I'll kill him right here!"

"Ming, for Christ's sake, the way he smells? Don't touch him if you don't have to." Ming slowly loosened his grip, but he didn't step away. "Smith, you should be happy, now I believe in your lunatic."

"Like I care what you believe. What the hell did you tell him? Did you screw this up? I swear to God, Lu—"

"Back off! Just back off. I didn't tell him anything. The kid talked to him. He told him you had a problem and to call back in twenty minutes. So go take a fucking shower and get back here. I want you to stop stinking up my place and I want you there to talk to him this time. Not the kid."

I took a breath, looked around. "The kid," I said. "Where is he?"

Lu rolled his eyes. "Down in the basement, washing the fucking dog."

I came out of the shower to find my shirt, socks, shoes, and a pair of jeans I'd never seen before on the chair beside the stall. The jeans weren't a bad fit. I wondered whose they were and how eager he'd been to give them up. When I got back down to the garish parlor I found Lu and his sidekicks, and Linus, Woof, and a pot of coffee. Three out of six ain't bad.

Woof, looking fluffy, stood and wagged a greeting. I asked Linus, "Did Kevin call again?"

"Not yet, dude."

Linus was drinking a Coke. I poured myself coffee. Maybe I should have waited for Lu to offer, but courtesy hadn't been a hallmark of our relationship.

"So," Lu said. "*Dude.* Tell me what the fuck is going on."

I ignored him, spoke to Linus. "Why the hell are you here?"

"I told you back at Nicole's. I go where you go."

"That's not real smart, Linus."

"Neither of you is real smart," Lu said.

I sat, tried the coffee. Not bad, for a whorehouse. "What happened with the cops?"

"Concerned citizen called." Lu seemed amused. "Nervous about cars by the water, worried it was a drug deal. Probably the dealer who owns that turf."

"What did you tell them?"

"Slacker here said the dog fell in."

"They bought that?"

"Who gives a shit? It made enough sense, they had no probable cause to search. They stuck their heads in both cars anyway, but nothing in plain sight, they had to leave us alone. After they were gone I told Slacker to beat it. I was explaining why that was a good idea when your phone rang."

"Kevin," said Linus. "I told Mr. Lu, lean in close."

I said to Lu: "So you heard him?"

"Oh, I fucking heard him," Lu said. "When I find him I'll fucking kill him."

"Did he give you anything?" I asked Linus. "Did you talk to Lydia?"

"No and no. He was kinda pissed it was me. I said you had a problem but he should call back. It was the best I could think of. He was mad he couldn't talk to you right then but he liked the problem thing."

I nodded. "That was good."

"Yeah, it was brilliant," Lu said. "After that I told Slacker to give me the fucking phone and get lost, but he wouldn't. Ming was going to just take it and dump them both in the river, him and the dog, but Jasmine didn't like that and she was starting to sneeze and all kinds of shit. So instead, here we all are. Now. Tell me what the fuck this is all about, who this cocksucker is, and where I can get my hands on him. Because he's going down slow and ugly. And then I'll decide about you. And Slacker. And maybe I'll keep the fucking dog."

I got up for more coffee. "Lu. If I knew where to find him, why would I be crapping around with the rest of this?"

"Because, like he says, it's a game."

"For him. Not for me. Once I find Lydia you can have Kevin and make it as ugly as you want. But if you screw this up before I find her, I'll kill you." We stared at each other stonily. Ming started to rise. Lu waved him back.

"I know I didn't just hear you threaten me under my own roof."

"I wouldn't be under your roof for a second if I knew where the hell to go."

"You think you could just leave?"

"You think you could make me stay?"

Now Ming did stand. And Strawman with him. And Linus said, "Dudes?"

Everyone turned to him. Lu spoke in disbelief. "*Dudes?*"

Linus flushed. "Fine, whatever. Just, maybe we could do this later, and do something else now? More constructive, you know?"

"Like exactly what?" I asked.

"Like, I dunno, that?" He pointed to the plastic bag.

I turned toward it, dumbfounded. A new collection of clues and I was busy playing bull elephant with Lu. *Jesus!* In two steps I was over there, knocking aside Ming's arm as he tried to stop me from getting near his boss.

"Let him," Lu said, and Ming subsided. "Let's see what this clue shit is about."

I tore the bag open and dumped it out on the carpet.

Only three things: a long silver screw, a printout of a photo, and a book. Lu cocked his head. "What the hell?"

"I don't know."

He leaned forward. "*Last Days of Old Beijing*? Maybe I should read that. Learn something about the homeland. Never been there, you know." Pointing at the photo: "Who the hell is that?"

"Chevy Chase, I think."

Linus wrinkled his brow. "You mean, the comedian?"

"Yes."

From Lu: "What the hell is that supposed to mean? Chevy, like, you're supposed to think of cars? Chase, like, 'Try and catch me'? Or some famous routine of his?"

"I told you, I don't know."

"This is what it's like? The other times? Bags of junk like this?"

"Every time."

"But you figured them out?"

I said nothing.

"That screw. You suppose it's just, 'Screw you'?"

I looked at him. "It hasn't been like that before. It's been real clues, not messages to me. But I wouldn't put it past Kevin. Then the book . . ."

Linus finished the thought I didn't want to: "Could just mean, Lydia's running out of time."

"And Chevy Chase?" Lu asked. "Haha, very funny, big joke?"

My heart sank. If this was just Kevin mocking me, if these weren't real clues, then time was slipping away, Kevin had gone to a whole lot of trouble for a laugh, and we were no closer. I stared at the screw, the photo, the book, trying to force them to reveal their secrets. Nothing. But I was struck by a different thought. "Lu. He's a client here."

"Who, your lunatic? Mama-san says he just came here once."

"And once to Junie's place, and once to Angelique's. And Lei-lei's. Maybe someone knows something about him."

"They usually don't leave résumés. And the cops have been swarming over all my cribs all day, thanks to you. I'm losing a fortune."

"Not thanks to me. Thanks to him."

"Funny, because they've been showing the girls pictures of you."

"The cops are way behind the curve."

"Yeah, well. If I knew what he looked like—"

"Shit!" That was Linus. "Why didn't I think of this already?" He had the iPhone out, was swiping at it. After a minute: "Dude? This him?"

I looked at the photo on the phone's screen. Kevin's mug shots from ten years ago. I felt a surge of fury at the sullen mouth, the accusatory eyes. I nodded. "According to Lydia he doesn't look like that anymore, though."

Lu took the phone from Linus. "This fat slob is the one who's making all the aggravation?"

"That's ten years ago," I said. "He's changed."

"Shit," Linus said. "Wish I had the iPhone Photoshop app. I can buy it and install it now but it'll take a little time."

To me that was gibberish, but Lu said, "Photoshop? That's what you need, kid? Ming, get one of the girls who knows how to work that."

Linus didn't look at all surprised that Lu had the technology he needed. I supposed I shouldn't be, either: the oldest profession, adaptable as always.

Ming came back with not just one of the girls, but Jasmine. Dressed in tight jeans and a rhinestone-studded T-shirt, shag haircut still wet from the shower, she sauntered into the parlor and over to me, climbed into my lap, threw her arms around me and kissed me.

"Jesus, doll," Lu said, but without heat. "What did I say about giving it away for free?"

"He save my life. He get anything for free he want."

"I appreciate it," I said. "But not right now."

She pouted, turned to Linus. "What about you? You busy guy, too?"

Linus flushed to his scalp, muttered something, shook his head. Lu laughed, which made Linus flush darker.

"Listen, honey," Lu said to Jasmine, "all he wants right now, that kid, is Photoshop."

Jasmine unfolded herself from my lap, strolled over to Linus, laid a hand on his shoulder. "Computer make you happy? Come. We go make you happy."

"Just the computer!" Lu said as Linus hesitated, then rose to follow her. "Jasmine, did you hear me? No samples!"

"Don't worry, dude," Linus mumbled. "Totally do not worry."

"He a virgin?" Lu asked me as Linus, Jasmine, and Woof disappeared upstairs. "Maybe I'll break the no-freebies rule for him, this works out okay."

Ming snickered. I said, "I have no idea." I did have some idea how that might go over with Trella, but I kept it to myself.

"This lunatic of yours," Lu said. "What's his beef with you?"

"He hates me." I drank coffee, too tired to go through it all with Lu and not giving a shit, really, if he knew or not.

"Not hard to believe," Lu answered, and then sat straight up, as I did, when my phone rang. He handed it to me.

"Not a sound," I said to him, to Ming and Strawman. Into the phone: "Smith."

"On speaker again?"

"Not a lot of places I can go besides the car, Kevin."

"Oh, poor you. I heard you were in trouble. Charlie Chan Junior told me. Hi, Charlie."

"He's not here. I dropped him off. This was getting too hot for a kid."

"Oh. Well, that's okay, you still have fat Hal, you need any help. What kind of trouble?"

"Jesus, what do you think? Cops!"

"But you did maneuvers? Evade, resist, escape?"

"I managed. What the hell comes next, Kevin?"

"Well, that depends. Did you get the bag?"

"Yes."

"Yes! Yes, he got the bag! Then it worked? Jasmine?" He suddenly sounded as excited as a kid. "That was great, wasn't it? You know how hard it was to build that thing? Did it work? Tell me it worked!"

Lu growled something. I shot him a warning glance.

"You mean, did one end dump the other in the water? Yes, you son of a bitch. Yes, it worked."

"Oh, swee-eet! You loved it, right?"

"Fuck you."

"You're really no fun, you know that? But anyway, you have the clues? And Jasmine's in hooker heaven? Wonder what they do up there. I mean, the hookers get their choice of studs all day, or what?"

"The cops'll be all over this, Kevin. Sooner or later some girl at some whorehouse is going to tell them there's a difference between you and me."

"Well, they don't have a photo of me, so that's not so scary."

"You don't think those places have hidden cameras?"

Lu knit his eyebrows in a look that said I was crazy. I shrugged. I knew there were no cameras: high-class clients would vanish like smoke if they had a glimmer of an idea they'd been taped. I was just trying to rattle Kevin.

"Oh. Oh. Hmm, you think they do? Well, you know what, that's okay. Even if they know my face they're still not gonna find me. It makes the frame fit you not quite so tight, but it's still good. Yeah, what the hell. Hope I looked good, though. In the photos."

"Suit yourself. But I don't get it, Kevin. Jasmine, the seesaw, it doesn't follow the pattern. The other times there weren't clues with the bodies, or bodies with the clues."

"Well, Jasmine wasn't a body when you found her, was she? You made her one!"

"Still."

"Still. Still. Still, Bill, kill. *Kill Bill.* Hey, you see that flick? I loved it. Thought about you the whole time. That scene in the rain, man, that was hot, that girl-on-girl stomping action—"

"Kevin!"

"Hah? Kevin, what? Who're you yelling at, white man?"

The drugs, the strain, I didn't know what was getting him, but he was less organized, wilder, every time we talked. His twelve-hour game clock still gave me five hours, but Kevin might unravel before the clock ran out.

"Kevin," I said calmly. "Are we playing, or talking movies? Because I don't give a damn about movies. Why was the pattern different this time?"

"God, you're boring!" He let out a huge theatrical sigh. "Well, game fans, the reason it was different was, now we're in overtime."

"What does that mean?"

"Overtime? See, that's when there's a draw at the end of the fourth quarter, so you have to—"

"I know what the fuck overtime is! What are we doing? You and I?"

"'You and I.' See, not 'you and me,' like normal people talk. No, Big Brain knows best! Well, here's the deal, Big Brain. Even though it's *not* overtime, technically, because there's no draw because I'm way ahead, but even though that, I'm cutting you some slack. But no more running around, finding bodies and clues, all that shit. I'm tired of that. You have almost all the clues you need now to find your girlfriend."

"I do?"

"In that bag, the one you got from Jasmine. Poor kid. Did she kick and squeal and struggle? I wanna hear about it! What was it like?"

I was silent.

"Oh, poor genius can't even talk about it? Must've hurt, watching her die because of you. Aww. Too fucking bad."

"Are these clues, Kevin? The stuff in this bag? Or just a way to mess with my head?"

"Your *head*? I'm supposed to give a shit about your head? No, Big Brain, that bag, what's in there, you need one more thing to tie it all up. I just call one more time to tell you that one more thing, and then all you gotta do is put it together right."

"Why call again? Why not tell me right now?"

"That's for me to know and you to find out. No, seriously, I'll call you when everything's ready."

"Let me speak to Lydia."

"Not that again! You're a drag, you know that?"

"I followed the clues. I found the girl."

"What a whiner. 'I did what you said, now can I have my reward please?' Well, you know what? No. She's fine. She's right here. But I don't feel like it. Later for you, asshole."

"If I don't speak to her—"

"Oh, don't start that bullshit again! You'll keep playing because you love little Kewpie Doll here. You lurrrrve her. Right? Or maybe not. Maybe you're banging Charlie Chan Junior, and you don't give a shit about her. Well, it doesn't matter, because think about this, Prince Asshole: you *need* her. You need to find her. Because right now the *po*-lice are thinking you killed four Chinese hos. Cutie Pie here is the only one who knows that ain't so. Say it ain't so, Joe! Say it all you want, but until you got a witness—can I get a *wit*-ness!—you're just totally fucked. And she's the only witness you got. So even if you're like, soooooo over her, you need to keep playing."

"Kevin—"

"Oh, Kevin this, Kevin that. I'm sick of it. You just be a good little genius and sit there with your thumb up your ass until I call again. Peace."

After that, nothing. In the silence Lu whistled. "You know? That really *is* a lunatic. What are you going to do?"

"Let me think!" I yelled. Lu raised his eyebrows at my tone, but he didn't say anything.

I rubbed a hand down my face. "Check around," I told him. "See if you're missing any other girls."

"He says it's all about your partner now. No more running around."

"Yeah, and he's real big on the truth."

Lu sat for a moment, as though lost in thought. He called out something in Chinese. The mama-san came instantly into the room. They exchanged a few sentences; she bowed and left.

"Drives me up the wall when she bows," Lu said conversationally. "Like this was fucking Shanghai or something."

After that, some moments of quiet, of nothing; then Woof plowed back downstairs and bounced over to me, wagging and pawing. Linus followed more slowly, crimson as Jasmine walked behind him, rubbing his shoulders.

"He good boy," she told Lu. "Even I say it's okay, he don't want, even tiny kiss. Anyway that picture, make me out of the mood."

"Dude." Linus strode over, leaving Jasmine pouting, and showed me the results of his work. "She says it's him."

"Jasmine?" Lu asked. "That true? This is the guy you went with?" He leaned toward me, to see Kevin: older, thinner, grayer, harder. Jasmine bit her lip and nodded.

"How did you do that?" I asked Linus.

He shrugged. "It's only a program." He turned to Lu. "The picture's on her computer. In case you wanted to send it around. To where the other girls, you know, live."

"Good thinking, kid." Lu opened his mouth to call the mamasan. As if reading his mind, she came flying back into the room; but she didn't give him a chance to speak. She poured forth a stream of agitated Chinese. Lu rose from his chair, speaking in short, clipped phrases. He crossed to the window, peeked out. Then came the unmistakeable pounding of police fists on the door.

20

"You son of a bitch," Lu said to me, but this time more exasperated than murderous. "You brought this on."

"Or it could have something to do with you running a string of hookers."

Inside, a bell started tinkling. Galloping commotion erupted on both floors as girls and johns leapt up and threw their clothes on.

From outside, more pounding, then, "Chinatown Vice! Open the damn door!"

Chinatown Vice: that would be Mary's friend Patino. And possibly Mary, too.

"We've got the back covered," the voice called. "And the roof. So forget it, just open the door."

The mama-san and Lu exchanged quick words. She protested, he insisted; she threw me a snarl, then she went to the door and screeched in English, "Hey, who making so much noise?"

"Oh, who the hell do you think, Mama Zhu? It's the police. Open up!"

Teapots and sweets appeared on trays rushed into the parlors by nervous young women. Musical instruments were whipped from cases. Woof joined in the excitement, barking like mad.

"Oh! Police! Okay, just one minute, hold your horses!"

Hookers and johns streamed down the stairs to sit artistically in the parlors as the fists thumped again. "Forget one minute! There's nowhere to go and I'm getting impatient. Just open the door!"

Nowhere to go: bad for the johns, worse for me. They could try to sell the idea they'd all been sitting around listening to pretty girls sing. I had nothing to sell. I also didn't think for a minute this raid was a coincidence.

The voice called, "We have the ram, Mama Zhu. Should we use it? Ten, nine . . ."

The mama-san pointed at me, spitting something that was a curse in any language. She turned back to the door. "Hey, police! You have warrant?"

Lu said to me, "Come on."

"Where? They're out back, too."

"Damn tootin', we have a warrant!" the cop yelled.

"Kid?" said Lu. "You want to come, you want to stay? Do your street cred good, you get picked up in a high-class joint like this." Lu was grinning, talking over his shoulder, heading down a set of basement steps under the staircase.

Jasmine hurried with him as though this was old hat. "Come on, cute boy!"

Linus stared; being swept up in a whorehouse raid or going down into the dark with Jasmine was not a choice he'd woken this morning expecting to have to make. "Damn, dude." He shook his head in wonder; then he shoved the new clues back into the orange bag and he and Woof followed. Ming gave me a push, but I didn't need it. I knew what would happen if the cops picked me up now; I'd take my chances with Lu.

The basement was about what I'd have thought: dim, dusty, mold-scented, scattered with old furniture and low-ceilinged with pipes. We followed Lu through it, feeling the chaotic pounding of cop feet overhead. Lu strode on with purpose and without panic, around hot water heaters and past the giant mound of an oil tank. In a dark corner of a far wall he moved aside a rusting bedspring to reveal a door.

"You have a priest hole down here big enough for all of us? And the dog?"

"What the fuck is a priest hole?" Lu asked, ducking through the low opening.

I was about to come back with something brilliant—"A hiding place, jackass" was on my mind—but when I followed Lu, Linus, and Woof through the doorway I didn't find the abandoned coal bin I was expecting. Or the wall separating Lu's building from the building next door, either. I could barely see Woof's wagging tail up ahead as he vanished with Lu and Linus down a tunnel. I moved along and Ming climbed in behind me. Strawman crowded in, and Jasmine shut the door on us with a cheery "Bye-bye!"

The rough-walled tunnel wasn't quite high enough to stand up in. Lu, in front, and Strawman in the rear danced penlights through the darkness. I glanced back and got a cold kick out of Ming and Strawman, who were stuffed in the passageway like ten pounds of trash in a nine pound bag.

"Where the hell are we?" I asked, crouching along as the tunnel bent, turned, and headed down. I was surprised to hear the answer come not from Lu, but from Linus.

"It's the Chinatown tunnels! Mr. Lu, dude, am I right?"

"You're right, kid."

"Oh, awesome! Dig, I always thought these were made up! They're real?"

"You're in one. One of the reasons I bought that building."

"What about Jasmine?" I said. "How's she going to explain popping up out of the basement?"

"She doesn't pop up. She hides there until they find her and then just looks embarrassed. They haul her out like she's a find, search the basement for more girls, and that's that. You're just lucky all my girls have papers."

"They're all legal?"

"No, they just all have papers."

Suddenly Lu stopped, played his light on a surface in front of him. We all barely avoided piling into each other. Lu pulled out a jangling keyring, scraped it into a steel door. The thunk of a bolt, the creak of hinges, and he stepped forward, the rest of us close behind. The walls and ceiling fell away into a space dank and lightless but obviously much bigger than the cramped tube we'd been in.

"Oh, awesome!" Linus breathed, stopping, trying to see around him. "Tell me it's the opera house."

"Hey, kid, not bad. You know your history."

"Yeah, but I didn't know it was history! I thought it was fairy tales."

Lu played his light over an underbrush of benches and toppled stools. A low platform stood against one wall. Lu walked forward. "Watch your step here," he said. "There's still junk around."

We picked our way through dusty wreckage that rolled or cracked or clanged when you kicked it. I caught up with Linus and asked him what the story was.

"All the old men tell you. Different tongs and gangs, back in the day. No one liked to be trapped anywhere. They dug tunnels under every place. But they got filled in, mostly. Or some, they were never there."

"And this? The opera house?"

"They put it down here because no one could afford this much space on the street. You know, where you could put stores. Dig, dude, they had a gang war down here one time! Big ambush, guys shooting each other up while the people were singing. Cops came in the front door maybe two minutes later. Upstairs, I mean, the real door. No one went out that way but no one was here when they got here except the bodies! Everyone, the actors, the whole audience, even the ones not in the war, they all ran out through their own tong's tunnels!" He added matter-of-factly, "But then the CCBA built their building, with the auditorium, and everyone stopped using this down here."

"Except me," Lu said, unlocking another door at the far end of the space. Brightness briefly dazzled, though the small corridor we stepped into was, in truth, lit only by a single fluorescent strip.

The corridor led nowhere but to a flight of stairs, so we climbed. Ming and Strawman seemed to know just what they were doing. I guessed they'd been around for a police raid or two before. At the top of the three flights, Lu pulled open another door, and there we were in a Chinatown commercial corridor, standing among barbershops and noodle shops, jewelry stores and junk stores.

"So." Lu grinned. "Not bad, huh?"

"Terrific," I said. "Thanks, Lu. See you around."

"In your goddamn dreams. Where the hell are you going to go?"

"Not your problem."

"Wrong. Last thing you're going to do is catch that lunatic without me."

"I told you. When I find him, you can have him. After he gives me Lydia back."

"I hate to say this, because I hate to sound like your lunatic, but I don't trust you. You could turn him over to the cops to help you kiss and make up with them. Or you could kill him yourself. No, my friend, whatever you do between now and then, Ming will be right there to help."

"I don't want him."

"Did I ask you?"

Breaking into this standoff, a familiar melody, and an "Oh, shit," from Linus. "Bad Boys," Mary's ringtone. "Dude? What do I do?"

I nodded, eyes still on Lu. "Answer it."

Linus frowned, and Lu did, too, but I wanted to know if I had, really, been the point of the raid on Lu's crib.

"Hey, Aunt Mary," Linus said, sounding less chipper than the last time he'd talked to her. "Uh . . . Um . . ." He covered the phone. "She wants to know if you're here."

"Tell her no. Give her the number of one of the new phones."

He dug one from his cargo pocket, gave her the number, listened, winced, said, "Yeah, 'k, well, gotta go," and clicked off.

Lu said, "What are you doing? Who the hell was that?"

Linus told him, "A cop."

"In the middle of this shit you're—"

I batted Ming's hand away when the new phone rang. I lifted it, said, "Mary?"

Lu held a palm up and Ming backed off.

"Where the hell are you?" Mary asked fiercely. "And is Linus with you, or why did he cover the phone?"

"He was here, gone now. I told him to split. I'm in Chinatown. I'm telling you that because I know you can trace this call to a Chinatown tower. But that's all I'm saying and by the time you get here I'll be gone, too."

"How did you get out of Lu's?"

"How did you know I was at Lu's?"

"Chinatown telegraph."

"What?"

"I wasn't thinking Lu's, because I didn't know you were pals. Last I heard he wanted to kill you. But I thought you might turn up here someplace, trying to track Lydia. I asked the old ladies, if they saw you, to tell me."

"They know me?"

"Lydia's partner? Chinatown's only PI, with a non-Chinese partner her mom doesn't like? You're kidding." Her tone shifted, got low, insistent. "Bill, you have to come in."

"No."

"This is police business now."

"I can't. I'm close, Mary."

"Oh, yeah, and you're doing great! One hooker dead, one half-frozen, one nearly blown to bits. Two cops and a garbageman hurt. A hysterical widow, and a luxury condo with a big hole in the side. Just great! And you haven't found Lydia, have you?"

I couldn't argue with that, any of it. Except: "Another hooker you don't know about. Supposed to be dead, but alive. Three alive, because I found them. Not because I'm so smart. But he's leaving *me* clues, Mary. Not you. Me. Mary, he's crazy. And he's high. The only way to do this is to string him along. He's making mistakes already."

"Like what?"

"He doesn't know those women aren't dead. He's getting wild and sloppy."

"And what has that bought us?"

"He says I have almost all the clues, he's just going to call once more. You guys have to back off."

"No. No, you have to back off. You have to give us everything you have and let us do it."

"You can't do it."

"And you can?"

"I don't know. Maybe. I hope. But I'm the one he wants. Without me, he'll stop. He'll walk away and we'll be nowhere. *Lydia* will be nowhere. You can't keep me out of jail, can you?"

"To get the clues? I can try. I can explain—"

"One hooker dead, two cops hurt, an explosion—explain what? No, if I come in that's it. You know it is and it's not what he wants. If he can't play this game with me he'll walk away."

"We'll find him."

"*How?* Mary, you know if I thought you could I'd be there in a second. It has it be me. I have to do this."

"We know who he is."

That stopped me. "You know?"

"Kevin Cavanaugh. An ex-con. Nicole White told us you were asking about him. We checked; it fits. You should have told me, Bill."

Linus made a T with his hands. I said, "I couldn't risk it."

"We're closing in."

"You won't find him. He knew you'd be coming. He says he's got his tracks covered."

"Yes, we will find him. This is what we do."

"Yeah." A wordless moment. "It's what I do, too." I hung up.

"Whoa," Lu said. "That was a cop? You got better pockets than I do."

"Special case."

"Well, good for you. Now, what's your next move? You and Junior and Ming?"

"Not Ming."

He sighed. "You're a pain in the ass. Let me explain the situation you're in. The only use I have for you, or Junior, or fucking biscuit-breath here, is finding me this bastard. Now: we're in my backyard. We have cars. We"—he gestured around—"have guns. You don't."

"Come on, Lu, there are people everywhere. You're going to shoot us right here?"

"No. You can take off if you want. But if you do, you'll always have a problem. All of you. Always. You'll have to look out for me every time you open a door, because I might be on the other side. I can carry a grudge for a long, long time." He smiled. "But look on the bright side. You take Ming with you, whatever happens, happens. You're off the hook. All three of you." Still smiling, he leaned over and scratched Woof's ears. The dog wagged his tail, licked Lu's hand.

Linus paled, but stayed silent. I said, "Jesus, Lu, you're as crazy as Kevin."

"Could be."

Looking at Ming, I spoke to Lu. "He'll take orders? He won't go charging in like he's Genghis Khan?"

Ming scowled, but Lu said, "Sure. Pretty much. As long as you're reasonable. That okay with you, Ming? You're the lieutenant. He's the general. And this"—he pointed at Linus and Woof—"this is the fucking marines."

Ming's face darkened some more, but he finally nodded. "Great," Lu said. "Ming, take the Audi."

"No," I said.

"What are you thinking, going back for the kid's car? It's parked too near my place. Besides, your cop who has your private number, and the kid's, they must know his car."

"You don't think they know all your cars? Thanks anyway. Linus, call Trella."

"I texted her already," Linus said. "They'll be right here."

21

Our corridor had an entrance into the Elizabeth Street garage. When Joey's town car rolled down the ramp, Trella hopped out and got in back. She sat in the middle, the ham in the Linus-Ming sandwich, while Woof scrambled in at their feet. I took shotgun. After a few soft words from Lu, the garage attendant waved us straight through. Joey pulled out the other side, onto the Bowery.

"So," said Trella, "come on, you guys! What's happening?" Turning to Ming: "Hi. I'm Trella. Who are you, and can you move over a little?"

"Ming," growled Ming, and to his credit, shifted his bulk an inch or so.

"Thanks. Well? Guys?"

"Oh, dudess—!" Linus began, but I interrupted.

"First, Trella, did you guys find anything? Any likely building?"

"I'd have called," she said, a mild rebuke. "There are a lot that could be. With basements, areaways, windows that might catch the sun for a short time. But none of them are near any of those places we were looking for—kids' clothes stores, that kind of thing.

A couple of times I got out and tried to see in the areaway windows, but I didn't get anyplace."

"Shit," I breathed in frustration, though I hadn't really expected any different. She'd have called. I turned to Joey, who drove expertly and expressionlessly. "I'm hot," I said. "She told you that? You can get out of this, just say the word."

He shrugged. "No problem."

"Well, thanks. I appreciate it. I know you don't have a horse in this race."

"Hey, something different, you know? Besides," he grinned suddenly, "I always back Trella's horses. Where to?"

"I think we just drive around until he calls. Least chance of me being seen." I added, "I guess we can work on the new clues until then."

"You got new clues?" Trella demanded.

"Right here," Linus said. "But he says they're not complete. He called again, the crazy man, and he said he'd only call one more time. With the last and final clue."

Plastic rustled. I turned in the seat to see Linus and Trella with the contents of the bag spread across their laps.

"Only three things?" Trella said. "Usually there are more."

"This is different," I said. "For one thing, they're not complete. For another, this is overtime."

"This guy," Joey drawled. "It's really a game? Like Trella says?"

"Only to him, but yeah. Four quarters, now overtime."

"Did you get anywhere with these?" Trella asked.

"Not really," said Linus. "Cops came and we had to escape. Second time today!"

"Can't wait to hear," she said. "But let me look at these first. But . . ."

"But what?" I asked.

The briefest hesitation. "Anyone else dead?"

"No."

"Phew." She turned back to the clues. "You guys must have come up with something. Some ideas?"

"Well, only, maybe they're not clues." Linus explained our reasoning. Trella's lips scrunched in distaste.

"You think? It's way out of the pattern. And didn't he say they're clues?"

"He's losing it," I said. "Coming apart. Even if they are clues, leaving them with a victim is still outside his pattern."

She considered. "Maybe he's losing it now. Long day, I guess. But wouldn't he have left these hours and hours ago? Pretty much when all this started?" She picked through the items, turning the screw in her fingers, riffling through the book. "I think they are clues. I think they mean something."

"What, then?"

"I don't know."

We drove, exchanged theories, fell silent, tried other theories, fell silent again, and all jumped when my phone rang.

I put it on speaker, answered calmly, "Smith."

"*YOU MOTHERFUCKER!*" Kevin's scream was so loud that Woof sat up and yipped. Linus grabbed the dog's jaw, but Kevin didn't seem to catch the sound, just howled on. "*You cocksucking son of a bitch!* You cheated, you cheated, you cheated! You've been cheating all along, motherfucker!"

"What the hell are you talking about? How could I cheat?"

"*Those girls aren't dead!* Not Angelique, not Junie, and I bet not Jasmine, either! You son of a bitch! You lying son of a bitch!"

"Jesus, Kevin!" Rage blazed in me, matching his. I tried to force it down, to speak reasonably to this lunatic. "You told me where they were, you sent me there, what did you think I'd do, just stand back and applaud?"

"They were supposed to be dead! You told me they were dead!"

"No. You asked if I'd seen Junie's arms and legs flying and I said no."

"Oh, clever, clever, clever, aren't you clever! You *saved* her! You fucking saved her, you lying bastard! You ran away with her in your goddamn superhero isn't he wonderful Prince Asshole arms!"

Everyone in the car was staring at me, at the phone. Even Joey, still smoothly driving, was wide-eyed.

"Kevin?" Certainty settled on me. "How do you know? How do you have any idea what happened?"

"Oh, you think you're the only team that has a bench? You're the only guy in the world that has some asshole working for him? Fuck you, pally!"

"You're not doing this alone."

He laughed wildly. "The light dawns! Hey, maybe you're not a goddamn super genius after all! No, asshole, no, I'm not doing this alone. I've got an assistant. And I just talked to my fucking assistant. And my fucking assistant just totally fucked up! That explosion, that explosion—" Kevin's fury choked off his words. It was a moment before he found his voice again. "That fucking explosion was supposed to happen when you got there! As soon as you were on the street, so you could see it!" I met Linus's eyes: that's what we'd thought. "But my stupid goddamn assistant didn't see you go in, just come out. So when you came out, came running out, the fucking idiot thought, 'Doh, this must be the time.' Jesus! Can't anyone do anything right?"

"Kevin—"

"Oh, shut up! *Shut up!* Now I'm pissed. Now things are different. You lied and cheated, you didn't play the game right and now things have to change."

I took a deep breath, another, forced myself to speak quietly, as though this were acceptable, as though negotiating for Lydia's life with a madman who was accusing me of cheating by saving other lives were on any level okay. Quietly, I asked, "Change how?"

"I don't know how! I have to think of how! Now it'll be different, some kind of different. You have to wait until I think of how. And then I'll call you back. And you're lucky, I'll tell you that, you're really lucky I'm going to keep on playing. Because I could just declare a forfeit. If one team cheats the other gets a forfeit. Did you know that? Did you know?"

"Yes, I knew."

"So is that what you want? You want to forfeit?"

"No."

"No. I see. You want to keep playing?"

"Yes."

"Say it."

"I want to keep playing."

"No, you don't!" He cackled. "No, you don't, you want to stop and have me just disappear and then you get your girlfriend back and they lived happily ever after! *That's* what you want! You hate this game, right?"

"You know I do."

"Well, boo fucking hoo! That's not gonna happen! Hahaha! We're gonna keep playing until I'm ready to stop. Me, you get it? Me! So what you do now, all you can do is, you just wait, you just drive around and try to keep out of trouble and wait until you hear from me again."

The click of a broken connection. For a moment, the world dead calm, silent, airless. Then sounds and sights and smells flowed back into the car: the street, the day, real life. I held the phone, stared at it, unable to put it away. Linus released Woof's jaw and scratched the dog's ears, mechanically telling him he was good. Even Ming looked astounded.

Finally I slipped the phone into my pocket, lit a cigarette. "Head uptown," I told Joey.

"Where to?"

"The Village."

"Dude?" Linus tried tentatively. "What are you thinking?"

"Hal," I said savagely. "Hal's what I'm thinking. The assistant."

Linus swallowed, nodded. "Me, too. That's what I thought."

"Hal?" Trella said. "Your cop friend?"

"Ex," I said. "Ex-cop, and ex-friend, and he blames me for it."

"For what?"

"I'll tell her," Linus spoke up quickly. "You just, you know, smoke and stuff."

It was good advice and I took it.

After the explosion Hal had called me from a bar on Hudson Street. If I knew Hal, he was still there. With luck—thin on the ground lately, but always a chance—he was still conscious. With Linus narrating what Trella and Joey had missed, we drove uptown, finally reaching the cross street to Jim White's rented apartment. The street was open now, though narrowed by orange cones until the city could send a crew for the glass triangles and twisted window steel littering the asphalt. On Hudson, just around the corner, Joey pulled over in front of the White Horse, a famous

Village tavern and the only bar right there. I slammed the door as I got out and was surprised to find Linus on the sidewalk with me.

"What the hell are you doing?"

"You know what I'm doing."

"Get lost."

"No."

"Shit!" I left him to follow, yanked the bar's door open. The bartender and half-a-dozen drinkers turned to stare. None was Hal. I strode through both rooms, came back and pushed into the men's room. Empty.

"Hey, buddy, you looking for something?" the bartender barked. A square-shaped guy stepped off a barstool, probably the bouncer.

"No," I said. I swept past Linus, who stood apologetically in the doorway. Back out on the sidewalk I stared up and down Hudson, trying to pick out another place to drink. Coffeehouses and dry cleaners. "Goddamn it!" I exploded.

"Dude?"

"*What?*"

Linus pointed to the side street, to a paint-flaking basement storefront near the corner. The only thing that gave it away was one dusty Bud sign low in the window. This had to be a relic, left over from the Village's funky days. The bar owner was probably the bartender, too, and he likely also owned the building or he'd have had his rent raised out from under him long since.

Two steps into the stale-smelling interior showed me I was right at least about the vintage of the place, and the vintage of the bartender and the two regulars on their rickety barstools. It showed me, also, what I'd been looking for in the White Horse: Hal slumped at a booth in the back, too wasted to even look surprised when he saw me.

I slid in across the table and Linus sat down beside him, boxing him in. That was overkill, though; Hal wasn't in any condition to bolt.

"Get you something, fellas?" the bartender called across the small room, his voice louder than needed, a warning.

"Coffee," I said. "And one for him."

"And a Coke," Linus added.

Hal finally reacted to the invasion, barely able to form words. "Hey, buddy."

"Hal," I said quietly. "When this is over I'm going to kill you. First, though, and I mean right now, you're going to tell me where Kevin is."

He stared blankly. "What?" Sloppily, he slid the stare to Linus. After a moment: "Where's the pooch?" He began to chortle.

I lunged across the table, caught him by his shirtfront. "Stop the shit!" I dropped him back, righted the empty glass I'd knocked over, as the bartender appeared, two coffees and a Coke on his tray.

"Not in my place, pal," he growled, a short, pale man whose tattoos had fuzzed blue along his wiry arms.

"Sorry," I said. "I'll get him out of here as soon as he can walk." I dropped a twenty on the tray and he nodded and walked away, both of us understanding I was getting no change.

"Where's Kevin, Hal?" I said when we were alone.

"Kevin. Motherfucker. Poor kid, she didn't want to go." He reached for the empty glass. "Fuck," he said, peering into it. "Hey." He raised his voice for the bartender but I waved him off. I took the glass away, pushed the coffee toward Hal.

"Drink that."

"Fuck you."

"Drink it or I'll pour it into you."

He muttered something, lifted the cup, managed to down half before he dropped it and spilled the rest. "There. Happy? Now I want another drink."

"I'm not happy and you're not getting another drink. Where's Kevin?"

A beat late: "Left. The fucker left."

"*He was here?* Son of a bitch! When did he leave? When?"

Hal blinked blearily. "Pretty girl. Chinese or something. Didn't want to go." He rubbed a hand over his face, kept doing it, an endless loop. I reached across, yanked his arm down.

"He left here with a girl?"

He stared at me, then looked around. "Where? Who?"

"Kevin! Goddamn you, Hal, where did Kevin go?"

Linus had been mopping up Hal's spilled coffee. Now he slipped out of the booth, walked to the bar. Hal looked at me through drifting eyes. "Smith?" As though he'd just noticed me. "What are you doing here?"

"Hal," I said, low and slow, "you've been working with Kevin all along. I don't how he sucked you in but if you don't tell me where he is, where he has Lydia, I'll kill you right now."

"What?" With an obvious effort he focused on me. "Where Kevin is? Inside, where he belongs. No, wait, he got out, didn't he . . ." He trailed off, didn't pick up again.

"You've been helping him, you son of a bitch. You're his eyes and ears."

He stared. "Me? You think . . . me?"

"I know, you."

"Me?" He shook his head, trying to clear it. "No, see, a thing you gotta understand." He spoke clumsily, using his tongue the way you would an unfamiliar tool. "You gotta understand. I hate that motherfucker."

"You hate me, too, and so does he."

"Because you're another motherfucker. That don't make him, doesn't make him not one." He nodded, satisfied with how he'd explained things.

"You were at Jim's apartment. You set the explosion off."

"Explosion. *Boom!*" The bartender, Linus, and the regulars turned to look, but when Hal went on in a softer, slurred voice, no one moved our way. "Saw you. Yelled at you. You didn't hear me."

Yes, I realized, I had. My name, someone calling my name just before the blast.

"Called in a ten-thirty-three, a ten-fifty-four. Told the super, move people away from the building. Asshole was crapping his pants." As Hal went on jerkily detailing his actions after the explosion, Linus came back and sat down.

"Crazy Man wasn't here. Bartender says. Dude's been drinking by himself all afternoon."

"Doesn't mean he didn't call. Hal! Hal, shut up!"

Hal was muttering disjointedly about an EMS tech. He stopped, looked at me, blinking.

"Give me your phone."

He didn't move. I reached across the table, searched his coat pockets.

"Hey, what the—?" He watched me flip his cell phone open, but didn't try to reach for it. I realized I had no idea how the thing worked, so I passed it to Linus.

"Check incoming and outgoing."

Linus poked some buttons, then some more. "Dude." He shook

his head. "In, a restricted number, must be Mr. Crazy, but just the one call. Around when we went up to Harlem, so must be the one with the song lyrics. And a couple from you, before and after. Nothing else from the restricted number, and nothing out."

"Nothing? Kevin said he just talked to his assistant."

"Well, not on this phone. And he wasn't here."

Hal had been trying to follow this, swiveling his head between us, always a few seconds behind. "That's my phone."

"Where's the other one?"

"Other what?"

"Stand up."

Linus slid out but Hal didn't move. I went around and grabbed him, tugged him out of the booth. It was like manhandling a mattress. I pushed him against the wall, started going through his pockets.

"Hey!" the bartender came around the bar gripping a baseball bat. "I told you, not in here!"

I shoved Hal back to his seat. "Ex-cop," I said. "In this condition I didn't want him carrying a piece."

The bartender frowned. "Is he?"

"Carrying? No."

"You on the Job?"

I shook my head. "I'm private. Old friend. He has a problem, I'm here to help. Listen, did he talk to anyone here? Did he use your phone?"

He shook his head. "Couple cell phone calls, like I told the kid. Been sitting there drowning his troubles, hours now. Not sure he even got up to piss. Only guy here he talked to's me, when he wanted another. I was about to cut him off, before you came."

"Okay," I said. "Thanks. Won't be any more excitement."

He hefted the bat, gave it a look that was almost wistful. "Okay." He walked off.

I sat down again, said to Linus, "No other phone." Turning to Hal: "When you talked to Kevin, where was he?"

"Kevin. Lay down your six-gun, it's coming. I don't know where he was," he added mournfully.

"What did he say to you?"

He raised his arm, tried to signal the bartender. I pressed his hand down to the table. "What did he say?"

"Six-gun. Broken dream. Stupid shit."

"After that. When you talked to him after that, what did he say?"

"After that, when?"

"Hal—"

"Dude." Linus interrupted me. "Dude, it's not happening. It's not him."

I stared at Linus, at Hal. I released my hold on Hal's arm, sat back against the booth. "No," I finally admitted. "You're right. Goddammit. It's not him." You might think that would make me feel warmer toward Hal. Sympathetic, even contrite. Looking at him slumped in his seat, his brain soaked in booze and his eyes seeing nothing, what I felt was a strong urge to smash his doughy face.

"Come on," I said to Linus. I stood, needing movement.

Linus stood up, too, and Hal watched us as though this standing thing were new to him and he didn't get it at all. He raised his glassy eyes to mine. "She shouldn't have told him."

"What?"

"The pretty girl. She didn't want to go with Kevin. She shouldn't have told him."

I was ready to walk out, leave Hal to replay the past as many times as he wanted, but Linus asked, "Told him what? She shouldn't have told him she didn't want to go?"

Hal stared at Linus. "Saving herself for marriage. She shouldn't have told him *that*." He shifted his eyes to me. "Got him going. Always. Virgins, you know? Their maiden voyage. He always said, he liked to take them on their maiden voyage." He shook his head, moved a sloppy hand around reaching for something, maybe his glass, but it wasn't there. "She didn't want to go."

When I pulled the front door open the bartender yelled, "Hey! You said you were taking him with you!"

"I said, when he could walk," I answered. "My guess, day after tomorrow."

22

I didn't want to get back in the car. Being confined, forced to sit still, not even distracted by doing the driving—it sounded like hell. But no, hell was wherever Lydia was.

"Wasn't him," Linus reported, edging Woof off the backseat. Linus and I slammed our doors and Joey pulled out.

Trella frowned. "You're sure? He's not just a convincing liar?"

Ming said, "You want me to go in and make double sure?"

"No fucking way!" I snapped.

Linus threw me a glance, and then said to Ming, "Uh, thanks, but I don't think so, dude. We checked his phone and we talked to the bartender. Besides, you should see him. I don't think a guy that wasted could get it together to lie."

"*In vino veritas,*" said Joey.

"What?"

"What you said. Truth is in the wine."

We chewed on it for a while, who the assistant could be. It gave us a way to pretend we had steps to take, something positive to do beyond drifting around downtown mapping areaway windows and waiting for my phone to ring.

"The ex," Linus said. "Megan Beer Stine."

"You didn't see her," Trella said. "She wouldn't help a baby bird find its mother. And especially, she hates Kevin. What would be in it for her?"

"A friend he used to know," was Ming's idea. "Who stuck with him, whatever."

"Chinese kind of answer," Linus acknowledged. "Dude?"

"He never had a lot of close friends that I know about," I said. "Maybe Jim White, only he killed him."

"What about Nicole?" asked Linus. "Pretending she didn't know anything?"

"You saw her. That was one hell of a performance, if it was fake." I was trying to stay patient. "And if they were working together why would he have needed the camera there?"

"Nah," said Joey. "It's someone from inside."

I nodded. "That's what I've been thinking."

"This Kevin asshole, he's flush?"

"Probably. He was when he went away. He couldn't touch it while he was in, so no reason it wouldn't be waiting for him."

"So I bet he hooked up with some guy he met inside. Cellmate or something."

"He was in ten years," I said. "According to him, four different places. That's a hell of a lot of guys."

"Aunt Mary could trace them," Linus said. "Could start, anyway."

"And finish next week." But it wasn't a bad idea. Or maybe it was, but bad ideas look better when you're desperate. "Joey," I said. "Borrow your phone?"

"Whose phone is this?" Mary asked when she knew it was me. "Ready to come in?"

"No. Listen. Kevin has help. We think it's someone from inside."

"Who's we? You still have Linus with you?"

I could have kicked myself. "No, and that's all I'm saying. Can you track down Kevin's prison buds?"

"How do you know he has help?"

"He said."

"Why are you giving it to me? Why not do it yourself, Lone Ranger?"

"You know I can't."

"What if I find him, the helper, and he gives Kevin up? And we find Lydia and everything you've done turns out to be one big, dangerous mistake?"

"He won't give Kevin up. Kevin won't have told him enough. But it'll jam Kevin's gears. He'll have to improvise. Maybe he'll make bigger mistakes than mine."

We didn't speak much more as we drove around downtown, checking on the basements and areaways Trella had identified, finding others that might be likely. It was hopeless, doing it this way, but I had no other ideas. We kicked around the new clues a little, but no one came up with a breakthrough.

And as much as my phone was what we were all waiting for, we all jumped when it finally rang.

"Smith," I said, flipping it open, as though this were just any phone call. I put it on speaker and held it so everyone could hear.

"Oh, no shit? Damn, and I meant to call the White House!" Kevin sounded better: a little less wild and a lot more cheerful. I wondered if that was good or bad. "Hey," he said. "No 'Hi there, what's shakin', how you doing?' Aren't you happy to hear from me?"

"No."

"Oh. You want me to hang up?"

"I want you to tell me what comes next so we can finish this."

"Yo, what's up with you, Grandpa? You were a hell of a competitor, back in the day. Always up for a game. You turned into a couch potato while I was away? I guess that's what happens when you get old."

I didn't say a word.

"Well, lucky for you, this is almost the last time."

"The last time for what?"

"*Almost* the last time. For me to call you. Happy now?"

"You know when I'll be happy."

"Maybe never. Now listen close. Your mistake, Mighty Prince Asshole, was, you missed the whole point of the game."

"What does that mean?"

"You thought it was all about you. You, and your girlfriend. But that was only half. And you never figured that out, did you?"

"I don't know what you're talking about."

"I *know* you don't! That's what I'm saying! I'm talking about the other prize, that's what I'm talking about."

"What other prize?"

"Oh, I'm not going to tell you. The one I get to keep."

"You'll have to spell it out," I said. "I'm not following."

"I know. And I'm lovin' it. Now, here's what happened: I moved it, the second prize. I took it somewhere else. Actually, it's not second prize. It's first prize. And it's mine."

"Okay, Kevin," I said calmly. "You moved the other prize, and it's yours. What am I doing?"

"Yeah, it's mine, and it's first prize," he repeated. "Should've been mine, now it *is* mine. Your girlfriend, she's second prize. Actually, between you and me, she's not much of a prize at all, is she? Got an attitude, I don't like that. If you never find her, well, I wouldn't worry too much. Genius hero like you, you can do better, that's for sure. Even at your age, probably."

"Kevin?" My voice rasped; I brought it under control, measured each word. "The final clue. You're calling with the final clue, right?"

"Oh, so wrong. No final clue."

"What the hell do you mean? These three, you said they weren't complete. You said I needed the final clue."

"Well, yeah, I did say that. But that was before I found out what a lying cheating sack of shit you are! So I changed my mind, good buddy. No more clues."

"But then—"

"But then what?" he interrupted, suddenly loud and fast. "But then you're stuck, right? You hit the wall, you're screwed, you don't know what to do next? That what you mean? Like if I hang up now, poof, it's all over, the whole thing, the whole game, everything? Over? That what you're worried about? I'll bet you are! And you ought to be. Because check it out! Here I go!"

I yelled, "*Kevin!*" but it was too late. He was gone.

I went cold to my core. Over? No. No. Impossible. To end like this, out of nowhere? *Lydia!* No.

The phone rang again.

"*What?*"

"That was pretty good, right?" Kevin cackled through the car. "Did you like that?"

"No," I said, in a voice that didn't sound like my own.

"No? Really not? Shit, I thought it was great! Make you nervous, just a little?"

"Yes."

"More than a little?"

"Yes."

"A lot?"

"Yes!"

"Wow, he's yelling! Don't tell me your game face is slipping, bro. Gotta keep that game face, keep your cool. You gonna do that for ol' Kev? You gonna try?"

He was racing. He must have done a line between calls. I breathed deep. "Why, Kevin? If we're stopping the game?"

"We're not stopping. Who said stopping?"

"You said no more clues."

"That's not the same as stopping. I mean, I already won and you're the big fat loser, because I already have first prize and even if you find your girlfriend, which I doubt if you can do but even if, that's still only second prize. But if you try to keep that game face, I'll think about going on. You gonna try?"

"Yes."

"Yes what?"

"Yes, I'll try."

"Atta boy. So I guess you still want to find her, your stuck-up girlfriend?"

"Yes."

"Fuck knows why. But okay. Yeah, I guess okay. We'll keep playing. There, that made your day, right?"

"Yes."

"And making your day, you know that's what I'm here for. Well, it's fine with me. I mean, this's been fun, I'll give you that. So, you ready? Oh, don't answer me, I know you're ready, you're Ready Freddy. Now, the game's still on, but I changed some stuff. Because, you know, of that cheating thing you did. That okay with you?"

"None of this is okay with me, Kevin."

"Oh! I thought you wanted to keep playing. You want to stop? I could hang up for real this time."

"What I want is to have it out, face to face, you and me."

"Not happening. Two choices: go on, or hang up. Up to you."

"Go on."

"You sure?"

"*Goddamn it—!*"

"Tsk, tsk. What did I say about keeping cool?"

"Yes," I said through gritted teeth

"Don't you think you should apologize?"

"I'm sorry."

"No, you're not!" He cracked up. "You're steaming! Old guy like you, you want to watch that. Blood pressure, you could stroke out! Now, should I tell you what to do next? You want to hear?"

"Yes."

"Yes. Nice and calm, see how easy it is? Well, right now, right *now,* Prince Asshole, your girlfriend's waiting for you, watching the clock, all by herself, back where I left her, and what you do is—nothing!"

Lydia alone, Kevin somewhere else? I glanced at Linus and Trella. "What the hell does that mean, nothing?"

"Hard word for you? What I said! Nothing! You sit there and do fucking goddamn nothing while I take a walk."

"A walk?" On the street, in the open?"

"Yeah, time for me to check out this great city, pal. Drink it in one last time, make some memories. Because when this game's over, I'm blowing this hellhole and I'm not coming back. Taking what should've been mine and it's mine now, starting a new life. A real life. The life I should've had, that you stole from me. Prince Asshole."

Steadily, I asked, "How do we finish the game?"

"Now that's a great question. Overtime, see, it's gonna be fun! When I get back to where your girlfriend is, her and me, we're gonna party."

"*You—*"

"Don't start that shit. As long as you keep playing, I'm a gentleman, I don't touch her, that what you were about to remind me? Hey, but you cheated! *You* cheated, not me! So now the rules changed! You don't like it, you shoulda thought of that! So here's what's gonna happen. Her and me, we're gonna party. And you're gonna watch."

The icy cold returned, flooding me. "The hell I am, Kevin. I'm going to kill you."

"You're gonna watch, and I'm gonna know you're watching, because I'm gonna talk to you every now and then and you're gonna answer. You're gonna tell me what you're seeing."

A few deep breaths, then, "All right. Tell me where to go." To watch I'd have to be there. If I was there—

"No, Grandpa." As though Kevin were reading my mind. "You just find yourself a computer. I have a webcam where your girlfriend is. You know what that is, a webcam? Just like I had at Jim and Nicole's. You know?"

I looked to Linus. Eyes wide, he nodded, and I said, "I know."

"Great. So go settle in your rocking chair and wait for me to call. That'll be the last call. I know you like that, right? Here's how it's gonna go: If you watch, and talk to me, and I'm happy about the whole thing, then when we're done I'll tell you where she is. She'll be kinda tired, worn out, you know? Maybe a little sore. But really, pretty much okay. Then you can go rescue her. Won't that be great?"

"No. I'm not doing this, Kevin."

"Well, up to you. But if you don't, her and me, we're gonna party anyway. And then I'll just split. Take first prize here and leave town. And you'll never know where she is and she's gonna die. That better? What, you have nothing to say? *Is that better?* Asshole?"

"No." I could barely get the word out. "Not, that's not better."

"I knew it! You're so dependable, I just love ya for it, bro. Okay. Talk to you later. Oh! One more thing. You better hope I don't get stuck in traffic or anything. Or see too many cops around. Cops kinda spook me, you know? And when I'm spooked I stop walking and hide someplace. You don't want that."

"I don't control the cops, Kevin."

"No, but you can hope. You can pray real hard. See, you want me to get there kind of soon. Because your girlfriend, I think she's got maybe two, three hours of air left. Tops. After that, sayonara! Hey, what a great exit line! It's good, right? I think I'll use it. Check it out, asshole: *sayonara!*"

He hung up. I sat for a few seconds, paralyzed, hearing nothing but the silence and the fading echoes of Kevin's sneer. Then my own voice exploded. "*MOTHERFUCKER! Goddamn motherfucking son of a bitch! I'll kill him, I'll kill him!*" I slammed my fist against the door hard enough to send fiery pain streaking up to my shoulder.

Linus grabbed my jacket from behind. "Dude! Dude! People are looking!"

The driver beside us was staring into the car. So was a passenger in the car ahead. I grabbed the strap above the door as Joey made a quick left through the yellow light to get away from curious eyes. Linus toppled into Trella, righted himself.

"Dude! That's not gonna help."

"*What is?* What's going to help? You heard him, what he wants.

Fucking bastard, fucking Kevin, I'll kill him, I swear I'll kill him, slowly, as bad as I can make it. After all this shit, that bastard—"

"Dude. Dude! We gotta think here. This time it's air. He's up to air, did you catch that?"

"I caught it! Great, he's down to the end! So? Think about what? What? Motherfucking Kevin—"

"Yeah. Okay. Stop. Have a smoke. We gotta think."

The smoke was a good idea and I lit one up. But think? "Linus, you get an idea, you tell me. That Webcam, that's not connected to anything, right? Anything we could trace?"

"Might, but it would take hours. Maybe days."

"Fucking lot of good that does! What else? What the hell else can we do?"

"Dude? He's on the street. Sooner or later he'll head back there."

"We don't know where he is and we don't know where there is."

"There is here. Somewhere here, downtown."

I pulled in smoke. He was right. At least it was something. "But what the hell are we supposed to do, just drive around and hope we get lucky enough to spot him?"

"Better than nothing."

"Not by much."

"Would this be the time to bring in the cops?" Trella ventured. "They could be on the lookout, just to follow him, not to stop him. There are a lot more of them than us."

"He'd notice. He's looking for it; he'll notice. Every sector car that drives by, if the cop inside turns his head, Kevin will know. He'll either go to ground, or he'll try to and they'll chase him, take him up."

"Couldn't they, like, make him talk?" Linus asked. "Promise him immunity or something?"

"Immunity from what? What are they going to charge him with? Kidnapping hookers? Their word against his. Murdering Lei-lei? Their case against me is better."

"Kidnapping Lydia?"

"Jesus, Linus, how would you even begin to make that case? How could you even prove she was kidnapped in the first place?"

"We have the tapes. Of the phone calls."

"Can't prove it's him. Or her."

"Voice pattern matching?"

"It wouldn't be fast enough. They'd need a warrant. He'd shut up. All he has to do is sit there and grin for two hours, and if he's right about the air where Lydia is, then after that it won't matter about anything else."

A brief silence, as that sank in for everyone.

Trella shrugged. "Probably they wouldn't even find him. They don't know what he looks like."

"Well, I have that photo," Linus said.

"You do?"

"Not a real one, I mean. Photoshopped." He took out his iPhone. "Here. This is him, pretty much. According to, you know, Jasmine." He flushed. Trella gave him a curious look, then leaned over the phone, examined the photo silently. Linus leaned with her. Suddenly he sat straight and yelped, "*Yo! Twitter!* Hey, Trell! We can tweet it!"

Trella looked up, eyes glowing. "Yes! Yes!"

"We can make, like, a flash mob, but in reverse!"

"Yes!"

"With the photo on Facebook, and my Web site!"

Trella threw her arms around him, kissed his cheek. Leaning over her own phone, she said, "Send it to me. You are *so* brilliant!"

"Naw," he said, turning crimson for a second time. "Well, okay."

"What?" I said. "*What?*"

"Twitter," said Linus. He was feverishly working his phone. "You know what that is?"

"No idea."

"It's like . . ." He was groping for words, distracted by what he was doing. "Like e-mail, but it goes to lots of people at once."

"So?"

"No, but then everyone else sends it out, too. Dig, you re-tweet."

"I don't know what you're talking about."

"We send it out," Trella said, looking up from her phone. "I only have a couple of hundred followers, but Linus has thousands. Those are people who read the messages we send. Tweets."

"And, see," Linus picked it up, "all those followers, they have followers. And they have followers, too. So me and Trella, we send tweets that say, 'Dudes, it's life and death, for real, if you're in New York and you see this guy, take his picture and tell me where right now. We don't find him, he's gonna kill somebody. But don't follow him, don't stop him, don't spook him!' Course," he shrugged, "gotta be shorter than that." He started thumbing buttons and swiping at his screen.

"No." Trella sat up straight. "Wait. We can't say that. If people think they're chasing a killer they'll go right up into his face."

"No, only you would."

"But I *would,*" she said. "And there are bound to be other people in New York who would, too. He'll know right away."

The spark of hope I'd allowed myself to feel died out. Kids, day-dreaming a techie fix to a real-life disaster. But I was no kid. Why had I fallen for it?

I started to turn away, but Trella went on, "No. Look—a contest, we say it's a contest. Prizes. A promo, for, for—"

"For Wong Security! That's why the picture's on my Web site!"

"Yes! Perfect! We say, take a photo of this guy, send it to us. He's somewhere in New York. Like *Where's Waldo!* Random drawing. Only, if he spots you, you're disqualified. And only one entry per person, multiples to be discarded. So the photos will be sneaky, and no one'll follow him because once you send one, that's it for you."

"Wait," said Linus. "If it's a prize, why would people re-tweet? Only adds more players. Lowers your chances."

"Because," Trella said, "because there's a prize for the assist, too! If he's not in your neighborhood or even your city but it was you who re-tweeted and it's one of your followers—"

"Dudess!" Linus beamed. "*You* are the genius!"

Trella shrugged. "My dad says I have my moments. Prize?"

"Security sweep and any fixes, year's monitoring free, any installation, any size."

"Got it."

They both returned to their phones.

I watched, unsure whether to believe or not. Tentatively, I asked, "Can you send the photo?"

"Not on Twitter," said Linus. "But I just now put it on Facebook and my Web site and sent the links. And my phone number, to send the pictures to."

I responded to one of the few words I understood: "What pictures?"

"That people are gonna take with their cell phones. When they think they see Mr. Crazy."

"Linus, not all that many people can possibly need the prize you're offering. It's computer security, right?"

Bent over his phone, he nodded. "That's what I do."

"So why would people pay attention to your tweet, or whatever it is?"

"Dude, it's not about the prize. It's not even about winning. You want like a thousand people in Union Square in an hour, you Twitter it."

"That's a flash mob," Trella added.

"If I want them there for what?"

"Just to go. To be part of the flash mob. Then they all go away again. Dig, dude, people like to be part of shit."

"Friend me," Ming rumbled from the other side of Trella. He had a phone out, too.

"You're on Twitter?" Linus asked, eyebrows raised. "Whoa. Not sure I want to meet your followers."

"No. Just Facebook. But I'll post it. Friend me and give me your cell number."

Whatever that meant, Linus seemed to do it. Ming grunted and worked his sausage fingers along his phone's keyboard. Beside me, Joey dug his phone from his pocket. "I'm on Twitter, and on Facebook. And MySpace." He started thumbing his phone, steering with his wrists at the bottom of the wheel. "What's your number? Friend me, too."

Linus did for Joey whatever he had for Ming.

"What if Kevin's on one of these things?" I asked. "Won't he find out about this?"

Linus shook his head. "He'd have to be following one of us or one of our followers. Or a Facebook friend."

I didn't understand what that meant, besides "No." I gave up. I was surrounded by people thumbing buttons on cell phones and I had no idea what was going on. I half-expected Woof to paw a phone from his collar. Joey pulled into a bus stop so they could all focus. I lit another cigarette and watched the street. "What are we waiting for?" I asked. "I mean, how will we know if it's working?"

"We'll—" Linus's phone pinged. "Like that! Yo! Here comes something!" My heart pounded, but he said, "No. Shit. It's some other dude." He held the phone up to me. A city street, the face of a man with a passing resemblance to the photo he'd sent out, but not Kevin. I shook my head.

Joey, apparently done with his part in this, pulled the car out into traffic again. We rolled along for a couple of minutes; then Linus's phone pinged again. "Wait, here comes another one! Damn. No."

After a third wrong photo I turned away, resettled in my seat to stare out the front. I smoked, worked hard to keep my disappointment and anger bottled up inside. Like forcing the lava to stay in the volcano, but I did my best. The kids had tried; exploding at them wouldn't do any good. And it was myself I was furious with anyway, for falling for it, for getting my hopes up over the possibility of some stupid Internet trick. Maybe Trella had been right, before. We should call Mary. Or wait for Kevin to activate his Webcam and try to trace that, while it transmitted images I didn't want to imagine. Or pray for the one-in-a-million chance of spotting Kevin as he strolled by. Three bad choices, but they were all we had.

Ping. "Yes! Yes! Dudes, I think it's him!"

I whipped around in the seat, resolve blown. *"Dammit, Linus—"*

"It's *him*!" He held up the iPhone. A man's three-quarter profile on a city street, slanted and not quite focused, but my heart hammered when I saw it.

I nodded. "Son of a bitch. I think it is."

"It is! That's from Forty-first and Seventh, says the dude who sent it. Shit, he's gonna walk down from there? That'll take forever!"

"About an hour. He's going to burn up an hour walking down here," I said, thinking about Lydia, thinking about air.

"You want we should go up and get him?" That was Joey, ready to rocket.

Before I could answer, Linus said, "Another one! Next corner."

"Head up there," I told Joey. "But not to pick him up. Can we parallel him? He might lead us right to her."

"You sure you want to do it that way?" Ming asked. "Give me five minutes, I could get him to tell you whatever you want to know."

"Didn't work on me."

He shrugged. "You didn't know anything."

I regarded him, considering it. When I turned the offer down, it wasn't from benevolence.

"As long as he seems to be headed in this direction, our best bet is to follow him," I said. "For about an hour. After that, maybe we'll do it your way."

Ming gave a slow nod. He didn't smile but his eyes glinted.

Pings from the iPhone began to fill the car, faster and thicker as we drove uptown. The next two photos were of other people, and strangers' faces kept cropping up after that, too, but pictures of Kevin began to outnumber them in a big way. In shade and sunlight, sharp or blurred, close and from a distance, Kevin made his oblivious way downtown. From corners, midblocks, and the middle of the street, people who didn't know me, didn't know Lydia, most likely didn't know Linus, Trella, Joey, or Ming, clicked away on their cell phone cameras and sent photos of a pedestrian's progress to a stranger's phone number.

"Won't he see them?" I asked early on. "So many people taking photos around him? Even though you said to make sure he doesn't?"

"Dude." Linus gave me that pained and patient look. "Check out your window. What do you see?"

I turned and looked. "Point taken." Every third person was talking on a cell phone, thumbing a text into one, or, yes, shooting a cell phone photo.

"Fortieth and Seventh," Linus said. "Thirty-ninth. Wow, another one, same spot. Thirty-eighth. Wait, from the same dude. And same again. Trella, this jerk, send him a text: 'No joke, don't follow, you're about to disqualify yourself!' Thirty-eighth and Eighth. Mr. Crazy's heading west." Then, briefly, nothing.

"We lost him?" My heart pounded. "Maybe he ducked inside somewhere? Maybe he has Lydia in one of those buildings, not downtown at all?"

"I don't know. Could be there's just no one on that block—wait, no, here comes one! Still Thirty-eighth."

We were nearly there. Joey turned left, rolled us east on Thirty-eighth Street. My eyes roved over every inch of sidewalk, both sides of the street, never stopped moving. Was he really here, that son of a bitch?

Halfway along the block I was stabbed by an adrenaline spike. "*Shit!*" I exploded, then clamped my jaw shut, glad the windows were up. I pointed. Kevin Cavanaugh, sunglassed and baseball capped, sauntered along the sidewalk, sipping a takeout coffee. He was graying, big, and bronzed. He must have spent the months since his release working to erase his jailhouse pallor. He hadn't stopped hitting the gym, either. Muscles mounded his arms and shoulders, and the soft gut I remembered had been replaced by large pecs and a solid waist. *Jesus, you bastard,* I thought, *you should thank me, I did you a favor, you never looked so good!* But the face: even behind the dark glasses, under the shade of the brim, the arrogance, the challenge, the sneer were the same. I'd never wanted anything as much as I wanted right then to jump out of the car and beat him to an unrecognizable pulp.

"Dude? You okay?"

"Fuck. Yeah."

"Then let go the strap, you're gonna rip it out of the roof."

From Ming: "I'm saying again. You want me to go get him?"

As I watched, a pair of young women pointed their cell phones in Kevin's direction. A few seconds later, two pings sounded inside the car.

"No," I told Ming. "He takes us to Lydia. Then he's yours. If I don't get him first."

"You don't," Ming warned me. "Remember what Mr. Lu said."

I lit another cigarette. I didn't give a good goddamn what Mr. Lu said. I was having enough trouble following my own sensible, reasonable course, enough difficulty shoving aside visions of Kevin with his brains greasing the pavement.

We followed Kevin's path from a block over, or a block behind, or two streets down, circling, preceding, trailing. Time felt like it was racing and standing still at once, but it was really passing normally and we were still okay. Twice more we drove right past him. "It's a car service car," said Joey. "They all look alike, you know? Guarantee he won't notice." That was probably true but I was reluctant to push it. And we didn't need to. The pings were steady and so was Kevin's progress. In a little under an hour, we were almost back downtown.

23

"Trella." I turned to the backseat as we hit the college student anthill that was lower Broadway. We'd gotten down here by a winding route, weaving a complicated pattern required by one-way streets and Kevin's meandering. He was working his way south and east, but he wasn't in any hurry. The photos coming into Linus's iPhone showed him window-shopping, smiling up at buildings, buying peanuts from a street vendor. He looked like what he said he was: a man drinking in the sights and sounds of a city he was about to leave.

The photos and Joey's expert driving, paralleling, following, and pulling away, had been enough for a while. Here, though, we were getting close. The area covered by the cell tower he'd been using was a few blocks away. So I asked Trella, "You ever tail anyone?"

"No." She grinned. "But I bet I can."

"If this is where he has Lydia, somewhere down here, he'll duck into the building soon. Too much to hope for that someone'll take a photo of that. We could lose him." Ping. "I want you to go around the block, follow him on foot. Keep him in the corner of your eye, don't stare directly at him, even at his back. He'll feel it if you do. Okay?"

She nodded. Ming said, "She's an amateur. Why her, not me?"

I looked from Trella to Ming, the Goth teenager to the skinhead man-mountain. "You're kidding, right?" To Trella again: "Window-shop, talk on your phone. To me, the whole time."

"On this." Linus, a step ahead, handed me a new prepaid from his cargo pocket. I gave Trella the number.

"Smile, laugh," I said. "Try to look like everyone else who's on a cell phone and has no idea what's going on around them. If Kevin seems to make you, if he shows the slightest interest, dash into a store like the stuff it's selling is what you've wanted all your life."

Joey pulled over. Woof bounced out of the car to use the hydrant and had to be herded back in after Linus got out for Trella. Our last photo had come from Bond Street and Lafayette; Trella, face aglow, practically skipped in that direction.

I heard Ming muttering as Linus climbed back in, something about at least having room to breathe now, but he stuck to the pecking order Lu had given him and didn't argue with my decision. That was good. If he'd decided to go rogue I don't know how I'd have stopped him without creating a major ruckus that would draw every eye in our direction. But I'd have done it. No way in hell I was going to let things get screwed up now.

My new phone rang almost as soon as Trella was out of sight. "Got him. Lafayette and Bleecker. I'm about a block behind. He's stopped at the light at Bleecker. I'm window-shopping pots and pans. Okay, the light's changed. He stepped off the curb. I can make the same light. He's at the far corner, I'm where he was. Now I'm in the street. Do I really have to keep talking?"

"You can pretend I'm talking sometimes."

"Good. Hey, someone just took a cell phone picture of him."

Ping. "We just got it."

"Great. Okay, he's almost to Houston Street. Houston coming up, Houston real close. Light's red, he stopped, I'll stop back here. Wait, no, he's not crossing. He turned west. I'm going to pretend I'm texting. Okay, I'm back. He's waiting to cross again, I guess he wants to go down Crosby. Oh, hey, another photo!"

Ping. "Just came."

"Cool. Okay, he's heading down Crosby. I'm at Houston. This talking thing is tiring, you know? Okay, I'm crossing. I'm still a block behind, lots of people between us— Oh, *shit!*"

"What?"

"A car just pulled over! An SUV! Two guys are getting out, Asian guys! One normal, one huge. They're heading toward him! He saw them." Her breath started to come harder. "He ran into a store. Summit Sports, on Crosby. They're going in after him. I am, too."

"Trella, don't!"

"Already did. Lots of commotion. Emergency exit. Stairs up."

"Joey!" I shouted. "Pull over." He did.

I jumped out. Linus followed. I said to Joey, "Sit tight." Ming yelled, "What the hell?" Linus told Woof to stay. I told Ming to go fuck himself. Woof listened. Ming didn't. We all three raced down Lafayette and through on Jersey.

"You bastard!" I spat to Ming, and then, "Trella?" into the phone. "Trella? What's happening?"

"On the roof," was all she said.

"What?" shouted Ming. He looked genuinely perplexed. Running seemed to be even less his sport than mine. I was savagely glad to see him fall behind.

"Lu's there!" I yelled over my shouder. "You called him!"

Ming shook his head.

"Bullshit!"

"Dude! Come on!" Linus was in front as we exploded from the alley. "Didn't have to call! Probably doesn't even know! His phone! His GPS!"

Son of a bitch, I thought, dodging traffic on Crosby. Lu's SUV angled across a loading dock. Linus was likely right. Ming tracks the girls. And Lu tracks Ming.

I put on a burst, pushed past Linus, surged into Summit Sports. "Police!" I flashed a gold badge that looks great from a distance in a hurry. Our quarry's tracks were clear from the goggle-eyed customers, the shouting clerks, the knocked-over sneaker display. I charged to the rear, through the exit door and up the stairs. Four flights, and then, chest heaving, I yanked the roof door open.

"Whoa! Prince Asshole!"

I stood, frozen.

Lu, Strawman, and Trella all whipped around to stare at me, then turned back to what they'd been fixed on: Kevin Cavanaugh, arms wide like a condor's wings, balanced on the limestone parapet.

"Kevin," I said, breathing hard. Slowly, I stepped forward. "Come down. It's over."

"Over?" Kevin, grinning, cupped a hand to his ear. "Oh no, no way, your cocksucking highness. You hear any fat lady singing?"

Linus pounded through the door. Trella put out a hand to stop him. Lu saw the look that passed between them and snickered. Trella glared at him as Linus came to stand beside her. He moved no farther. We stood in a semicircle, the five of us, equidistant from Kevin as though at the edge of an invisible force field. Strawman held a gun trained on Kevin but Kevin didn't seem bothered.

A few feet to Kevin's right, a flagpole angled over the street from the face of building. I tensed as Kevin leaned to peer around the snapping flag—do I leap for him? can I make it?—but then he straightened, still grinning. "Jesus, it's been a long time, Prince Asshole." Marveling, he looked around. "How did you do it? How did you find me?"

"Come down, I'll tell you."

"I do not fucking think so. Oh, I do not. In fact, I think you all need to take a step back. Back! Good, that's better." He gave me a wide smile. "So, Prince, how're you doing? Gotta tell you, pal, you look like shit." He didn't look so great himself. Despite the smile, his pupils were pinpoints and his skin was mottled, blotchy.

Ming finally made his lumbering way through the door. Lu glanced back at him. Maybe because his entourage was now complete, he took a step toward Kevin. "Listen, you lunatic motherfucker—"

"Lu!" I shouted. "Stop right there or I'll throw you off this roof myself. What the hell were you thinking, coming after him?"

"You were getting close," Lu said mildly. "I was tailing you and I spotted him. You think I really believed you'd hand him over to me, if you were the one who found him?"

"This is about my partner!"

"And you believe he's going to give you your partner back? About who, let me remind you, I don't give a shit? The only reason Ming hasn't chucked him into the street already is I need to make sure this really is as idiotic as it looks, and Fatboy Cho or someone isn't behind it."

"Lu, I swear to God—"

"Hey, are you guys fighting over me?" Kevin said. "Aw, that's so touching. I feel the love."

I turned slowly from Lu, bringing myself down, trying to remember where I needed to be. "Not love, Kevin," I said. "But tell me where Lydia is, and I'll make sure the cops know you cooperated."

"Ain't that sweet. And that'll make *them* love me, I know it will."

"I'll do what I can."

"Oh, mighty Prince Asshole! Do what you can. Gee, thanks. Come on, admit it, bro, the truth is, you can do *bullshit,* you can do fuck-all about anything, that's what you can do. Isn't that what we've been proving all day? And speaking of bullshit, who are the Three Chinese Stooges here?"

"You want them gone? Lu, take your boys and get lost."

"No!" Kevin barked. Smiling again, "Did I say I wanted them gone? Aren't you listening to me? I really think you should listen to me. All I asked was who they are."

He was liking the audience. I pointed, said, "This is Lei-lei's pimp."

Lu frowned, and Kevin laughed. "Oh! Fo' shizzle? And these must be the Pimp's Gorillas! Howdy, fellas! Hey, bro, Mr. Pimp, you run some truly hot girls, I gotta tell you that. And look, thanks to the Mighty Prince here, three of them who're supposed to be dead aren't! Can't tell you how much that burns my ass. But it must make *you* want to show *him* the love."

"Not even a little," Lu said. "You, even less."

"Lu," I warned, "shut up and back off."

"Hey!" Kevin's face went crimson and his good cheer vanished. "Hey, motherfucker, *you* shut up! *You* back off! I was talking to him!" He swallowed, shook his head as if to clear it. "*Everyone* just shut up for a minute. No one talk." He stood motionless, balanced, with his eyes shut; then he snapped them open. "O-*kay,*" he said.

"Now. You, pimp. And the gorillas. And whoever this bitch with the nose ring is. And little Chop Suey over there. All of you, just shut up. I don't want to hear a single goddamn motherfucking word out of anybody anymore except Prince Asshole! Nobody, no-fucking-body. We all got that?" He waited. No one spoke. The wind died a little, letting the flag rest. "And you, Gorilla, put the gun away. It makes me nervous. I could fall or something." He flashed a fast and shaky grin.

Strawman looked to Lu. After a moment Lu nodded. Strawman tucked his gun in his belt.

From below, sirens wailed. Kevin glanced down again. "Asshole," he said with an accusatory frown, "this seriously better not be the cops."

"It probably is," I said. "You're standing on a parapet flapping your arms around. You think no one's going to see that?"

"Oh. Oh, you think? You mean you didn't call them?"

"Of course I didn't."

"Of course. Of course. I forgot how law abiding you are, how you follow the rules. Except when you're cheating. Well, whyever they're here—that a word, 'whyever'? Don't answer that, I don't give a shit—I don't want them up here." He dug a phone from his pocket, poked a few buttons. "Hi, 911? Well, the nature of my emergency is, I'm standing on a parapet on Crosby Street, and a whole bunch of cops and fire trucks are pulling up down there, and I really, really, don't want anyone up on this roof, know what I mean? You don't need to rescue me, I'm doing just fine, thank you, sweetie. I'm just standing here talking to some friends. But if anyone comes up here, I'll jump. For real. Helluva rescue, right? So-o-o-o embarrassing for New York's Finest, and New York's Bravest, and New York's whoever the hell the rest of you are. So just tell them all to stay down there, and everything'll be fine. Yes, I'm sure, thank you. I'll call if I need you." He clicked off and, turning, waved to the street below. Then he turned back to me. "Now," he said, "okay, now, motherfucking Prince Asshole, let's talk."

"About what, Kevin?"

"Maybe about what a lying, cheating, backstabbing cocksucker you are. No, that would take too long. How about, about your girlfriend?"

"Okay, let's talk about her. Where is she?"

"God, what a one-track mind. Where, where, where. She's hot, your girlfriend, right? Even if she can't cook. I bet she's great in the sack."

"What do you want, Kevin?"

"'What do you want, Kevin?' Well, what *do* I want? Hmm, let's see." He rubbed his chin and frowned, lifted his finger theatrically. "I want a condo! Well, or maybe a brownstone. I want a Ferrari, and a fast-track job with a six-figure salary and a mega-Christmas bonus and kick-ass perks. I want to go to Aspen and Ibiza and drink Grey Goose martinis and smoke Cuban cigars and eat ginormous Kobe sirloins. I want a hot wife and a hot secretary and I want little Cavanaughs all running around that I can teach to shoot hoops at my house in the Hamptons!" The smile dissolved and his face turned hard. He lowered the finger slowly until it pointed at me. "What I *want* is what I had! What I had, and would have had, except you stole it all! Except you buried me! I had a *life,* and you made me a zombie! A *life*! That, you goddamn son of a bitch, *that* is what I fucking *want*!" He stopped, panting as though he'd run a race. In a softer voice: "And now I'm going to have it."

His face lit up. "This game? I'm tired of it. It was fun for a while, but then you started cheating, and all these losers started crowding up the court, I mean, who asked them? Well, I guess you did. So I changed the rules again. That okay with you?"

"None of this is okay with me."

"Yeah, well, who cares? We're done. That whole party thing, me and your girlfriend? Never mind. I'm over sticking it to Chinese girls anyway. No offense, your pimphood. But now I'm going to go pick up my first prize from where I left it and get on with my life." He started inching along the parapet to his left. "The hell with you, asshole. This whole thing has gotten out of hand."

"No argument from me."

"Oh, good. Because you know how I hate it when you argue with me. Stay there!"

I'd stepped forward, not close, just trying to keep our same distance as he shuffled toward the next building. Now I stopped.

"Good. Don't move again. If you make me nervous, I could fall. Too bad for me, not that you give a shit, but too bad for your girlfriend, too, right?" He shook his head again. "See, when I got out, when I first got back into the world, I wasn't going to do it this way. My plan, I was going to settle things with you, just straight-up bust your motherfucking ass and get on with my life. Months ago, when I first got out, I came by your place. Did you know that? *Did you?*"

"No."

"No. Because you're not, you're just not all that fucking smart, really, are you?" Another few steps along the wall. "I came by, and you could've bought it that night, bro, that's what I had in mind. But I saw you with her. Your girlfriend. Your slanty-eyed mama.

You two walked right by me and it was like you knew I was there. It was like, 'Fuck you, Kevin, look what I got, only mine ain't dead so I'm cool.' I almost popped a cap in your ass right then, but it wasn't enough. Not enough, not enough. So I went back and thought and planned, and it took months, and it was excellent! Excellent! Because inside, you know, inside you don't get to think and plan. You get to do what they say. And here I was, thinking and planning and I worked it all out, this whole goddamn thing, and it was excellent and it's been lots of fun. Hasn't it? Oh, don't lie, you loved it. But you fucked the whole game up. You cheated and now look where we are. And it's not fun anymore. So it's over." He smiled. "You like that, don't you?"

"You know I do. Just you and me, face to face, that's all I ever wanted. Tell me where Lydia is, and we'll be even, and then you and I can have it out."

"Oh, no no no. Not happening. Didn't I explain that, how I changed the rules? New rule number one: You're not getting your girlfriend back." I went cold. "Whoa!" Kevin barked. "Check him out, how white he turned!" he shouted to everyone else. "Oh, I'm lovin' it. No, you don't get her back. See, I have an assistant, too. I told you that? Yeah, I thought I had. And my assistant's waiting for me to call." He held up the phone. "If I don't call soon, half an hour maybe, there's a phone number. My assistant calls the number, that activates this gas canister I have there. Where she is, your girlfriend. I know, I said she had a couple of hours of air left, but this is, like, my insurance. If me and her were partying and you were watching, then I was gonna call, tell my assistant, no, don't do it. And then, you know, I was gonna help your girlfriend use up some of that air. After that I was gonna split, give you a chance to find her. I was gonna be fair, asshole. I was.

"But I thought some shit like this might happen. You cheating. So I set it up, my assistant and the number, some nice poison gas. Dependable. Kinda like you. A lot like you. Dependable, and fucking toxic. So see, what I *could* do, I could call my assistant right now, and say, it's okay, don't make that call. If I did that, then you guys"—sweeping an expansive arm—"you could run around looking for her, your girlfriend, looking in every building in New York. Even the cops could help, I don't care anymore. You might even find her in time. You want me to do that? Call, so you have a chance?"

No sound but the flag snapping. Kevin waited, giving me an encouraging look as though my answer mattered to him.

"Yes."

"I know." He nodded sympathetically, a friend discussing a friend's bad situation, and took some more tottering steps along the parapet. "What you're thinking, you did all this shit, all day, you went to Red Hook and uptown and Harlem and all whatever shit I made you do, and now you're thinking this isn't fair. You're thinking, if ol' Kev doesn't give it up, then your girlfriend's toast and that's just not *fair* because you tried so hard. Tell me, am I right? Is that what you're thinking?"

I weighed my words, spoke as carefully as I ever had. Kevin's shaky mental state was echoed by his unsteadiness as he balanced. I needed to draw him back in. "What I'm thinking, Kevin, is, you were talking about a forfeit? That's what this would be. You and I aren't done yet. You walk off the court, I win. This game, you against me, is that what you want to do? Throw the game?"

More sirens, and shouting from below. From the corner of my eye I could see Trella edge toward the parapet, peer over. *Jesus, Trella, everyone,* don't move! Kevin glanced at her, then back to me, doubt flickering across his face.

"You think?" he asked earnestly. He frowned, considering this new idea. "You think it'll be like that? Me throwing the game?"

"And I'll win again. An easy win, if you throw it."

"But how can you win, if you don't get the prize?"

"How can you win, if you quit in the middle?" He didn't answer. I pressed. "What's wrong, Kevin? You keep saying I got old. And look at you, you're an iron man now. Training all those years, what for? Don't you want a piece of me? Or you still don't think you could take me? Like before, you never could?"

"Fuck you! I took you then and I could take you now, Grandpa! I took badder guys than you in badder places than you've ever been."

"I don't believe you."

Blazing rage clenched his fists; then he relaxed, grinned like a skeleton. "And I don't believe you. You think I can't see through this shit? You think you can get me so pissed off I'll come down there to beat on you so all these motherfuckers can jump me?"

"They'll stay back," I said. I looked around the arc: Trella over by the parapet, Linus beside her; Ming, Strawman, and Lu in a row. Everyone nodded. "Just you and me, Kevin," I said. "If you think you can."

He didn't answer. He shifted his gaze, shifted it some more: Trella, Strawman, me, Lu. Over his shoulder to the street. Ming, Linus, me again. I tried to project a cool I didn't feel, the scornful calm of a champion facing a scared rival. Silence stretched, broken only by the sharp, random cracks of the snapping flag. Wind played around us, changing direction, shoving and pulling. The flag and the wind and Kevin's jerky eyes: that's all there was in the world, for me.

"You know?" Kevin started to edge along the wall again, nearing the next building. "You know what?" The wide grin came back, the glint in his eyes. "Fuck it. Fuck it, and fuck you, and fuck your posse here. And fuck your girlfriend. I'm gone, bro. I'm outta here."

In two more steps he reached the corner where the parapet hit the wall between this building and the next. That building was lower than this one. Just before he jumped down onto its roof, he cocked back his arm and, aiming out over the street, he let the cell phone fly.

24

I saw Kevin tense and I lunged forward just before he jumped. I had a half-second lead, a good push-off, and I stretched like Mr. Fantastic.

It wasn't enough. My hands reached for Kevin and closed on empty air.

As I slammed into the wall something crossed behind me, flying higher than I had, a blur of plaid and heavy boots. Then a cry: "*Trella!*" The voice was Linus's. The sky was blank. I scrambled up.

Linus raced to the parapet. "*Trella!* Oh, shit, Trell! Dudess! *No!*"

Torn in half, I glanced wildly from Linus behind me to the roof below. I saw no sign of Kevin. Strawman raced by, swung himself over the wall to the roof where Kevin had gone. "Don't kill him!" I yelled. Strawman hit the silver surface and didn't look up. I hesitated a second, then turned, ran to where Linus stood peering down over the street. Nothing but the flag and the wind, and Linus, wide-eyed, white.

Then, barely audible in the wind: "Linus, if you're really worried, maybe you could help me out here?"

Linus leaned out so far his feet left the roof deck. I stretched beside him. I was taller; I could see what he couldn't.

"Jesus Christ," I said.

"Whatever," Trella called, dangling over the street, arms wrapped around the base of the flagpole. "Can you pull me up, please?"

I yanked Linus away, leaned down. Five stories below, cops and rescue personnel swarmed the sidewalk like helpless ants. They had a net ready, because they had to, but this was just too far a fall for that. Any minute now they'd defy Kevin's ban and race up here. But Trella's grip might not hold that long.

A few feet down, a little above the flagpole, a cornice made a ledge just wide enough to stand on. I swung my legs over, slid onto it. One arm over the parapet, I inched along to the flagpole. If I let go and crouched I'd be able to reach Trella, take hold of her hand, but not to haul her up. I had no purchase; I'd fall with her.

"Here!" Ming's booming voice. I turned to see him, one leg over the parapet, leaning, offering me his right hand. His left was gripping Lu's above the elbow, as Lu, braced against the parapet, was gripping him. After a second I took hold. Ming's grip was crushing but the pain reassured me. If I could hold Trella like that, no one would fall.

"Trella?" Welded to Ming, I crouched. "Come on, it's okay." I could see the firefighters below maneuvering the net. Trella uncoiled one arm from the flagpole, whooped, "Whoa, cowboy!" and grabbed my hand. I wasn't sure I could pull her up but when I started to, she said, "No, don't. Just give me a handhold."

I did what she said, just gripped her. With the deliberate absorption of a rock climber, she walked her feet up the wall, left arm still wrapped around the flagpole. Using me for leverage, she spidered along, and I moved over, until her feet had come up the wall to where the flagpole connected. She slid her right leg over the flagpole and straddled it, back to the building, facing out into the wind. "Phew," she said, grinning.

Then, using my grip for balance, she rose to her feet in a single move. Now she stood on the cornice ledge. Twisting, she reached her left arm up and grabbed the parapet. Her right hand let go of my hand, and she pivoted around to face the building. She took a measuring breath and leapt upward, grabbed the parapet wall, and swung over.

"*Awesome!* Dudess! Oh, awesome!" Linus, bouncing, wrapped Trella in a bearhug.

Trella had been elegant, graceful, and sure-footed. I was standing on rubbery legs on a narrow cornice five stories above the ground, attached to a Chinese goliath. I half climbed, was half-hauled by Ming, who wouldn't let go until I had both feet back on the tar paper roof.

"Thanks." I shook the pain out of my fingers. Ming nodded, Lu shrugged. My heart raced, my skin sizzled with the adrenaline surge. It took a few moments for my brain to clear, to remember where we were, what had just happened, and why rescuing Trella didn't make things okay. Unfairly, but I had no way to be fair, it was Trella I blew up at.

"Jesus Christ!" I bellowed. Everyone jumped. "What the fuck was that? What were you thinking, you were Supergirl? You were going to grab that son of a bitch Kevin out of the sky, is that what you were thinking?"

Trella looked at me, big eyes wide. Her glowing grin, which matched the one on Linus, faltered. "No," she said. "I was thinking about this."

She stuck her hand in her pocket, brought it out and offered me Kevin's phone.

My heart stopped.

"We needed the phone." Trella spoke in that tone that said she was explaining the obvious to me. "I mean, I knew where the flag-pole was."

"Dudess!" Linus hugged her again. I snatched the phone, stared at it. Then, afraid to screw something up, I passed it to Linus.

"The assistant," I managed.

"I know, dude, I know."

Linus poked buttons. Lu said to Trella, "Damn. You're something else. Who exactly are you?"

"Trella. I work with Linus."

"You want to work with me?"

"You're not serious? Your girls—"

"Not that way. I always have room in the organization for someone with skills like yours."

"Mr. Lu?" Linus looked up from the phone. "She has a job."

"This is a better job."

"Dude—"

"Thank you." Trella smiled sweetly. "And thanks for the assist just now. But I have a job." She hooked her arm through Linus's. He flushed to his scalp.

Lu shrugged. "Well, if it's like that. Listen, maybe I could use you, too, Junior. Show Jasmine a thing or two about the computer. And she could show you a thing or two, too."

Trella looked inquiringly at Linus. He focused single-mindedly on the phone. Turning it so I could see the highlighted number on the screen, he said, "This one. Gotta be. Press the green button."

Before I could, Ming, leaning over the parapet, called out, "Hey. The cops. I think they're coming up here."

"Shit." Lu's phone rang as he strode over to take a look. He answered it, spoke briefly while he peered down. "Smith, you're a goddamn cop magnet, you know that? That was Strawman. He lost your lunatic."

I gripped Kevin's phone, heard cop feet pounding up the stairs. "I—"

Lu sighed. "Yeah, I know. Go on. We'll deal."

"Jesus," I said. "Thanks." I turned to Linus and Trella. "You guys stay—"

"I don't think so, dude," said Linus. Trella said nothing, just raised her eyebrows.

"No, I didn't, either," I said. "Okay, come on."

We headed for the roof to the south, the one Kevin and then Strawman had jumped to. I pocketed Kevin's phone, swung over the parapet, held on, and dropped about twelve feet. A second later Trella landed lightly beside me. We looked up to see Linus peering over. "Shit, dudes!"

"Just bend your knees as you land," Trella said. "It's fun."

"Oh, right," Linus grumbled, but he slid over on his stomach, scrabbled to hold on to the wall for a moment, then slipped off in a windmill of arms and legs. I moved under him, tried to catch him, but the best I could manage was to break his fall. We both went sprawling. From the silver-painted tarpaper he looked up at Trella. "Fun?"

"All in the technique. I could teach you."

He snorted. She stretched a hand to pull him to his feet. I stood up, Linus dusted himself off, and we all made for the fire escape at the back of the building.

"Smith!" I turned at Lu's shout. He was leaning over and smiling. "You owe me, that's all. You and Chin, too, if she makes it."

"*I owe you?* You're the idiot who—"

"Dude?" Linus called.

"Yeah. Fine. Whatever." I joined the kids on the steep steel stairs.

The fire escape landed us in a back alley—this involved another jump, from the fire escape ladder, which, though shorter than the first jump, still made Linus roll his eyes—and the alley landed us on Broadway. No sign of Kevin, or of Strawman. That was the bad news; the good news was, no cops on this street. I went a few yards north, stopped in a loading dock. I pulled Kevin's phone out and said to Linus, "Kevin's assistant. What do I do again?"

Patiently, he thumbed buttons until a number came up. "The green one."

I took the phone, pressed the green button. I turned my back to the street, the better to hear. Two rings, three. *Son of a bitch, come on, can't be too late,* can't *be*—

"Hello? Kevin?"

The voice was a woman's.

A girlfriend. Jesus Christ, what was wrong with us, why hadn't we thought of that? "This isn't Kevin," I said, trying to keep my tone even. "But I'm calling to tell you not to call the number he gave you."

Pause. "Who is this?"

"A friend."

"Of whose?"

"Yours and Kevin's."

A bitter laugh. "We don't have any mutual friends. Who the hell are you?"

Deep breath. "All right, I'm a friend of Kevin's and I'd like to be a friend of yours. Who are you?"

"You want to be friends and you don't know who I am? Where's Kevin? What's going on?" She had a ragged sound, someone just holding it together.

"Kevin's in trouble. That's why I have his phone. He said to tell you, don't call the number."

"Okay," she said tentatively. "What should I do, then?"

"Meet me. We need to talk about it. About how to help Kevin."

"Help him? Fuck him. Wait! No, all right, whatever you say. Where?"

"Where are you?"

"Home."

"Where's that? I'll come up."

"No. No, wait a minute. Who the hell are you? How do I know you're not a cop? What kind of trouble is Kevin in?"

Think, Smith. "That kind. The cop kind."

"Shit!"

"I think the only way to help him, the only thing we can do, is find the hostage."

"What?"

"She hasn't got much time before her air runs out, and Kevin's not talking." That part was true, anyway. "If she dies it's all over for Kevin. If we can find her they'll go easier on him."

"And then what?"

"I don't know, but whatever it is, his sentence will be lighter—"

"I don't give a shit about that. What about my baby?"

My breath caught. "What?"

"My baby. When do I get my baby back?"

The other prize. "Kevin has your baby?"

"Why the fuck do you think I've been doing all these sick things he wants? He didn't tell you?"

"About a baby? He didn't say anything."

"You're a friend of his and he wants you to get him out but he didn't tell you about my baby? That bastard! That motherfucking bastard! Well, get him to tell you. Make him tell you where he has Jason!"

"I can't talk to him."

"Why? Is he in jail? Then get the cops to make him! Make him tell!"

"He can't. He's been—injured. He can't talk. Tell me what happened. Who are you?"

"Jason's mother, goddammit. Who the hell are *you*? And what do you mean, 'injured'?"

I ignored that. "We can't waste time, if he has your baby somewhere. The other hostage doesn't have much time, either. Tell me where you are, I'll come to you. You have to tell me everything you know."

"No. No! I don't know anything and you can't come here." Her voice turned cagey. "Who are you? I think you're a cop. I think you want to arrest me because I helped Kevin. I bet Kevin's not injured and you're a lying bastard just like him. Well, fat chance. No cops! He said, no cops. If he finds out I helped you—no, no way, I'm not helping you!"

Her words were coming faster, uncontrolled. Praying I could calm her, keep her from losing it, I said, "I'm not a cop. I'll get Jason back, but you have to help me."

"You get Jason back, *then* I'll help you."

"I need to know things from you. I need to know everything Kevin said, anything that might help. We need to talk."

"*No we don't!*" She drew a long breath. "Okay, look, whoever the fuck you are. I didn't even know that son of a bitch was out of prison until he showed up early this morning and smacked me around. He grabbed Jason, he took my baby, and he said he was keeping him until whatever this is, whatever he was doing, this goddamn shit"—her voice cracked—"until it was over. He's messing with some guy's head and he needs someone to help him. I told him no fucking way, but . . . anyhow if I do what he says I'll get Jason back. He said Jason should have been his anyway, so he has a right to him and I was lucky he wasn't keeping him. That's what he said, that's every goddamn word he said."

I stared at the grafitti-blazed door in front of me. *Oh, Jesus, Smith!* "You're Megan. His fiancée. That's what he meant, the baby should've been his. Megan, it's Bill Smith. We met, back then."

A long silence. "Bill Smith? You're the guy? The guy he's doing all this to screw with? Whose girlfriend he has?"

"Yes."

Another brief pause. "Fuck me, why didn't I know that? Of course. Kevin has a hate on for a lot of people but no one more than you."

"Megan, I need your help."

"And I need Jason back."

"You have to help me find him."

"Ask Kevin."

"I don't know where Kevin is."

"I can't help. How can I help? I told you everything that happened. He said he'd call. He said when it was over he'd give Jason back. Find my baby!"

"I'll try. But—"

"No! Try! Try is bullshit. You find him. This is all your fault.

You and Kevin, what a fucking pair! What did you get me in the middle of your bullshit for? *You find him!* You find my baby. Then—" She drew a long breath and her words went sly. "Then I'll tell you where your girlfriend is."

A great rush, a wave of hope almost knocked me down. "Megan, my God, you know? Tell me now. Please. We can do both things at once. Find Jason, and find Lydia. Please, Megan."

"No. You find Jason. That's all I care about. How do I know you're not lying? How do I even know you're really Bill? Maybe you're a cop. You're a cop and you're lying."

"No. Megan—"

"*I DON'T CARE.* If you are Bill then why the hell would you look for Jason once you got your girlfriend back? No, I want my baby and that's what you have to do. And nobody's going to arrest me and Jason and I are going to disappear when you find him and you can all go fuck yourselves! *When you find him!*" A short pause, marked by quick breaths. "Deal: I won't make Kevin's phone call. Whatever bullshit it was supposed to be this time, I won't do it. You find my son. Call me when you do. How's that? You want to know where your girlfriend is? Then find Jason."

The line went dead.

25

"What, dude?" Linus demanded as I frantically tried for redial. "Dude, give it to me."

I stood facing the door, my back to the street and to the kids. I'd forgotten they were there, forgotten anything was there except Megan and, somewhere, Lydia. I spun around, handed the phone over. "Call her back."

"Her, who?"

"That was Megan."

"Megan, the ex?" asked Trella, eyes wide, as Linus thumbed buttons.

I nodded. "Kevin took her baby."

"Oh, my God," Trella said.

"Shit," said Linus, not looking up. "A baby?" He handed me the phone.

"Yes. That's the first prize, that he was ranting about. Jason." I pressed the green button again. "We dismissed her as the assistant because she hates him. But we never thought of something like this."

"But the baby—if it's first prize, he's keeping it. Did she—"

I waved him quiet as Megan's voice burst in my ear. "Hello? Bill? What? Do you have Jason?"

"Megan, I need to—"

"Bullshit! Don't call until you have my baby!"

She hung up.

"This button?"

"Yes."

This time I got voicemail. "Shit!" I snapped the phone shut.

"You could say you found him," Linus suggested. "Leave a voicemail, I guarantee she'll call back in thirty seconds."

"She'll want to see him. She'll want him back before she tells us anything. Fuck!" Again, I was thinking about air.

"Damn," Trella said slowly. "The baby. I knew she had a baby. But when I saw her on the street, she was alone. But the stroller was in the hallway. So where was the baby? It didn't even occur to me! God, I'm sorry! I should've—"

"No." I shook my head.

"Baby," Linus said suddenly. He looked at me. "Lydia called you 'baby.'"

I stared. "You're right. Oh, son of a bitch! Not kid's clothes or ob-gyns. She said, 'It's not just me,' and she called me baby. She was telling me she wasn't the only hostage. Telling me about the baby."

"And he said, remember Mr. Crazy said she was taking care of something else for him? That must be what he meant. Although."

"Although, what?"

"Well, dig, is he serious? He thinks he can just, I don't know, take someone else's baby and go have that life someplace, that life he thinks you stole from him? The condo and the car and the hoops and all?"

"He's crazy, Linus."

"Well, yeah." Linus seemed awestruck. "But still . . ."

"But guys," Trella broke in. "He said he moved first prize. That means the baby's somewhere else, not with Lydia now. And Kevin's on his way there."

I pressed into the shadows as a patrol car drifted by. Strawman had lost Kevin, but maybe the presence of so many cops would drive Kevin to ground, or at least slow him down.

"Guys?" Trella said. "Let's go."

"Go where?"

"Wherever. Don't you think we should get off the street? I texted Joey. He's here."

Another thing I'd forgotten: Joey, and the fact that we had wheels. I watched the Lincoln float to a halt beyond the row of parked cars at the curb. We dashed from the loading dock and piled into the car, Woof barking and climbing all over Linus and Trella in the backseat. He lunged forward and gave me a few slobbers, too, as Joey pulled out.

"Dog missed you guys," Joey drawled. "I hadda let him up front with me. Where to?"

"Dude." Linus frowned in thought. "When Mr. Crazy said he moved first prize, that was when we picked him up in Times Square."

"I had the same thought. Joey, head uptown."

"You got it. All that cop action back there, that was you?"

"Yeah." I took out my prepaid phone.

"You gonna call the ex again?" Linus asked. "From that?"

"No. You know Mary's number?"

"Aunt Mary?" He blanched. "No, but it's here." He took out his iPhone and read it to me.

A ring and a half; just long enough to yank a phone out of a pocket.

"Kee."

"Mary, it's Bill."

"Bill? *Where the hell are you?*"

"Lydia's downtown," I said. "In a basement. Kevin Cavanaugh was down around Crosby Street and now I think he's on his way uptown, somewhere near Times Square. Blanket the route with cops, you might pick him up."

"Why are you suddenly interested in us picking him up?"

"He's planning on making a stop and then leaving town without telling me where Lydia is. Mary, she's running out of air."

"I know. We're already searching. Where are you?"

"How do you know?"

"Lu told us. He said Cavanaugh said so. Who the hell was on the roof with them? The guys below said some girl was dangling from the flagpole until someone pulled her up, but when they finally got up there it was only Lu and one of his boys. Lu said it was him on the flagpole, trying to catch Cavanaugh. That's bullshit, right? It was Linus's girlfriend, it was Trella, wasn't it?"

"Doesn't matter."

"The hell it doesn't!"

"Mary? He took a baby."

"A *baby*?"

"About six months old. His ex-fiancée's. To force the mother to help him. Her name's Megan Collings and she lives at"—I looked at Trella, covered the phone. Trella whispered the address.—"at Three-twenty-three West Eighty-first. I don't know if she's there now. She knows where Lydia is."

"*What?*"

"But she won't tell me, won't even meet me, until I find her baby."

"She'll tell *me*! I'll come down on her like—"

"Yeah. Maybe. If you can find her. That's why I'm telling you about it."

"How do you know about it? About her?"

"Found her phone number. The thing is, she's already committed some serious crimes helping Kevin out. She's not sure anything I said to her was true. Part of her thinks I'm a cop trying to trap her."

"Why would—"

"She's not thinking straight. In fact I'd say she's halfway out of her mind, and she's waiting for me to call and say I have the baby. Until that happens I'm not sure she'll hear anything else."

"Give me the number."

I flipped open Kevin's phone and read it to her.

"If it has a GPS—"

"Kevin will have taken care of that," I said.

"Maybe. But if I can get her to talk to me and keep her talking—"

"Great, go ahead. Good luck. I'm not even sure she'll answer if it's not Kevin's number calling. But try it, that's why I'm giving it to you. We—I think the baby's somewhere near Times Square. That's where Kevin's heading. To get the baby."

"Where? Why do you think that?"

"Some things Kevin said last time he called. I don't know where. But I'm going to look."

"I'll send people up there. But it's a big neighborhood."

"So's downtown, where Lydia is."

"For God's sake, Bill! We won't stop one search because we're doing the other."

"I know," I said wearily. "And maybe you'll find Lydia. And maybe you can find Megan, and maybe you can find the baby. Maybe you'll spot Kevin and make him give it all up. But until then I'm not coming in; I'm going to search, too." I clicked off.

"Christ," said Joey, after a moment's quiet. "I know some wackos, I'll give ya that, but this shit—Jesus. A baby! Where we headed? His place? Up near where we picked him up before?"

"Up near there, but it's not his place," I said. "He lived in Queens when he got out. A halfway house. Hard to hide a stolen baby in a halfway house. Anyhow, the cops'll have been all over it by now. Anything to find, they'll have found it."

"You been there?"

"No, but I had someone there. Apparently his room's so empty you could just about believe he was never there at all."

Joey nodded in sympathy. "Probably he wasn't. I've known a couple, three guys like that."

I lit a cigarette, regarded him. "What do you mean? You've known guys like what?"

"Guys when they come out," Joey said, "Like, say, Cueball. Danny Santori, Trella, remember him?"

"Louie Leopard's brother-in-law? With the shiny head?"

"Yeah, him. He pulled a ten-year bid, served six and change."

"He ran a chop shop."

"Right. When he came out they sent him to a halfway house, finish out his sentence. Couldn't take it."

"Why, too many people around or something?"

"Nah, he was okay with that. Reminded him of stir, being crowded in with other guys. No, problem was just what you wouldn't think. House was too nice, Cueball's room was too big, too sunny. Too much to think about. Where to sit, where to stow your stuff, how to arrange the furniture. Sunshine kept getting in his eyes, he could hear birds singing. Shit like that. Tell ya, he couldn't stand it. He was there as little as he could get away with. In at curfew, out first thing in the morning. Rented a dump in the old neighborhood. Down the street from Louie Leopard, you know? Came rolling in every day, couple cappuccinos for breakfast, pasta for lunch, smoked cigars, kept the blinds down. Happy as a pig in shit. Like I say, I seen it before. Some guys, especially it's been a long stretch, just being back in the world's hard enough. They need to be in a place like where they came from, or they don't make it."

I'd been half-listening, focused out the window as though a neon sign might be flashing around the corner: BABY HERE! As I lit another cigarette, though, something penetrated. I turned to the backseat. "You guys hear that? Listen, what if Kevin never did anything but sleep at the halfway house? What if he's had another place since he came out? And he brought the baby there?"

"Yeah, okay, but where, dude?"

I had no answer. Tentatively, Joey offered, "With Cueball, it was in the old neighborhood. Dark and small, right on the street, you know? That's what he was after."

"But also," Trella said, "it's what he was used to. Not just from prison, from before, too. All those Santoris, they grew up in small dark dumps."

"You got that right," Joey agreed.

The car fell silent and I went back to looking at the street. What he was used to. What was Kevin used to? From the Upper East Side to ten years in prison. *I want a condo, or maybe a brownstone* . . . What you want, but is that the same as what you're used to? Kevin, what was it? If you couldn't take the halfway house, if you wanted what you were used to, where would that be?

"Dude?"

Disoriented for a second, I pulled myself back to the car. "Linus? What?"

"I don't know," he said uncomfortably. "Just, you're talking to yourself."

"Fuck!" I chucked the cigarette out the window, lit another one right away. "*Fuck!* Goddamn this shit! All day, no matter how deep shit we were in, Kevin was going to call again. We were—we were hooked in. Connected. Now we've got nothing. A baby, Lydia, both need help, both going to die and we have *nothing*! Nothing. *Fucking nothing!*"

"Dude? You're wrong."

"*What?* What do we have? One thing, Linus. Name me one fucking thing!"

"We have you."

"Oh, *fuck that*! Knock that shit off, Linus! All this, it's my fault in the first place. I'm not a fucking hero. I can't pull this out of the air!"

"Dude? That's not what I mean."

"Then what the fuck *do* you mean?"

"Mr. Crazy," he said slowly. "This whole thing, this whole game, was because of how you sent him to prison back in the day."

"Thanks a lot. You think that's news? Like I said, my goddamn fault. Jesus, I wish to God I'd left it alone, wish I'd let the cops screw it up and not tried to show off how smart I was. Son of a bitch!"

"No. Dude. Listen. Because of *how* you sent him to prison. The cops couldn't do it. You could, because you knew how he thought. You made it a game, to outplay him. You said."

"Yeah, me and him, great game players."

"*Dude!* You knew how he thought then. That's why it worked. So do it again. Know how he thought now."

I stared wordlessly at him. Both kids in the backseat kept their steady, confident gazes on me. I looked away, and after a moment rubbed a hand down my face. "Okay," I said quietly. "Okay. I'm Kevin." I nodded. "I'm out, after ten years. I've spent the whole time fixated on this guy I hate, and on getting my life back. Twin obsessions. I'm going to waste him, and then go about getting what I should've had." I shut my eyes, thought back to the days on the basketball court, the Kevin I'd known; and to the jagged phone calls, the elaborate setups of this day. "I'm out. And first thing, they send me to a halfway house. I can't deal. Why? Not because—not like Cueball." I opened my eyes and my words sped up. "Not it's too big, too bright. What it is, it's in Queens. That outer borough thing, Kevin was always ragging on the bridge-and-tunnel crowd. Didn't want anything to do with such uncool people. If I'm Kevin, I'm out and I want to be back in the *world*. If I'm Kevin, I came to Manhattan."

Linus nodded encouragingly, then prompted, "To your old neighborhood?"

"No. No, because the Upper East Side's old news now. I'm cool, remember, I'm hip? I'm erasing my ten years in prison, it never happened. I'm picking up where I left off. When I went in, the Upper East Side was hot, but now, only old farts live there. So my new place, it's in a neighborhood that's hot *now*. The hottest in Manhattan."

"The Meatpacking District," Trella said. "But there's not a lot there, and no rentals. Did you buy?"

"No. Because it's not permanent. I just have this one thing to do, get rid of this guy I hate, and then I'm going to split and start a new life. New York can go to hell. I'm going—shit, I'm going to LA. Movies, TV, be a big producer. That's where the coolest people are. No, I didn't buy in this town. I rented."

"Where, then? Maybe just south of the Meatpacking District, the Village?"

"No. Again, old news, and also, old buildings. Families and kids. If I'm Kevin and I'm renting, I want a loft, a new glass building or a luxury conversion. Big views. An address that the hip crowd understands, not familyland. Chelsea." I was stone certain. "North of the Meatpacking District. Galleries. Unmarked clubs with velvet ropes. The High Line. Big lofts, hot boutiques. The center of the action. That's where I am."

In five minutes, we were there. It's not a huge neighborhood, Chelsea, and I'd called Mary ("What the hell do you mean, he had a place in Chelsea?" "Mary, later. Send people there.") so there'd be a swarm of cops not too long from now. But now it was just us. And "not huge" still meant blocks and blocks, building after building of converted industrial lofts and costly new condos.

"Okay," I said. "We need to split up. All I can think of, we go building to building. The biggest ones, the newest. Look at the directories, ask the doormen—"

"Wait," said Trella suddenly. "There."

"What?" I looked out her side of the car. No CAVANAUGH BUILDING, no BABY HERE sign. A day care center? A foundling hospital? I saw nothing useful.

She pointed to the corner. I asked in disbelief, "What? The Chinese restaurant?"

"Grand Hunan," she said. "It's famous."

"It's fantastic," Linus agreed, but with a quizzical look at her. "Best in New York, as good as my mom's— Oh! Oh, dudess, I get it!"

I got it too, that same second. I jumped from the car, Linus and Trella with me. Inside, I didn't give the cashier a chance to say a word. I flashed my wallet badge. "Get the manager."

Taken aback, she hesitated, then called in Chinese to a waiter lounging in the back. He pushed through the swinging doors, returned with a smiling middle-aged man. Through the inset windows we saw a whirlwind hit the kitchen as everyone of dubious immigration status scrambled out the back. Customers watched us with brief interest, then went back to their meals.

"Yes, can I help you?" the manager inquired pleasantly, blocking my path to the kitchen and casting a skeptical eye on Linus and Trella.

"Deliveries," I said. "A big guy, looks kind of like me. Kevin Cavanaugh's his name. He's ordered I don't know how many times over the last couple months. He's a regular."

"Yes?"

"Where? I need to know where he lives."

"I'm sorry. The deliverymen, all out."

"All out back. I saw them go. Get them in here. We're not the INS. I don't care about their papers. I just need to find this guy."

Linus had been swiping at his iPhone; now he handed it to me with Kevin's photo on the screen, one of the ones we'd been sent from the street. The manager smiled again. "I'm sorry—"

"So's everyone else. He's a killer and he kidnapped a woman and a baby. They'll die if we don't find them!"

The manager paled, but still hesitated. Linus stepped up. "She's my cousin," he said. "The woman he kidnapped. My family, you know? They want me to find her."

The manager raised his eyebrows at Linus, then shifted his gaze to me and Trella.

"They're helping me," Linus explained. He added, "He's not a cop. It's a phony badge."

The manager frowned, but after a long moment he blew out a

breath. He spoke in Chinese to the waiter. The waiter trotted back through the kitchen doors, punching buttons on a cellphone. The delivery guys, I guessed, were waiting for an all-clear signal. The waiter crossed the nearly empty kitchen to the back door, returned a few moments later with four jumpy men. The manager said something in Chinese, which didn't relax them. To Linus, he said, "Go ahead, you may talk to them."

Linus spoke to the men in Chinese so clumsy even I could hear it. They all stared, uncomprehending. Linus turned to the manager. "They don't speak Cantonese?"

"Fujianese. Or Mandarin."

Linus looked abashed. "I can't . . ."

The manager pursed his lips in disapproval. He turned to the men and spoke, gesturing at Linus. Linus showed them the iPhone photo. Two of them shook their heads. The third man's eyebrows flew up. He started to say something. Then the fourth, a tall, hard-looking man, spoke to him sharply. They exchanged brief sentences. Color drained from the shorter man's face. He looked at Linus again and shook his head.

26

"What just happened?" I demanded.

"Dude, I'm not sure." Linus turned to the manager of Grand Hunan. "This guy recognized him but this guy told him not to."

The manager spoke to both men in Chinese, then came back to Linus. "Lo Shu says he made a mistake."

"Bullshit!" I exploded. "He knows him! He knows where he lives!"

The manager, raising his eyebrows, questioned the man again. "He says he can't help you."

"Dude." Linus grabbed my arm before I could lunge for Lo Shu. "Stay back. Let me try this Chinese-on-Chinese." He crooked a finger at the delivery man and walked to an empty table. Lo Shu, sweating, glanced from the tall man to the manager. The tall guy scowled but the manager gestured sharply for Lo Shu to follow. Barely reining myself in, I watched as Linus grabbed a paper napkin and set a pen racing across it. Lo Shu's brow furrowed as he leaned in to read; then, unexpectedly, he laughed. He spoke to Linus, who shrugged and offered him the pen. Lo Shu took it and flattened another napkin. They wrote Chinese characters at each other fast and furiously.

"What's he doing?" I asked Trella.

"He doesn't speak Chinese well."

"I know that!"

"But he can read and write it some. Poetry and the classics, from Chinese school when he was a kid."

"I remember he said that. But does he think—"

"I guess he does."

And he was right.

They wrote together for two or three minutes. By the time they put down their pens Linus was sweating as much as Lo Shu had been. Lo Shu, though, was grinning. They stood, Linus making a quick bow. The manager stepped to them and spoke to Linus, then Lo Shu. I watched the manager's head swiveling as his translation bounced back and forth. The tall man came forward, too, objected, but Lo Shu shushed him, jollied him along. After a dozen sentences Linus bowed to the manager, who rolled his eyes.

"Okay, dudes. Let's go."

Lo Shu was speaking low to the tall man, who fixed Linus with a suspicious glare.

"Go where? You got the address?"

"Those Tang poets," Linus said. "Useful dudes. These two guys have to come with us."

"Why?"

"Tell you on the way."

"Wait!" the manager demanded. "What are you doing? You already wasted their time. How can I keep up my deliveries if you take my staff?"

I slid three twenties from my wallet, gave one to each of the two men staying behind and one to the manager. "Tell these guys to ride faster."

The manager slipped his bill into his pocket. "Slow time of day anyway. All right." He spoke to Lo Shu and the tall man, and tapped his watch. Lo Shu nodded, but the other man still scowled.

"Tell them," Linus said to the manager, "they won't get in trouble with the law, and they'll get their twenties, too."

Linus, Trella, and I left the restaurant with the two deliverymen. Just before we took off sprinting Linus stuck his head in the car window and gave Joey the address. Joey pulled out to circle around. We were evidently heading downtown, against the traffic, so we went on foot.

Lo Shu kept grinning, waving his hands around, and talking to the tall guy, who didn't stop scowling but took out his phone and made a call.

"Why do we need these guys?" I asked as we jogged. "He's not sure about the address, he has to see the building?"

"No, he knows. And the baby's there."

I almost screeched to a halt. "Jesus Christ, are you sure? He saw him when he made a delivery?"

"No. The big guy. Ha Lin." He pointed. "His wife's there taking care of him. She speaks English. She can tell you the whole thing."

Of course. Kevin's son-to-be, his first prize. Part of the real life that would start as soon as he got rid of me. He wouldn't have left something that valuable all alone. First he had Lydia taking care of the baby. Now it was another Chinese woman's job.

"She's supposed to not let anyone in but Kevin. Lo Shu doesn't think she'd let him in. But her husband, she will. He just called her, to say we're coming and not to let Kevin in if he shows."

"Linus? How did you do this?"

"Took lines from famous poems, you know, that talked about

families, losing people, stuff like that." Linus flushed. "I thought maybe those, plus what the manager told him, I thought maybe he'd get it. Then if he could write back to me in poetry I recognized, and I could write back to him, maybe we could, like, bond, you know? Just so he'd trust me."

"What made you think he understood classical poetry even if he got what you were doing?"

"Wasn't sure he did. Wasn't even sure he could read and write besides 'orange chicken.' Most of the illegal guys, they're peasants. But a lot of them had a whole other life before they came here. Educated, dig, but not in anything anyone cares about in the New China. Or they have, like, political problems, better to not be there? Turns out, back home, Lo Shu was a Beijing opera star."

Two blocks down and one long block over, Lo Shu, wheezing behind, called us to a halt at a new, wide-windowed building of black steel panels with glossy copper accents, faux industrial, clearly expensive. I told the others to wait outside and gestured to the tall man. Lo Shu spoke to him with an easy grin. The tall man replied with ill humor, but he followed me in.

"Kevin Cavanaugh," I told the poker-faced doorman. "Eight-L."

"No Cavanaugh here. Eight L's Tony Stark," the doorman corrected me with a superior smirk.

Tony Stark: Ironman. *Jesus, Kevin!* "Cavanaugh's staying with him. And Cavanaugh's wife. In fact she's the one we want to see. With the baby? This is her brother."

The doorman narrowed his eyes in indecision, like he wasn't buying it but he didn't want to throw us out in case we were legit and Tony Stark got pissed off and didn't tip him at Christmas. "Hold on," he ordered. He clicked a button and we saw ourselves on a TV monitor behind him on the wall. He called upstairs, said a few words, and hung up. "Okay. She says go on up."

The elevator ride was the longest of my life. It took a week to run down the hallway and after I rang the bell it was a month before the door opened. When it did, a thin Asian woman stood in the entryway holding a sleeping blond baby.

She exchanged fast whispered words with her husband, eyeing me suspiciously. After something he said her eyes widened and she covered her mouth in shock. She nodded and put the baby in his arms; he took it the way you would someone's eggshell collection you hoped they'd come back for soon. Returning inside, she quickly gathered up her things: a handbag, a sweater. Meanwhile I had Kevin's phone out and was calling Megan.

"Bill? What?" Megan's rough voice demanded as the door shut behind us and we headed down the hall. "I swear to God, you'd better—"

"I do."

Silence. "You do? *You do?*"

"Where are you?"

"You have my baby?"

"Yes. Where are you?"

"Oh, my God! Oh, God! I'm— No, wait! How do I know? This could be a trick. How do I know it's not?"

"Jesus Christ, Megan! Tricks, games, all that shit, I— Forget it. Can you get photos?"

"What?"

"On the phone!"

"Yes. This phone? Yes."

"We'll send one in a minute."

The woman had taken the baby back from her husband, whose

relief was obvious. She fixed worried eyes on me as we waited for the elevator. "Baby daddy," she said uncertainly. "Steals baby?"

"He stole him, but he's not the daddy."

She looked at me blankly.

"The baby's mother's coming to get him. Do you know where Kevin—where the man who said he was the daddy was going?"

"No. Just, I take care baby, he come back tonight."

"Did he say anything else?"

She shook her head. "Just, come restaurant two day before, ask me I like baby. Say, good pay, I take day off today, take care son." Exiting the elevator into the lobby, she gave me a worried look. "In trouble? Ha Lin, me? Lo Shu?"

"No." In fact, the opposite. When this was over I was going to hire these three the best immigration lawyer in New York. "Linus!" I shouted as we burst onto the street.

"Dude! Oh, awesome!"

"Linus, take a photo, send it to Megan. She wants proof." I handed him Kevin's phone. He glanced at it, poked a few buttons, pointed it at the sleeping baby in the woman's arms. Then he poked some more buttons.

We waited forever. Kevin's phone rang.

"Megan?"

"Where are you? I'm coming there."

"Tell me where Lydia is."

"I want him in my arms. I'm hailing a cab right now. Where?"

"Megan—"

"*Where?*"

I gave her the address. Then I called Mary.

"Kee."

"It's Bill. I'm ready to come in."

"You are?" Her astonishment was clear.

"We found the baby."

"What? You did? Where? Is he all right?"

"He seems fine. Megan's coming here. She doesn't trust me. When I give her the baby she'll tell me where Lydia is. Getting her out will be something you guys will do better than I could."

I expected a dig and I deserved it, but all she said was, "Where are you?"

"West Twenty-sixth Street. Six-two-three. Kevin has an apartment under the name 'Tony Stark.' "

"*Ironman*?"

"Everything's a game to him. He may be headed here. Mary, keep your people out of sight until Megan tells me where Lydia is. Don't spook her."

I hung up, said to the woman holding Jason, "His mother is coming. You can go if you want. You can give the baby to me."

Her husband seemed ready to take off but she stood her ground. They argued briefly; she shook her head, was adamant. "No," she said to me, clutching the baby to her. "I wait for mama."

I nodded, turned to Linus and Trella. "Mary's on the way. When Megan gives us Lydia's location the cops will get her out. You guys, I think you should stay out of trouble if you can."

It took a moment for my meaning to dawn. Their eyes met. Trella smiled, like I was sweet but silly. Linus looked as if I'd told him to dance a tango. "Dude! You can't be serious."

"Why should you—"

"After all this? I know you don't mean that."

I was starting to argue, to tell them to get lost and I'd claim I hadn't seen them for hours, when a cab pulled up and a pudgy woman jumped out. In the time it took her to cross the wide sidewalk I had flashes: a fat woman in sunglasses in the deep shade, mouth open in a silent scream, outside Jim White's exploding apartment. A heavy woman elbowing her way through the crowd outside the tailor shop. A stocky woman trotting around the corner as I left my place when this all began. This woman. Megan Stine, fifty pounds beyond the woman I'd known, but I should've seen it. Then she was on top of us, her arms out for the baby. Ha Lin's wife met Megan's eyes, then smiled and handed the baby to her. Megan clutched him close and started to cry.

"We go now," Ha Lin's wife whispered to me. The three of them melted into the crowd on the sidewalk, Lo Shu waving cheerily and calling something to Linus.

"Megan—"

She jumped, stepped back when I spoke. "You bastard! You and Kevin. I ought to kill you for this."

"Megan, I'm sorry. None of it was my idea. If I could make it up to you I would. Please. Tell me where Lydia is."

She leaned over Jason, who was fussing, waking up. She spoke softly, kissed him. He opened his eyes, blinked, filled his lungs, and bawled.

"Oh, honey, sshhh."

"Megan."

"He's hungry. Come on, sweetness, Mommy will feed you." She stepped to the curb to hail another cab. I grabbed her arm. She tried to shake me off but I was locked on.

"Megan! Where's Lydia?"

"Let me go."

"You have your baby. Lydia's still in trouble. Where is she?"

Unable to pull away, Megan stopped struggling, turned to face me. Malice and triumph glowed in her eyes. "You stupid bastards. You and Kevin both. Well, fuck you. How would I know?"

My heart turned to ice. "What?"

"Are you insane? You think Kevin told me anything like that? He didn't even tell me I was setting off a bomb, or that this was about you. I was his robot, his little machine. I don't know anything about this bullshit. I don't know where your girlfriend is. Now let me go."

Linus and Trella had stepped up behind her. I saw their faces go white. "You said—"

"And you fell for it. Good for me. Come on, would you have given a shit where my baby was otherwise? Would you have looked for him if you didn't think I could help you? It's your fault Jason and I got all messed up in this. Sorry about your girlfriend, but it's not my problem. Let go of me."

"No. Megan. I—"

"Oh, *fuck*!" Wild-eyed, she stared up the street. "Are those cops? You son of a bitch! Unmarked cars, oh, you bastard!" She yanked against my grip some more. I turned, saw what she'd seen, three black Tauruses idling up the block. And a Fusion: Mary's car. Mary jumped out and dodged traffic to reach us.

"Something wrong?"

"Yes!" Megan screeched. "This creep won't let go of me!"

"Quiet!" Mary ordered her. Megan blinked in disbelief. Mary said, "Bill?"

"She doesn't know," I said. My voice was dry, lifeless. "Where Lydia is. She doesn't know."

27

Cops and CS techs trotted in and out of Kevin's building. They bagged shoes to check for one-of-a-kind dirt, pawed through papers for store receipts, parking tickets, anything that might start a trail. Detectives interviewed neighbors, porters, the super, the doorman. Other cops cruised the area in case Kevin was on his way. A Mandarin-speaking officer had been sent for, to question the staff at Grand Hunan. Child Services had taken custody of Jason while Megan, alternately weeping and screaming, was hauled back to the Fifth precinct to answer questions, and the DA decided whether or not to charge her.

All good police work, proper procedure. It would probably yield results.

In the end.

Long after Lydia's air ran out. After the clock ran down and the whole thing was over. After nothing mattered anymore.

I was under arrest.

Mary had made the collar, fast, and shoved me in the back of her car. She'd scooped up Linus and Trella, too, in the general confusion, stuck them in there with me. I knew not to argue. A guy as wanted as I was, all these cops around, no way she could let me walk.

And where would I have gone?

So here we were, me, Linus, and Trella, in the backseat, Mary up front, with the last of Kevin's plastic bags, trying to salvage something.

Or that's what we told ourselves. We sat still and silent, staring at the book, the screw, the photo. Maybe the others were furiously trying out ideas, following paths, putting pieces together in their heads. I was empty. I had nothing. I smoked, looked at the bag and the incomprehensible junk that had come out of it, looked through the windows, looked inside myself. Nothing, anywhere.

Mary's cop radio kept up a low, staticky stream. Trella and Linus, pressed together, whispered occasionally to each other, then shook their heads. I smoked.

Patino came over, stuck his head in the window, spoke to Mary. I roused briefly—had they found Kevin?—but he walked away and Mary went back to fingering the screw, peering at the photo, turning the pages of the book.

Lighting the fourth cigarette off the butt of the third, I suddenly exploded. "Fuck!" I threw the car door open, climbed out. Mary, maybe thinking I was about to run off, jumped out with me. She had nothing to worry about. If I'd had a direction, I'd have split in a heartbeat. But I didn't. There was only one place I cared about right now, one place I would have given anything to be, and I didn't know where that was.

"Bill?" Mary spoke more gently than I expected. That made it much worse.

"No! Don't talk. Don't talk to me." I slammed my fist on the hood. "*Fuck!*" A couple of cops turned to stare but Mary waved them away. "That motherfucking *bastard*! No, I know, don't think about Kevin, think about Lydia. Do something clever, come up with something, fill in the missing clue, *goddamn it*! I can't! God-damn son of a bitch." I sagged against the side of the car. "Goddamn son of a bitch."

"Dude?" I hadn't noticed Linus getting out, but there he was, with Trella, standing beside me. "You were right the first time. Don't think about Lydia. Think about Kevin. Think *like* Kevin."

I shook my head. "I can't. I can't anymore, Linus. I'm sorry. I'm . . ." *What, Smith? Drained? Exhausted? And no one else is? These kids aren't? Lydia isn't, wherever she's sitting, alone, waiting, with the air getting foul?* "Shit," I heard myself say, "I wish I had a drink."

"No," said Mary.

"Oh, back the hell off! *Yes!* I wish I were shit-faced. Falling-down drunk. So fucked up I could forget all this. Not feel it, not even *know* it. That's what I wish."

"Yeah," Linus said, "like your cop homie, Hal. That's someone to look up to, for real."

"Linus, goddamn it! I never wanted anyone looking up to me! That's not my— I'm not—" I swallowed, shook my head. As though someone were interrupting me, as though there were too much noise, I put out my hands to stop it. I whispered, "Wait. Wait."

Linus and Mary exchanged looks. "Dude?" Linus asked cautiously. "What?"

"I . . . Hal . . . falling-down drunk . . ." I didn't know what I meant, kept shaking my head, to clear it. No. Not clear it. Falling-down drunk. "When you and I talked to Hal at his place," I said carefully, "he was halfway wasted. At the bar, he was far past that. So smashed he couldn't walk."

"And?"

"Something he said. State-dependent memory."

"I don't remember he said that."

"No! He didn't say it. It's what he was. What he was in."

Linus glanced at Mary. "Dude, you're not making—"

But Trella was nodding. "Yes. It's like, something you learn when you're, say, terrified, and then it doesn't come back until you're terrified again. Or you saw something when you were stoned, and you don't remember what it was until next time you get stoned."

"Or you hear something," I said, "when you're drunk. So drunk you can't walk, can't get up and stop a girl from going off with a son of a bitch. What Kevin said, Linus. What Hal said Kevin said about the Lin girl, the girl he killed in the park." I paused, groping in my mind. "An odd phrase he used. Hal was completely wasted, and he was quoting Kevin."

Linus's forehead crinkled in thought but he shook his head. "I don't remember what he said, exactly."

Goddammit! Think, Smith, you useless bastard. I told myself that, and nothing happened. Likely, there was nothing anyway. Likely I was grasping at straws, and Hal hadn't said a goddamn word that mattered. I tried to steer my thoughts into some other channel, somewhere they might be useful, but they wouldn't budge. They were stuck on Hal, his slurred words and that dark bar. I felt my fists clench. *Look at you, you stupid son of a bitch, in the end you can't even control your own thoughts! God, Smith, you are one fucking loser, you know that? Not just a blind game player like Kevin Cavanaugh. A total and complete loser.* The world went red as a hopeless rage burned through me.

Then a moment like a thunderclap. "*Shit!*" Unable to stop myself, I began to laugh.

"Dude?" I heard. "You flipping out?"

"No!" I was close, though. I shut my eyes, opened them again, brought myself down. "No, not flipping out. State-dependent memory. 'Maiden voyage.'"

"What?"

"I just needed to get as mad as I was in the bar, at Hal. Now I remember what he said." I shook my head in wonder. "He said the Lin girl should never have told Kevin she was saving herself for her husband because Kevin liked to take girls on their maiden voyage."

"Dude? And?"

And? For a moment, nothing. But there *was* something. The power of the itch to remember what Hal had said, the depth of relief when I'd scratched it. Why did it matter?

"Oh, God in heaven!" I yanked the car door open. "Let's go. Tell you on the way."

A brief hard pause from Mary. Then, "Get in the car," she said, and the kids did, and we were rolling. Patino glanced our way as Mary pulled out; none of the other cops paid any attention. Kee was transporting her prisoners, fine, they had their own jobs to worry about. They probably didn't give a thought, either, to Joey's town car slipping away from the curb a block up, just as Mary didn't notice Trella sending a text silently from the backseat.

"All right, where?" Mary asked.

"Downtown. Near South Street. Give me that stuff." I gathered the things from Kevin's bag. "*The Last Days of Old Beijing.*" I held up the book. "Beijing—in the old days, Peking. The South Street Seaport has a schooner called the *Peking*. It's docked down near the end of Maiden Lane."

"Oh, dude!" Linus's face lit up. "Oh, you think? You think so? Some 'maiden' thing, that was the last clue he was gonna give us, before he decided not to?"

"I don't know if it was. The last clue may have been something else. But you have to know 'Maiden Lane' would just crack Kevin up. The question is, does the rest of this fit? You guys, this photo. Chevy Chase. What if it's not about him, or his routines, or cars or anything, it's about one of his movies? What movie would this be from?"

"Shit, dude, I don't know. He's not a guy I follow, dig?"

"Then we need to go through his filmography," Trella said.

"Oh! Duh! We can IMDB him!" Linus had his iPhone out again. "Give it here, dude." I had no idea what he was doing but I passed him the photo. He muttered, "Filmography, huh?" and Trella smiled. They leaned together while he swiped small square pictures down his screen. "Here! Dude! Damn, it's right in front of us! It's the thumbnail for something called *Fletch*." He looked hopefully up at me. "That help?"

"Goddamn it, yes! Fletcher Street is three blocks long, runs parallel to Maiden Lane, a block away!"

Linus whooped. "And the other thing? The screw?"

I held that in my palm, waited for lightning to strike. And waited. "I don't know," I finally said.

Mary swung the car around Battery Park and up the FDR, pulled in at a NO STANDING sign under the highway by the seaport. "You'd better be right."

I had no answer. It was true: I'd better be.

We left the car, crossed South Street to the foot of Maiden Lane. "What now, dude?" Linus was ready for instructions, and Mary let me be the one to give them.

"You two take Fletcher. Go slowly. Look for what we talked about before: areaway windows, slots between buildings."

"And you'll be on Maiden Lane?"

"You got it."

On the way down, Mary had called it in, telling Dispatch to send cars but keep them back until she asked for them. Now she walked silently beside me, her eyes, like mine, searing the façades of the buildings lining Maiden Lane. Trying to burn away their secrets. To outsmart them. Though if you asked me they could keep every secret they ever had, all but one. There was no one I ever wanted to outsmart again, nothing I wanted to figure out anymore, except this one thing.

The first two blocks west from the river, nothing. No calls from Linus and Trella, either. Maybe I was wrong; this wasn't the place. Maybe we were wrong, wrong as could be about everything: the location, the areaway, the windows, the sun. Maybe I'd gotten the clues, and everything Lydia had said to me all day, totally wrong.

Then we crossed Front Street. And there it was.

"Mary." I grabbed her arm. "Look."

"What?" She squinted where I was pointing: a turn-of-the-last-century brick building squatting along Front Street, taking the entire block between Fletcher and Maiden Lane.

"New Jersey Zinc. Above the door."

"New Jersey—"

"Zinc! Galvanized, the screw is galvanized! That's why it's silver. It's coated with zinc!" I was across the street before I was done talking.

New Jersey Zinc showed signs of ongoing work: boarded-up windows, blue tarp draping the parapet, scaffolding over a blocked-off sidewalk. The eastern façade, on Front, met the sidewalk hard, no areaway, no basement windows. The Fletcher Street wall was on the north; it wouldn't get sun. But the southern wall ran along Maiden Lane itself. And the quoins on its corner were lit, right then, by a disappearing slice of sunlight. Earlier in the day that slice would have briefly fallen right in the pebbled glass windows of the areaway that spanned the building's length.

I called the kids while Mary called Dispatch. "Be right there, dude!" Linus promised and we heard the sirens start up and grow nearer but we didn't wait, Mary and I. Inside, where plastic tarps and orange warning cones cut off half the dusty lobby, a startled security guard looked up from his newspaper when Mary barked, "NYPD!" She held up her badge. "I need the building manager. Now!"

The guard blinked. "Manager's gone home."

"Then the night super!" Mary shouted at him, as though he should've thought of that himself.

He spoke into his radio. Thirty seconds later by his desk clock, thirty years by my heart, a heavy man in a blue uniform came through a door across the lobby.

"Looking for me?" He addressed me, but Mary answered, flashing her badge again.

"NYPD. We have reason to believe a kidnapper's hiding his victim in your basement."

He turned his stare to her, examined her badge as though there were any way he'd have known a real one from a fake. "In here? No."

"Take me down there. Now."

"Building's being renovated, in case you can't tell. Half empty. No one's using the basement, except my workshop's at the other end."

I asked, "You been down there today?"

"No, not for a couple days now."

"Well, we're all going down there now," Mary said fiercely.

More stare. "You have a warrant?"

"Get out of my way." She started to push past him.

"Okay, okay," he said with a shrug. "Reflex question. No skin off my nose. Come on."

Over her shoulder Mary told the guard, "I sent for backup, but don't let them downstairs until I say so." We followed the super along a corridor and down a flight of stairs.

"How long has this renovation been going on?" I asked.

The super grunted. "A year. I don't know why everything's gotta move like molasses in this city. No work a whole damn month now, some permit bullshit. 'Scuse my French," he said in Mary's direction, not looking like he cared much whether she was offended or not. "Okay, here you are. Gorgeous, huh? What do you want to see?"

He'd flipped the switch for a row of construction-caged lightbulbs. The stairs had brought us down to an open area where three plastic-draped, dusty corridors branched in different directions. Piles of construction lumber, stacks of Sheetrock, bags of dry cement crowded each route, looking malevolently ready to disorient and trap you and keep you wandering until you dropped. The super unclipped a flashlight from his belt, played it over the debris. "See? Like I said." He spoke as if this mess proved his point, and shifted his weight, ready to leave. To me it suggested just the opposite and Mary and I ignored him.

"I'll take that way," Mary said.

"No," I said, calm and sure. "Come with me. This leads to the south side. Where the areaway windows are."

We lifted a tarp and stepped into a shadowed wasteland of hanging wires, scattered wood scraps, sawdust, and half-framed walls. Wordlessly I held out my hand for the super's flashlight. He hesitated, then passed it to me. As I started forward Mary clutched my arm.

"Booby traps," she said. "Kevin might have it wired. Collapsing ceiling or something."

"No." I was stone certain. "If he has Lydia here, it's one day only. Last thing he'd want is some carpenter getting clobbered and the place swarming with rescue personnel."

Still, we moved in slowly and carefully. After a moment the super followed, muttering. I was aware every second of the hot, close, dusty air. I wanted to race along, pounding on doors, shouting Lydia's name. What kept me steady was Kevin's tank of poison gas, set to be released by a phone call, but maybe not only by that. The corridor might not be booby-trapped, but if I were Kevin the room would be a different story.

Like most commercial building basements, there was nothing straightforward about this one, wouldn't have been even if it hadn't been in the middle of construction. The hallway bent and branched, threw up dead ends and doorways like a stream with dams and tributary brooks. At each doorway, I inspected the jambs, the head, the threshhold. The first seven or eight were clearly not sealed, not airtight. Still, using my keys so the sound would be sharp, I tapped anyway, tried each handle, called Lydia's name. Some opened, some didn't, but the dust and grime hung heavy and undisturbed everywhere. We kept going. Then, after a jog to the left, the hallway widened as though the stream had been blocked and created a pond. The three surrounding walls each had a door. Two were full height, like the others we'd passed. The last was half-size, access to a machine room or some such. The full-height ones were ill fitting, with gaps at head or jamb.

The half-size one was sealed.

Caulking clogged the meeting of door and wall, door and floor, smeared flat by a finger, hard up against backer rod where the gap was too big for caulk alone. Mary's eyes met mine.

"What's this to?" I asked the super.

He peered, shrugged. "Beats me. Never been in there. Nothing the building uses, anyway. Old coal bin?"

"Is it on the drawings?"

"For the renovation? No idea. Never saw them. Not my job."

I clenched my teeth. "You have them?"

"The drawings? Could be there's a set in the office."

"Go get them. You have the key?" I leaned, looked more closely. "Shit, forget it. Glue in the lock." Meaning Kevin was never really planning to come back?

As the super's footsteps faded and my heart sped up, Mary got on her radio. I wasn't waiting, though. I squatted by the door. Steel, with chipped paint, dented knob, scabby rust dulling its hinges. I dug out my keys, rapped on the steel, called Lydia's name, stopped to listen.

No answering call.

We had to be right. This had to be the place. Stretching Kevin's time limits to the outside only gave us half an hour before Lydia's air ran out. We had no time to start over.

Again, I called, louder, banged the keys on the steel harder, paused.

Again, no anwering call.

But an answering tap.

I shot a look at Mary. "Did you hear that?"

"What?"

Was I wrong?

I rapped the steel once more, stopped once more.

Doubtfully, Mary said, "I don't hear anything."

"Wait! Listen."

Silence. Then—

Yes! *Yes!*

Rhythmic tapping, fainter than mine, but unmistakable. Not weak: the taps seemed sharp enough, just at a distance. She couldn't reach the door? Chained, tied? No answering call: gagged?

But alive.

I felt a surge of relief so powerful I almost thought I could burst right through the steel door. I was about to try, but light flared behind me. Shadows rounded the corner and became people, three guys in gray visored helmets and thick ballistic vests. With them was a cop I knew: Tom Sweeney, Mary's captain.

"Kee," Sweeney nodded.

"Captain," she responded.

Sweeney scowled at me. "You, later." But he didn't throw me out. "Kee, this is Kennison. Bomb Squad."

The guys in gray had put down their loads: boxes, a duffel bag. One started setting up a light stand; another, a broad-shouldered black man, stepped up to shake Mary's hand.

"Heard of you," Mary said.

"Hope so," Kennison grinned. "I don't do this for the money."

"It's not a bomb in there," Mary said. "It's poison gas."

"So I hear. Cell phone trigger. We have the number, Verizon's got it blocked."

"Could be another trigger, too," I said. "Couple more, maybe."

"Heard all about that, too. Talked to the Chinese kid upstairs while we waited for you to call us in. He said your bad guy was tricky. What's he, the kid, gang unit or something?"

"Civilian," Mary answered. "Damn good, though."

If this ever ended I'd have to remember to tell Linus that she said that.

"Robbie's on his way. The robot," Kennison explained when Mary looked blank. "Might not turn out to be his gig but he likes the exercise. DEP has an infrared heat sensor they use in the tunnels they're sending over, too. We came ahead because you seem to be in a hurry."

"The victim may be running out of air. Kidnapper said that would happen."

"But she's still with us now?"

"Yes." Mary nodded tightly. "You tap, she responds. But you can see how the door's sealed."

"Windows outside, too." Kennison squatted as he spoke, ran his fingers along the door jamb, explored the head and sill. He glanced up at her. "What, you thought we were just sitting around waiting for you? Did all the prelim recon already, you're welcome. We have lights out there." He gestured vaguely toward the building's exterior.

"She knows you're there, then," I said suddenly. "Lydia."

"The victim? Yeah, if she can see she'll know something's up, can't miss us. We can't see inside, though. Panes are all soaped up. But we can see wires on the glass. Like for an alarm. Might trip the gas, might not. Might be plain ol' dummies. Can't be sure yet. Look," he said, lifting a stethoscope from the duffel bag, "I have to ask you guys to step away. You, too, Captain. Me and my brother Darryl and my other brother Darryl here, this is what we get the big bucks for. We let you guys hang around, you'll steal our secrets."

"Move it out," Sweeney said to Mary and me, starting to step away.

"I—"

"No." Sweeney grabbed my arm.

For a second I resisted. *What the hell, Smith, you're going to mix it up with Sweeney? That would sure help Lydia.* Every bit of me wanted to stay but I let the captain pull me along. We retreated around a corner, far from any catastrophe the Bomb Squad guys might set off. Four other cops waited there, and three EMS techs with a gurney, oxygen, burn blankets, all the disaster supplies you might need. For Lydia's sake I was grateful to them all but it was too many people. I stepped away. I wiped a trickle of sweat from my neck as I thought about Lydia behind that door, in some small, rank space, seeing the lights, hearing my taps. *Hang on,* I thought, *hang on!* From where we were I couldn't see Kennison and the others, but the scene was vivid in my mind: the lights, the vests, Kennison's stethoscope, his big fingers exploring the caulk, the knob, the hinges.

Son of a bitch.

The hinges.

That door, so carefully sealed and Super Glued, wasn't the door Kevin used. Even a couple of trips, a couple of openings and closings, would have scraped some rust off the hinges. But they were scaly and dull.

There was another door.

I needed a look at the building's plans but if the super had found them the Bomb Squad guys would've had them. "Mary!" I lifted the tarp that led to another of the branching corridors. If I was right, one of these would split again farther along, and swing back to the left. I picked the middle one, the one most likely.

"What? Bill!" Commotion as she pushed through after me, two more cops on her heels.

"There's another way in," I shouted over my shoulder without slowing down. I jumped a pile of paint cans like a steeplechase horse.

"How do you know?"

I didn't answer, just paused for a moment at a branch in the hallway, chose a path, raced on. Another twist, to the left as it should be, and, a few feet along, another branch. If I was right, this would be just about the spot. I went left again.

There was a door.

I held up my hand for Mary and the others to stop. I stepped to the door to examine it, to check the caulking and to rap on it, see if I could hear Lydia answer. I played the flashlight on the floor: footprints in the dust. On the lock: this one wasn't glued. This one, the tumbler was new. The hinges: on the knuckles, the telltale gleam of recent use.

I pulled out my keys and rapped.

No answer.

Wrong. This had to be it, this had to be the same room. And Lydia had to be still alive. No answer was just wrong.

I pounded the door with my fist.

No answer.

I lifted my fist for another, harder go, but made contact with nothing. The door flew open, a hand grabbed my arm. With a powerful pull it yanked me inside.

28

I nearly stayed steady but a foot hooked mine and the hand pulled harder. As I stumbled forward something smashed the back of my head. I lost my balance and a second later my shoulder slammed the concrete floor. I heard a heavy clunk, maybe a bolt being thrown, but I wasn't sure. And I wasn't sure I cared. My head throbbed, swam, and I lay on the edge of a soft darkness, a cool comfort waiting to swallow me up. All I had to do was go with it.

Seriously? Dude!

I pulled in a ragged breath. The air was fetid, stale. I rolled over, struggled to my feet. From outside I heard shouting and the pounding of fists. I straightened, blinked, tried to register what I saw.

Unnaturally bright light streamed in from above, dividing the room into freakish washed-out pales and sharp black shadows. I squinted, worked at resolving the swimming jigsaw. Gradually, it sharpened.

High walls, grimy with ancient coal dust, rising on one side to high strip windows. The door I'd been pulled into, on my right; the small, sealed one behind me.

Across the room, eyes blazing, standing, but mouth taped, hands cuffed behind her, and locked to the wall by a short chain at her waist: Lydia.

In front of me, just out of reach, with an automatic and a huge grin: Kevin Cavanaugh.

"Well!" he drawled as I fought to stay standing. "Well, well, fucking well. Prince Asshole. Nice of you to drop by. Call them."

"What?" My head still buzzed; I was having trouble following.

"That army brigade you have outside, all your bench, your B-team, whoever the fuck they are. Little Chop Suey, is he there? Call them, tell them to cease and desist or everyone in here is d-e-a-d dead as a doornail. What the hell's a doornail, anyway? Who gives a shit? Call them right now, asshole. That gas, it ain't very nice, I'm told." He pointed to the floor behind me. A canister like a fire extinguisher stood on end, wired up—one set of wires ran to the small door—and not seeming too stable. "Do it now. Because if I hear one fucking word from any of them, that damn megaphone blasting or some shit-eating sweet-talker telling me everything's gonna be okay, I'll shoot us all. And then set off the gas," he added as an afterthought.

My vision was double and wouldn't clear. I blinked, shook my head, almost caved in under a wave of nausea. I turned to Lydia, met her eyes. Kevin saw the look that passed between us and his grin grew. Without taking his gaze off me, he swiveled the gun to her. "Now? Asshole?"

"Okay," I rasped. "All right." I fumbled for my phone. I forced myself to stand straight, which wasn't any harder than climbing Everest. Slowly, I grinned, too. As I dialed Mary, I said, "Finally."

Uncertainty clouded Kevin's smile but I didn't give him a chance to speak.

"Mary?"

"Bill?"

"Back off. It's Kevin. He's in here with Lydia. He says back off or he'll trigger the gas."

"Is she all right?"

I threw another quick look Lydia's way. Even with my vision off, I could see: blood on her cheek, a bruise on her arm, her face drawn and streaked with coal dust. But she was standing and her eyes burned. "Yes."

"Is he listening?"

"No. Back off, Mary. All of you. Kennison's door is wired to the gas."

"We have a hostage negotiator. He'll call your number. Put Kevin on."

"No."

"Bill—"

"No. It'll be okay. Unless you guys screw it up." I thumbed off, lowered the phone, looked Kevin in the eye, smiled. I tossed the phone to the floor. Reaching in my pockets, I pulled out my prepaid and Kevin's own phone, chucked them away, too.

"Wow, asshole. You're really wired up, huh? Hey, that looks like mine!"

"It is yours."

"Woo-hoo! Damn, your team's good, bro, I'll give ya that."

"They are. But I don't need them anymore. Now that I have what I want."

The confusion again; then the smile. "*You* have what *you* want? What would that be?"

"You and me," I said. "Face to face. I've been telling you all day, Kevin, that's all I wanted."

"Oh, sure. That's all, besides me cutting your girlfriend loose." He turned, made exaggerated kissing noises at Lydia. Her face darkened and she pulled against the chain.

"And you sure fell for that."

Kevin whipped back to me. "What are you talking about?"

"Oh, come on, Kevin, you don't really think I give a shit what happens to her? She's fun, but for Christ's sake, there are a billion of them. From the beginning, I said: You and me, face to face. And you said, no, I had to do all this bullshit about finding Lydia. Obviously there was no way to stop you from hiding behind her, so I did what you wanted. I knew it would bring us together in the end."

He took a step toward me. Lydia's eyes widened. I knew what she was seeing: a swaying, beat-to-shit veteran whose head was ringing, taunting a younger, hate-filled, drug-stoked iron man.

"Hiding behind her?" Kevin sneered. "What the fuck's that supposed to mean?"

"What part don't you understand? Her? Behind? Or, hiding? Isn't that what you've been doing all day?"

"What I've been doing? I've been setting you up! I've been jerking you around by the balls!"

"You believe anything you want. You know I'm right."

"I don't even know what you're talking about."

"You still playing? Well, suit yourself. Kevin Cavanaugh, big scary psycho killer. Bullshit, Kevin. You're a punk. A loser, a wannabe. You were scared of me so you came up with this crappy game. What a waste of time."

"Me? Scared of you? You're the one who's scared! Scared all day I'd hurt your precious girlfriend."

"A punk, and stupid besides. How the hell else was I going to get up close and personal with you? Since you wouldn't step up like a man. I played you, Kevin, and it worked. Now we're face to face in a locked room. What I've wanted for years."

"Years? What years?"

"You think you're the only one's been obsessing since way back then? I've thought about you a lot, Kevin. Every fucking day, in fact. Every fucking day of my life."

"Bullshit! It took you hours to even figure out it was me. You said you didn't remember!"

"You bought that? Shit, you really are a jerk. I knew it was you right away, of course I did. It's been eating at me for ten years, how that shitbrain Hal Ross got you a soft, cushy sentence. I had you all set up to do some serious hard time, until he fucked it up."

"Hard time? You don't know what hard time is, asshole! You'd have been crying for your mama, you did a day of the time I did."

"Crap. In those country clubs? I had you bound for Attica, you candy-ass. Until Hal came along."

"No. No." He shook his head. "This was all my idea. This is my game."

"See, that's your problem right there. 'Game.' You're a punk and you think like a punk. When you started with that bullshit, when you insisted on this 'game' and wouldn't cut to the chase, I finally caught on that you were too chicken to meet me. So I played along. I stage-managed it all. So it would end up like this."

"Oh, that is such bullshit!" Sweat gleamed on his forehead.

I grinned. "Then why would I be in here? The cops are outside. Why didn't I let them save Lydia, now that we have you cornered, instead of making like a hero and ending up locked in here with you?" *Damn good question, Smith, but it's too late now.* "No. I did it because it was what I wanted. Now we're here. Now we can have it out.

I was worried you really were on your way out of town when you said you were, but I thought no, not Kevin, he won't be able to resist."

Kevin stared. "I was! But you fucked me up. You stole my first prize! Or I'd have left. I wouldn't have come back here."

My grin widened. "I know that, Kevin. That's why I did it."

His eyes jumped and darted. A bead of sweat rolled down his jawline. Then his smile turned crafty. "Well. Well, if that's the case, then you won't mind if I, say, blow her away. Your pretty girlfriend." He pivoted the gun to Lydia again.

"Go ahead. If you think you can afford to waste your strength like that."

"What?"

"Come on, Kevin. You get off on it, right? You got off when you killed the Lin girl, and each one of those girls today, you felt it in your pants. You shoot Lydia now, you won't be able to lift a finger when I come at you. Girls sap your strength, Kev. Didn't they teach you that in high school? Pull that trigger, pull your own trigger at the same time, right? Think you can fight me then?"

He stared, then laughed, filled the room with that funhouse cackle. "Fight you? You're not serious, Grandpa. You want to fight?"

"Bring it on."

"You're fucking kidding. Look at you. Look at *me*." He turned to Lydia as though to a judge. "You believe this? He can hardly stand up, and he thinks he can fight me."

Lydia's eyes flared and once more she pulled against the chain. I spoke to her, also. "He never took me, not once. I broke him down one-on-one every time. *Every* time. On offense I scored on his sorry ass over and over. On D, I moved him around, powered him right into the double-team. Whatever he says, that's what happened."

Kevin spun back to me, face crimson. "You lying sack of shit! *I* used to muscle *you,* I used to—"

"Oh, Christ. Talk, talk, talk. You want to weasel out, you're scared to fight me, come on, just say so."

Kevin looked at the gun, at Lydia, at me. "Well. Well, asshole. If that's what you want."

"You know it is."

"Okay. Why not? You want a beat-down, you got it. Then you can watch me and your girlfriend have that party we've been waiting on."

"Kevin? You're still talking."

He hesitated another moment, then knelt to put the gun on the floor behind him. But he stopped. "Oh. Wait. That was almost a mistake. You'd have liked that, huh? You'd have cheated and gone for the gun. Maybe that's your plan?"

It had occurred to me. I tried to keep that off my face but standing was hard enough.

"Haha! Oh, poor asshole. No, you said fight, now you're gonna have to fight." With a smile and a cold click, he pulled the magazine from the gun. He emptied the chambered round, put the bullet and the magazine in his pocket, then skidded the gun across the floor. He crouched, spread his arms, twitched his fingers. "Okay, Grandpa. Show me what you got."

What I had was a head that rang, eyes that couldn't see straight, ribs that ached with every breath, rubbery legs that had lost a step long ago.

What he had was youth, drugs, muscles, and hate.

We circled each other. I feinted at him. He didn't bite. A few steps later I did it again. Same thing. The third time he couldn't hold out, not Kevin: he rushed me, threw a right. I saw him cock it and I ducked, nearly avoided it, just barely got my ear clipped by a blow that would've knocked me over if it had connected. I jabbed up with my left while his arm was still out. I caught his chin and followed with my right, a hammer to his nose. But he jumped back and I didn't make much contact. Good sense would have told me to jump back, too, especially since the shot he'd landed, weak as it was, seemed to have made my vision not just double, but now blurred. I stood against another wave of nausea. Good sense would have told me not to fight him in the first place. I charged, throwing everything I had at his head, gut, ribs. He grabbed me in a clinch, laughing. His iron arms pinned mine. I couldn't hit but neither could he, or so I thought until he let go to pound the back of my head where he'd clobbered me when I came through the door. I saw fireworks, sparks; I heard myself howl. I dug my feet in, lowered my head like a bull, and tried to get my legs to work. Tightening his grip again, Kevin wrapped me like a steel band. I pushed hard on the concrete floor, moved us a few steps, but Kevin didn't care, just laughed and took a big step back in the direction I was pushing, dropping me off balance.

"God, Grandpa! This all you've got?"

Taking my weight on my left leg, I swept my right forward and in, hooking his ankle. It would have been a miracle if I'd unbalanced him and I managed only to pull his foot over a few inches, opening his stance. He stayed firmly upright, and he laughed. Another blow to the back of my head, another burst of lights. Then another howl.

His.

The iron grip slacked. I'd been waiting for that. I pulled away, then threw a roundhouse to his jaw and a hammer that this time found his nose. Both were pretty feeble but that was okay; they were more icing than cake. One more to the stomach and he went down. He moaned as I kicked him in the chin. I went for his stomach again. It was all available, all open to me. The hands that should have been protecting him, should have been pounding me, were between his legs, where, after I'd moved him around, powered him right into the double-team, Lydia had kicked him in the balls.

29

In a haze, I stared at Kevin on the concrete floor, bleeding and moaning. Then I dropped to my knees and started to hammer him. I pumped my arm like a pile driver, though an increasingly weak one. I didn't have much left but everything I had I poured onto Kevin. Over and over, I pounded: his face, his kidneys, whatever his writhing brought under my fist. I kept going after he stopped moving. I could've gone on forever but a pain in my ribs interrupted me. When it happened a second time I stopped punching, pulled back. The pain came again. I looked up: Lydia was kicking *me*.

I blinked, stared at Kevin motionless on the floor. I rose onto rubbery legs, pulled the tape from Lydia's mouth. She drew a deep breath and rasped, "What the hell took you so long?"

I had no idea what to say.

So I kissed her.

It all vanished: the room, the lights, the coal dust. Lydia's chain, the battered lunatic on the floor, the shakiness in my legs. No, not the shakiness. That kept going, but now it came from a different source.

After—what? an hour? a day? ten seconds?—Lydia pulled away.

"I know," she whispered. "But we're not done yet. Don't you think you need to let them in before that thing goes off?"

I didn't think anything; I was beyond thinking. She nodded toward the gas canister. I looked at it dumbly.

"Bill," she said. "The door. Go unbolt it. Then you can fall down."

Falling down seemed like such a good idea that I staggered over and unbolted the door.

After that, for a while, jumbled sounds and images, like a highlight reel: some slow-motion, some still, some jerky fast.

Mary, Sweeney, lots of other cops bursting through the door, guns sweeping in all directions, voices yelling. "Police!" "Hands up!" "On the floor!" I complied easily, though involuntarily, with that last one.

Then everyone out in a fast-receding tide. One of Kennison's men, with bolt-cutters, clipping Lydia's chain; two cops dragging Kevin; Mary and someone else helping me up. Left behind: Kennison in a Darth Vader mask, examining the canister. Soon after: Darth Vader in the crowded corridor, bowing to applause.

Fading orange sunlight, deep blue sky. Blue-and-white police cars, white-and-orange ambulances. Kevin, dazed, disbelieving, on a gurney, loaded into one ambulance. Lydia, IV in her arm, squeezing my hand as she's rolled to another. Me, last because I said so.

• • •

Mary's friend Patino: "Just FYI, Smith, you're off the hook for the homicide. From what went on here, and what your buddy Lu tells us, chances are you'll be free and clear for the cops you assaulted, too. I don't suppose"—hopefully—"you want to press charges against Lu? Kidnapping, assault? Because otherwise, after all this, I still don't have anything I can use on Lu."

Me, shaking my head, thinking about the Chinatown tunnels, and the ledge, the flagpole.

"Didn't think so. Well, I'll nail his ass some other time. Meanwhile, like I say, you're good to go. Maybe even for the Sanitation guy, if I get my playoff tickets."

Me, lifting the oxygen mask to croak: "Courtside. Can I come?"

Patino, considering: "If I have to be seen with you, you're buying the beer, too."

"Done."

"And listen, just between us, from what I hear, if I were you I'd send a crew to clean Kee's living room floor. As a goodwill gesture."

"You think that'll work?"

Patino, glancing at Mary giving orders, confering with her captain: "It's a start. Oh, and Lu wants Linus Wong's phone number. For some girl—Jasmine?"

Me, lying: "I don't have it." Me, smiling innocently: "But go ask Trella."

Linus, holding Woof's leash, sticking his face in the ambulance's rear doors.

"Dude! You okay?"

Oxygen mask off again. "Hey, Linus. She said you were good."

Linus's brow wrinkling. "What are you talking about?"

"Mary. Told another cop. Said you were damn good."

Blanket wrapping me in case of shock. After the blaze of Linus's grin, though, I didn't need it.

The next words I heard from Lydia came late the next afternoon, and were the same as the first ones she'd said when I'd ripped the tape from her mouth.

"What the hell took you so long?"

This time, though, she wasn't talking about saving her life. She was talking about answering the phone.

I was in my darkened apartment, befuddled with painkillers, aching all over. Lydia and I had each spent the night in the hospital, she because Mary had demanded it to be on the safe side, I because the neurologist wanted to see if my concussion would develop into anything more exciting. It didn't, and they'd let me out once I promised to go back for a checkup later in the week and not to engage in any strenuous physical activity in the meantime. I'd come home, slept most of the day, gotten up, and was considering breaking the strenuous activity rule to make a pot of coffee. I thought I'd better work my way up to that, though, so I was sitting on the couch smoking, an arduous warmup.

I'd been knocking the ash off my cigarette, which involved more movement than I was happy about, when my phone rang. I sat looking at it, knowing it already held three messages from Lydia. Just before voicemail kicked in, I surprised myself and answered it.

"Oh, you're there? You're alive? You're not going to make me leave another message?"

"You sound good," I said. "Are you home?"

"Home, alive and fine, thanks to you."

"Not me. Linus. Trella. Mary. A piece-of-work pimp and his boys. And don't forget Woof, canine superhero."

"And you."

"No." I brought the cigarette to my lips, an impressive achievement. "The opposite. I was the reason you needed all of them."

"Don't start that."

"You know it's true. Kevin didn't have anything against you. Or any of those hookers, either, except they were Chinese. And that was to get to me. If it hadn't been for me—"

"Am I really going to have to listen to this?"

"You know it's true," I said again.

"What I know is, you did some pretty incredible stuff and saved my life."

"If I hadn't gone after Kevin years ago—"

"Right, you should have just let him walk away from beating a girl to death."

"What I should have done was let Hal beat Kevin to death."

"You're not serious."

"Wouldn't that have been better?"

"Who made you God?"

I started to shift on the couch, stopped when I realized there was no percentage in it: comfortable was just something I wasn't going to be. "Every time I take a case," I said, "every time I come down on one side or the other without knowing the consequences, aren't I playing God?"

"If you were God you'd know the consequences."

"That's what I said: playing. Like Kevin."

"No. Kevin was playing because Kevin's insane. Make sense, Bill. When do we ever know the consequences? Every time you walk out your front door, you could be changing someone's life. Are you going to stay home forever, then? Except maybe *that* will change someone's life. Oh no! Now what?"

I lifted the cigarette again. "I'm too out of it to argue with that."

"Then try this: I don't blame you for anything that happened. Neither does anybody else."

"Mary?"

"Anybody."

"Lu, for Lei-lei?"

"Anybody."

"Your mother?"

"You think she knows? Are you crazy?"

"Where does she think you were all day? Or last night when you were at St. Vincent's?"

"Working, and at Mary's. Don't change the subject. No one blames you. But—"

"I knew there'd be a 'but.' "

"But, if you start this stuff again, kicking yourself, doing the it's-all-my-fault dance? Avoiding me the way you do when things go wrong? Then it's over."

"What are you—" *Dude? You know what she's talking about.*

"I can't deal with that anymore. If you disappear to meditate on what a screwup you are, this time you're gone for good."

I brought the cigarette up. After such a massive effort there was no point in a polite puff; I drew in a lungful, coughed it out. I closed my eyes, and when I opened them, the room seemed sharper, brighter.

"Where are you?" I said.

"I told you. Home."

"That bakery near you. The Tai-Pan. They still make that great coffee?"

"Why wouldn't they?"

"Well, could you pick me up one on your way over?"

A pause. "I'm coming over?"

So many answers, so many possible games to play. But only one thing I really meant, so I said it: "I hope so."

Made in the USA
San Bernardino, CA
17 January 2017